05313843

THORP GREEN

A Tale of the Brontës

THORP GREEN

A Tale of the Brontës

Terence Kingsley-Smith

The Book Guild Ltd
Sussex, England

First published in Great Britain in 2004 by
The Book Guild Ltd
25 High Street
Lewes, East Sussex
BN7 2LU

Typesetting in Times by
Keyboard Services, Luton, Bedfordshire

Printed in Great Britain by
Antony Rowe Ltd, Chippenham, Wiltshire

A catalogue record for this book is available from
The British Library

ISBN 1 85776 803 5

To Michael and Jan Durney, my brother and sister-in-law, for their interest and support in bringing this novel to publication.

We wove a web in childhood,
A web of sunny air;
We dug a spring in infancy
Of water pure and fair;

We sowed in youth a mustard seed,
We cut an almond rod;
We are now grown up to riper age—
Are they withered in the sod?

Charlotte Brontë

FOREWORD

In a masterful compilation of the secret journal of turbulent Branwell Brontë and the diary of his sister Emily, Terence Kingsley-Smith's flight of fantasy takes us into nineteenth-century Yorkshire. Branwell leads us down a path pebbled with passion, heartbreak and sex to failure and self-destruction. This well-conceived novel both absorbed and intrigued me.

Joan Fontaine
California, June 2004

PREFACE

The Brontë Parsonage on Church Lane south of Keighley in Haworth stands at the edge of the Yorkshire moors.

It is a Georgian house of local stone constructed in 1778, the year General Burgoyne was defeated in the American colonies, the year Captain James Cook discovered the Sandwich Islands for his Majesty King George III.

The parsonage is attached to a shaded graveyard that is part of the Church of St Michael and All Angels. This place of worship with a dark tower was originally constructed in 1655, the year Oliver Cromwell suppressed an uprising against his Puritan government.

In 1820, the Reverend Patrick Brontë was appointed curate to this parish in Haworth, a land of rugged hills, emerald meadows and thriving woollen mills.

The Reverend Mr Brontë brought his wife, six small children and two servants to live in the parsonage. It was the month of May. The hills beyond wore a patchwork of wildflowers.

Soon the mother, Maria Branwell Brontë, died of uterine cancer. Afterwards the two oldest daughters, Maria and Elizabeth, died of consumption, fuelled by the harsh conditions at the Clergy Daughters' School in nearby Tunstall, an institution catering to clergymen of the Evangelical persuasion.

The remaining Brontë children – Charlotte, Emily, Branwell and Anne – banded together in this stone parsonage on Church Lane to create their own fanciful world, a literary kingdom from which *Jane Eyre*, *Wuthering Heights* and *The Tenant of Wildfell Hall* would emerge to haunt future generations.

I, Terence Kingsley-Smith, a lover of the Brontës and their literature, believed that there was nothing more to reveal concerning this remarkable family.

I was soon to discover otherwise, in a circumstance so mysterious that I must often remind myself that it was not simply a figment of my fevered imagination, and that ghosts do indeed exist.

PART ONE

THE DISCOVERY

A friend of my youth, Tom Tegart, worked in the British Branch of Bank of America. A bonus of his London employment was a gratis apartment on Cadogan Square, an exclusive area in Chelsea where the famed Lillie Langtry had once cavorted, her digs now a neighbourhood pub.

Tegart was to be transferred back to the States in early February. If I was to take advantage of a free London flat to stay, it would have to be the cold month of January or never. I booked a flight and arrived in England during the second week of the month.

I had been in England decades before with my parents and also on a student tour. This time, after the ritual of plays and museums, I decided to rent a car and drive south to Land's End, then north to the Lake District, the home of William Wordsworth, the celebrated poet, who was a favourite of my youth. Perhaps I would spy the famous Lucy who 'dwelt among the untrodden ways.'

In Rye, a charming village in Sussex, I spent the night in the historic Mermaid Inn and chanced to speak with a friendly Yorkshire couple. A mention of their romantic homeland brought to mind the Brontës.

It was the haunting movie versions of *Jane Eyre* with Joan Fontaine and Orson Welles, and *Wuthering Heights* with Laurence Olivier and Merle Oberon, and the Classic Comic Book versions of my youth that led me to the original novels and immersed me in the sisters' literary world of Yorkshire from which my imagination has never escaped.

The woman told me that the fabled parsonage was now

a museum and that I would find Haworth, the Brontë home, by first venturing into Keighley.

I had had no intention of travelling there, but now my course was set. I would circle down from the Lake District during my journey back to London.

There are no tourists in England in January. Many of the castles, country homes and inns are closed until the spring. Even my rented vehicle was lonely for other autos along the country roads. I cannot even remember now what kind of car it was. Small economy cars all look alike. At least it got me where I wanted to go – which eventually was Haworth, the site of the Brontë Parsonage.

Although Tom Tegart had predicted unfriendly weather for my unseasonal trip through the British countryside, the pale sun had spurred me along my route. It was only when I ventured into Haworth via Keighley that the sky grew dark and a numbing cold descended upon the town like the first raw breath of a new Ice Age.

The Brontë Parsonage is situated at the foot of the cluttered graveyard that stretches mournfully from the small church where the Reverend Patrick Brontë, father to the celebrated writers, was minister.

It was almost closing time. I shivered as I stepped inside the brick Georgian house and stuffed my hands in my pockets for warmth. I could almost see my breath against the frosted air. No wonder the Brontë sisters and brother had succumbed one by one to the ravages of consumption. I doubted if a roaring fireplace in every room could heat this drafty edifice. Already I felt as if my lungs were being affected.

I was the last tourist of the day. The others had departed. I promised the grandmotherly curator that I would hurry through the chambers and moved from room to room, each one smaller than the one before, the bedrooms upstairs not much larger than furnished cells. Only in Branwell's room did I feel a pang of the nineteenth century engulf me. When I heard a tortured cough, I whirled around to face the empty bed, but nobody was there. Still, I felt a presence, something or someone reaching out to me in a way that I did not yet understand.

The distant tinkling of the curator's bell, signaling the final closing of the parsonage, brought me back to the twentieth century where my eyes came to rest on Branwell Brontë's portrait of his three famous sisters. This was obviously an artist whose soul longed for greatness, but whose hands had not fulfilled it. There was promise in his work that had not been realised. It was clear that he had painted out his own figure from the centre of the composition so that only a shadowy apparition remained.

I hurried through the north wing, added later after all the Brontës had died. These are exhibition rooms that contain many items of Brontë interest including original Victorian dresses worn by the sisters, draped on tailor's dummies the size of pre-adolescents of a modern age. People used to be smaller. I suspected that even Branwell would not have reached beyond my shoulder.

Once again the bell rang. I thanked the patient curator and stepped outside into sudden darkness. Sombre clouds had engulfed the village. I stood transfixed in front of the parsonage, watching from the street as the curator rushed from room to room, plunging the brick building into night, before she locked the front entrance and hurried off – no doubt, for a warming cup of tea.

Lightning streaked the sky. I caught a fleeting glimpse of a figure staring down from the window that had been Branwell Brontë's room. He appeared to be a man of about thirty years of age. His forehead was pale and high and crested with red curls that fluffed at the sides of his head. He wore some sort of nightshirt and a robe that suggested he was still being confined owing to illness.

In an instant all was dark once again. The street lights had yet to begin their nightly glow. Another arc of lightning. This time there was no one in the window. In fact, I was no longer certain that I had seen anyone at all.

I hurried past the graveyard where naked trees suggested they would never produce leaves again. I had parked beside the church where the Brontë sisters and brother had once sat in attendance to their father's Sunday sermons. Thunder followed the lightning with such ferocity that my ears rang from the volume of it. When I attempted to unlock my car, I dropped the keys onto the stone street. As I retrieved them and stood up once again, I saw a candle move across the window of the ancient church, a flicker of flame that wavered frantically. Could it be the kindly curator locking up this edifice as well? I longed to tell her what I had seen in the parsonage window. Perhaps the Brontë household was famous for a male ghost and she would share this knowledge with me.

The door to the church was unlocked. It was a small building, the only illumination provided by the flickering light of the candle that had been set in a niche beside the bare altar.

'Hello? Anybody here?' I called.

No one responded.

I was drawn to the candlelight as I had been drawn to glance up at Branwell Brontë's window. It suggested the only warmth in the cold damp chapel. Long and white, the candle was placed in an old-fashioned copper holder, circular at the bottom with, beneath the candle, a place to crook your finger.

I approached the niche with trepidation. I had to stoop to read the words carved onto the stone floor: 'The Brontë Chancel'. Beneath the place where the candle actually rested, the Brontës were buried, the stone covering them cracked as if it had once been disturbed. The mortal remains of the celebrated sisters rested, side by side, under the cold stone floor. Suddenly a rush of wind blew through the church and extinguished the candle.

I stumbled hurriedly towards the door, falling against a pew in the process. As I stepped outside into the swirling wind, the church door blew shut behind me.

One more bolt of lightning, an even louder clap of thunder, and rain descended with the fury of a heaven scorned. I scurried to the car and managed to start the engine. The windscreen wipers could barely cope with the cataracts the skies unleashed.

My plan had been to drive back to London, but I was scarcely outside Keighley when I realised that I would never be able to proceed through such a torrential downpour. But where to spend the night? I was already beyond Keighley and I hated to turn back and retrace my steps.

No other car was in sight. My headlights were the sole illumination against the pelting rain. Occasionally there was the solitary light of a distant farm. The rain would not let up. It maintained its steady pace. The road was growing muddier. Soon I would be mired in slush, trapped in a small car with a heater that only gave warmth when the engine was running.

Beyond lay Bradford, which, according to the map, was too great a distance to travel. I had never encountered such a dramatic storm in California. Perhaps only this fabled isle produced weather of such inclemency.

Another explosion of lightning filled the unfriendly sky with dramatic light. I caught momentary sight of a 'Bed and Breakfast' sign fastened to a mailbox at the end of a solitary lane. My car seemed to turn in that direction of its own accord, as if it craved respite from the rain even more than I.

The country lane, seemingly interminable, suddenly ended before a two-storey stone farmhouse that reminded me of

Wuthering Heights in the William Wyler directed film, when Heathcliff, in the handsome guise of Laurence Olivier, ran off in the rain because he felt Merle Oberon's Cathy had rejected him. Could the ghosts of Cathy and Heathcliff be lurking somewhere about the premises? Would Cathy attempt to clutch my hand through a broken window as she did Heathcliff's in the Emily Brontë story?

A faint circle of light emanated from the upper window, something that came not from electricity but perhaps a lantern.

I parked my car, grabbed my suitcase, and dashed to the front entrance as quickly as the rain would permit. Fortunately there was an eave over the doorway which protected me from soaking as I banged desperately against the door. In the distance I heard the bleating of a sheep, but I could see nothing in the darkness.

At last the door was opened. A woman somewhere in her sixties held a candle, its flame moving the wrinkles about her face. Her long greying hair had been swept up and fastened on the top of her head. She was wearing a bulky woollen sweater and heavy trousers, clearly dressed not for style but warmth. She stared at me a moment, suspiciously, her hazel eyes searching my face to decipher if I was friend or foe. 'Are you lost?'

'I'm afraid I need a place to stay.'

'American?'

I nodded. 'I saw your sign on the road.'

'That's during the season. We're off season.'

'But I ... it's cats and dogs out here.' Did I sound as anxious as I looked?

'My husband doesn't like me to take anybody in when he's not here to tend to things himself, especially not after what happened to Mrs Frazier down the road.'

'What was that?'

'If I told you it might give you ideas.' She wasn't actually smiling, but I doubted that she would have told me her husband was away if she thought I looked like someone who could do her harm. She studied me another moment, then stepped back to give me space to enter. 'Come in, then.'

I no sooner stepped inside and she closed the door when I heard a frail voice call weakly from somewhere deep in the house. 'Who is it then, Brenda?'

'A lodger, mum. He wants his bed and breakfast!' Brenda shouted loudly to the rear of the house.

'In January?'

'That's what I say!'

Brenda placed her lamp against a large book on the table in the entrance hall. 'You'll have to sign the book first.' She opened it to the proper page and handed me a pen. 'What brings an American tourist to Yorkshire this time of year?'

'The Brontës.'

Brenda looked up at me at the mention of their name, as if there was more to it than the celebration of their novels. She shook her head. 'Did any of those sickly girls ever have the notion they would be such an attraction a century after their death?'

'I doubt it.'

I signed the book in the pale lamplight. The rain was beating against roof and window and the wind was howling loudly. The last entry was dated October 14, 1994. Truly January 1995 was the cruelest month of all in Yorkshire, and only such as myself would have ventured so far north out of season. 'Electricity is out,' she said as if it was to be expected. 'Usually happens this time of year.'

'As long as I have a bed and a warm blanket.'

'That comes with the price,' she replied, bending down to study my name, before looking back up at me, her eyes widening in a show of surprise. 'Terry Kingsley-Smith,' she repeated, for that was what I had written. 'Would that be "Terence Kingsley-Smith"?'

'The same.'

'Inspector Hume's Terence Kingsley-Smith?'

I was somewhat astonished that she would know of my books. Popular though they were in the States, I had never had a big readership in England. Inspector Hume was a former Scotland Yard detective. He had purchased a double-decker London bus, shipped it to San Francisco and converted it into a houseboat which he kept docked in Sausalito. Soon he was solving mysteries centred around the windswept city across the Golden Gate Bridge. I had created the character to be part of one of those revolving television mystery series, and when NBC turned it down, I developed a series of mystery novels instead. Inspector Hume was not as lucrative as one might think, but he did pay my bread and butter and a tourist class ticket to London as long as there was a free place to stay. Now television wanted my character, but I refused to sell. I didn't like the way talent was treated on television, especially by those with absolutely no talent at all. Inspector Hume would remain in my readers' imagination. He would not be broken into ten minute segments between panty hose commercials.

Brenda led me into the library, which I gathered was usually off limits to a bed and breakfast boarder. Bookcases stretched to the ceiling and were crammed with volumes. 'Mum loves mysteries. Most of these are mysteries.' She held her candle next to a particular shelf. I recognised my Inspector Hume books immediately, all six of them, still in their covers, but gathering dust. 'He's mum's favourite detective. She went to San Francisco once and she never forgot. A night like this makes her wish she'd settled there herself.'

'I wouldn't live anywhere else.'

'But Yorkshire's home.' Brenda pointed to another shelf. 'James Herriot's her favourite as well.' I glanced at his books.

Herriot hadn't written as many volumes as I in his celebrated Yorkshire veterinarian series, but each one was a gem. In my estimation, my Inspector Hume paled in comparison. 'Would you sign these copies for my ol' mum? Actually she's my husband's mum. This farm's been in the family since the time of the Georges. Used to be quite a spread at one time.'

'I'd be happy to.'

'Have you had your supper?' Brenda questioned. She had definitely warmed to me.

'Famished.'

'You can sign these books on the kitchen table while I see what I can come up with without electricity.'

'So it's not just bed and breakfast, is it?' I smiled.

'Only for a celebrated author like yourself.'

'Mum wants to meet you before she nods off,' Brenda informed me after I had swallowed the last of a cold mutton sandwich. The British are content with just a slab of meat and a little butter on their sandwiches, but fortunately there was mayonnaise in the fridge. There was egg custard as well, and of course hot tea, the water for which Brenda boiled in a pot over the kitchen fireplace. The rain continued to beat furiously against the house. I feared my rented car would drown before morning. The thunder and lightning had ceased but the pelting of water against the windowpanes was noise enough.

'I would be happy to meet your mother.'

'She's that excited to have you here.'

Brenda lifted the kerosene lamp and led me through the kitchen to the rear of the house. 'The stairs got too difficult for mum, so we fixed things up for her back here.'

The light flickered across faded paintings on the walls of the hallway that led to the back of the farmhouse. The door to the bedroom was open. There were candles at either side of the bed where the ancient woman was stretched out as if she were the leading player in a wake. There was a strong smell of medicinal ointment that reminded me of the Vick's Vapor Rub of my youth.

Mum wore a nightcap. The face that protruded from beneath its folds was ancient and looked as if it was carved from an apple that had now shrunk to its core. Her eyes were closed. 'Here he is, mum,' Brenda advised, stroking the elderly woman's hand.

The old woman's eyes snapped open immediately and surveyed me with curiosity, taking me in from head to toe. 'Looks older than that picture on the back of the book.' Her Yorkshire accent was even thicker than her daughter-in-law's.

'I need a new one,' I offered, knowing I would never get around to it. I hated to have my picture taken because photographers always made me look older than I saw myself in the mirror.

'Have you written another Inspector since *The Mystery of Pebble Beach*?'

'My Carmel mystery,' I corroborated. 'That one got me a few new readers. There are a lot of frustrated golfers out there.'

'Thought I figured it out, but the Inspector did me one better again.'

'He has the benefit of weeks of my mulling it over.'

'What I like,' she pointed out in a loud scratchy voice that reminded me of a used 78 rpm record, 'is that Hume doesn't get all bloody. That Patricia Cornwell is always in the coroner's office cutting up all those revolting bodies.'

'That's her speciality.'

'Have you got a new one?' she asked hopefully.

'Half done as we speak.'

'What's this one called?'

'*The San Francisco Opera House Mystery*.'

She nodded her head, pleased with this. 'I never cared

much for opera, but I saw the outside of that fancy place when I took the tour.'

'You might remember that Inspector Hume likes to listen to opera on his stereo.'

She nodded, her long chin touching her chest. 'Listening is better than seeing. I've always liked Vera Lynn myself. *I'll Be Seeing You*, that's what my Freddy and I used to listen to before he went off to fight the Hun and never came back. Had to sell off most of this place and run the rest myself.' She indicated her daughter-in-law, 'Till her Charley was old enough to know what's what.'

'My husband has been very successful with sheep,' Brenda boasted.

'He's a good boy,' the old woman agreed, her eyes closing a moment to reveal lids as wrinkled as the rest of her. She opened them once more and fastened her grey pupils on me. 'What happens in this new one? Somebody in the opera get murdered?'

'The tenor, the soprano and the conductor.'

'Could you tell me the story?'

'Mum!' Brenda obviously felt this was an untoward request.

'I'm an old woman!' the mother protested. 'Who knows if I'll live long enough to read the next! With no electricity or telly tonight, I have to have something to put me out!'

'I'd be happy to tell the story,' I volunteered, looking down at the bed. 'If you can figure out who done it before the Inspector, then I'll know I'm in trouble.'

The old woman snuggled deep beneath the covers in anticipation. 'Bring us some tea, luv,' she ordered her daughter-in-law. She motioned me to sit down. 'Now don't go rushing through it. I don't want you skipping over any of the good parts.'

* * *

Tea had turned cold before I finished the telling of *The San Francisco Opera House Mystery*, Inspector Hume's latest foray into the world of California crime. Brenda had absented herself, saying that she needed to prepare my bedroom, adding she would read my new mystery when it arrived in bookstores in the autumn.

The old woman seemed pleased and reached out and squeezed my hand. 'It's a good yarn,' she complimented, her head bobbing against the pillow. 'It puts me in mind of that ol' Ingrid Bergman movie where Charles Boyer was after the jewels in her mother's old costumes.'

I was surprised that she would remember. 'That's where I got the idea.'

'But I never really suspected the first violinist,' she admitted. 'Especially since he and the conductor were fairies together.'

'It took me a long time to work that one out.'

She hadn't let go of my hand. She clutched it even tighter as she looked up at me. 'Is it true what Brenda said?'

'What?'

'That you're here because of them Brontës?'

'It certainly is,' I confirmed, telling the old lady of my fondness for their literature. 'I wished they'd picked better weather for me.'

'Did you learn anything about the brother when you were traipsing through the parsonage?'

'Branwell?' How curious that she should ask about him.

She nodded her chin to her chest. 'The one who was always getting himself soused at the old Black Bull Tavern.'

'It was almost closing. There wasn't really time to...' I stopped myself and moved my chair even closer to the bed. 'Of all the Brontës, why do you ask about him?'

'Maybe he's the one who sent you here, and maybe that sister too – Emily.'

I couldn't help but tell her what had transpired at the

parsonage: the sound of a man coughing, the figure at the window and the candle in the church.

She accepted all of this with a strange equanimity, as if somehow it had been pre-ordained. 'It's as if he drove your car himself.'

'Why would he guide me here?'

'Why indeed?' was her enigmatic reply as she regarded me strangely. 'Perhaps now is the time after all,' she added finally, before calling out in a sudden strong voice that was louder than the rain buffeting against her window. 'Brenda!'

Her daughter-in-law came along the hallway and into the chamber. 'Is the story over, Mum?'

'It was a corker, Brenda.'

'I'll look forward to reading it.'

'You know why he's come here, don't you, luv?' the mother asked the daughter-in-law.

'He saw our sign.'

'Sent by that Brontë. After all these years, I think that Brontë wants to be published.'

The younger woman was taken aback. 'Mum!'

'Tell her what happened at the parsonage,' the mother instructed me, still clutching my hand, her white bony fingers squeezing into my flesh.

I had no choice but to comply, telling it slowly and, in truth, enjoying this additional audience.

Brenda's eyes widened at its conclusion. 'Take him up to the attic and let him have it,' the mother instructed her daughter-in-law. 'A writer like himself will know what to do with it and if it should be published.' As Brenda stood a moment in silence, looking from her mother-in-law to me and back again, the old woman spoke once again. 'It's been under this roof long enough!'

'It was her grand-dad,' the daughter-in-law volunteered slowly.

The old woman released my hand and placed her palms

over her chest. 'He was the one who done it and we've kept it hidden away ever since. Back then they were afraid of what they would do to him if they found out. They should have given it back when grand-dad died, but grandma decided to hold onto it – sort of the family way of holding something back if everything failed and they needed the money. Praise the good Lord this family never did go under, even if we had to sell off most of the farm to make ends meet.'

'Mum, are you sure?' Brenda asked quietly.

'Surer than I ever was!' She was vehement. 'Before I die I want those books out of the house!' The old woman reached for her cup of tea and her daughter-in-law held it to her lips. After a healthy swallow, the old woman returned her attention to me. 'When grand-dad was still a lad he thought he'd leave the running of our farm to his dad and older brother. He apprenticed as a stone mason. One of his jobs, around 1880, was the rebuilding of the Brontë Church where people still attended service. My grand-dad stayed late one night to finish up his job and some of the scaffolding fell and crashed into the Brontë chancel. I don't know what made him take the little tin box out – curiosity I suppose – but take it grand dad did, and it's been in this house ever since … waiting for somebody like you who'll know what to do with it.'

'You have something of Branwell Brontë's?' I could scarcely get the words out.

'It's his own little book in his little writing. And one of Emily's too. I read them once and it was that hard on the eyes. Those Brontës wrote small. I suppose they didn't want to waste too much paper.'

'Are they novels?' I couldn't control the excitement in my voice.

'Whatever they are they're sad stories,' the old woman sighed, before turning her head to face her daughter-in-law. 'Give him the letters too.' She looked back at me.

'They explain why she buried these things.'

'I...' I didn't know what to say. I couldn't believe that this was happening. The entire evening was stranger than a dream. When would I awake?

The old lady was growing tired. She wanted to sleep. 'Take him up to the attic and give it to him.'

The daughter-in-law hesitated. Then she lifted the kerosene lamp and led the way out of the chamber.

The dark attic, tucked under the eaves of the farmhouse, was almost a full story unto itself. The kerosene lamp spread shadows across generations of remembrances. There was scarred furniture, faded mirrors, limp dolls, discarded parlour games and a steamer trunk with peeling labels that suggested it had crossed the English Channel on more than one occasion. It was on top of this that Brenda rested her lamp and fished a key out of her pocket before reluctantly fitting it into the lock and turning it slowly. 'My husband should be here for this,' she said not looking at me. 'But when mum gets a notion in her head...'

She opened the trunk. Homemade costumes from some forgotten party hung on drooping hangers. Fancy shoes were littered beneath. Brenda opened one of the small drawers slowly – hesitantly – as if she didn't want to expose its contents to the light. The rusty tin box was all by itself. This was its special hiding place. Neither gloves, ties, tarnished jewelery nor old scarves interfered with it. Brenda lifted it out and placed it in my hands. There was no lock on the box. It was a simple container to keep its contents safe from harm and degradation.

A hallowed feeling came over me, as if Branwell Brontë, in his nightshirt and robe was there in the attic with us, and his sister, Emily, as well, waiting for me to open the lid of this ancient container. I hesitated, but as I found the courage to lift the lid Brenda stopped me. 'No, not here. Wait till you get to your room. I'll make sure you have plenty of light to read straight through if that's what you want, and I'll brew another pot of tea.' She indicated my glasses. 'I hope they're good and strong. A hen could scratch bigger with one of her claws than these Brontës.'

We left the attic in darkness as we descended the circular back stairway that creaked with memory. I felt as if Branwell Brontë was following behind me, winding with us around the steps, and I felt his sister's presence as well, the wind outside somehow finding us and hurrying us along. After I finished reading the manuscript, would the rain stop? Would the sun once again shine over Yorkshire?

I had always loved wearing pyjamas, even during the summer when California can be hot and others love luxuriating in their nakedness beneath the sheets. I especially love the winter months when it is cold enough to wear my flannels and I feel warm and contented tucked in my bed away from the outside world.

It was into these pyjamas that I burrowed like a furry creature escaping into his hovel from the rain. I snuggled beneath sheet, blanket and comforter on a wrought-iron bed. Kerosene lamps, their cylindrical glass shades radiating warmth, were turned up to their highest.

I opened the small metal box. On top of composition books was a faded white envelope, not brown with age, but grey with neglect.

I was careful in extracting the paper from the thin envelope. Fortunately, the letter within had not fallen to pieces. One day soon it would have to be pressed between glass for safety.

Like a hungry suspense reader skipping to the end of an Agatha Christie, I glanced first at the closing of the letter to determine its writer. The name 'Charlotte' was as legible as the rest of the letter. Her handwriting was pleasing to the eye: a simple small flowing script that Charlotte Brontë must have learned at the Clergy Daughters' School at Cowan Bridge, on the borders of Lancashire and Westmorland, the detestable boarding establishment that she pictured with such harrowing fervour as Lowood in *Jane Eyre*.

The words must have been scratched in India ink, its black pigment standing the test of time so that I could read the letter addressed to both brother and sister.

May 30, 1854

My Beloved Sister Emily and Brother Branwell,

It is with the heaviest of hearts that I must write to you, my departed sister and brother, rather than speak with you in person and hold your hands, as we were wont to do in our happier youth. No matter how much I long for it, neither sunset soft, nor moonlight mild can bring that hour again.

I will never know whether you left behind these secret parts of your short lives because of forgetfulness during your last days of illness, or because you wished to share these tortured, yes, sadly, sometimes sordid, periods of your precious lives.

Certainly you never wished for father to read what you have transcribed here. I have hidden this journal and this diary away from him: for assuredly, if he read these, he would weep even more for his dearly departed than he has done already.

I cannot bring myself to destroy what both of you have written; yet nor can I share your hidden thoughts with any living human being, not even my dear husband-to-be, the Reverend Arthur Nicholls, whom I fear would be shocked and certainly not understand how writing to the Brontës was as necessary to us as prayer is to him. Even I am aghast at how little I truly knew my younger sister and brother. How close we were and yet so far apart. It is only in these private musings that you dared to tell the truth.

There has been too much interest in us Brontë Sisters since our unmasking as the celebrated authors: Currer, Ellis and Acton Bell. The public has become overly curious and I shudder to think what would be written if they ever discovered what you have left behind.

Perhaps in some future generation when we are gone and forgotten, someone will discover what I have hidden here. If someone were to read what you have transcribed here now, not father, nor I, nor my husband-to-be would ever be able to hold up our heads, not only in Haworth but in all of England.

At least, as long as I am living, your precious reputations are safe with me, even though you, Darling Brother, already did much to sully your own in the last years of your short life, a period of which I was not as tolerant as I should have been, because I too burned with a desperate love – for Monsieur Heger – an uncontrollable emotion which I deplored in you.

I forgive you now: because of what you have written, I am better able to understand.

I rest assured that our youngest sister, Anne, has joined you with God, and I can only hope that in this after-life you are now enjoying you have found the contentment and happiness that were denied my beloved sisters and brother here on earth; that one day our family will be reunited in our own Glasstown.

When the dead in their cold graves are lying
Asleep, to wake never again;
When past are their smiles and their sighing,
Oh! why should their memories remain?

Though sunshine and spring may have lightened
    The wild flowers that blow on their graves;
Though summer their tombstones have brightened,
    And autumn have pall'd them with leaves;

Though winter have wildly bewailed them
    With her dirge-wind as sad as a knell;
Though the shroud of her snow-wreath have veiled them,
    Still how deep in our bosoms they dwell!

The shadow and sun-sparkle vanish,
    The cloud and the light flee away;
But man from his heart may not banish
    The thoughts that are torment to stay.

The reflection departs from the river
    When the tree that hung o'er is cut down,
But on Memory's calm current for ever
    The shade without substance is thrown.

When quenched is the glow of the ember,
    When the life-fire ceases to burn,
Oh! why should the spirit remember?
    Oh! why should the parted return?

Because that the fire is *still* shining,
    Because that the lamp is still bright;
While the body in dust is reclining
    The soul lives in glory and light.

Your loving sister,

Charlotte

I reached first for the small unlined notebook where

Branwell had perhaps scribbled his attempt at immortality. Beneath was Emily's diary.

Branwell's writing was minute, but the ink was still dark. I was able to decipher the sentences.

As the wind howled outside and the rain added dots of punctuation against the window, I turned up the kerosene even more and perused the first page of Branwell Brontë's Journal.

I read straight through, never closing my eyes, until both books were devoured and in the morning the rain had stopped and the sun shone once again.

PART TWO

THE JOURNAL OF BRANWELL BRONTË
AND
THE DIARY OF EMILY BRONTË

(Intermingled so the reader can better interpret the events in the order in which they transpired.)

The Journal Of Branwell Brontë

5th September, 1845

As a starving man needs porridge, I crave paper and pen.

I must write it all down or surely strangle from keeping silence; for I can speak to no-one of the tragic events of these past two years.

I can no longer escape to my imaginary world called Glasstown, the mythical African literary kingdom created by my sister, Charlotte, and I, when we were merely children: a world of imagination perpetuated by my younger sisters, Emily and Anne, and rechristened Gondal.

Hitherto I could escape by transporting myself to this magical land and creating a new adventure for my hero, the Earl of Northangerland; but, to quote my favourite poet, William Wordsworth:

The world is too much with us; late and soon,
Getting and spending, we lay waste our powers:
Little we see in Nature that is ours;
We have given our hearts away, a sordid boon!

Cruel reality has come crashing down like stinging rain on this childhood world: and my fiendish contribution to this cruellest of realities, is the most unforgivable thing of all.

As I sit here in the back room of the Black Bull Inn, a stone's throw from my father's parsonage, the myriad days leading to my destruction crumble before me like endless leaves. My pen scratches into my notebook of its own volition and finds its way to my inkwell of its own accord. Perhaps it is the whisky that gives me courage, and the warm comfort of what is becoming known as 'Branwell's room' at this familiar watering hole. I am drinking away the last of my wages until there is not a sixpence left. Of what the future promises afterward is anybody's educated guess.

I am sitting in my special chair here at the Black Bull Inn. It is oaken, resembling a school desk, which makes it agreeable for writing, although, in truth, I never attended a proper school. I was instructed by my Reverend Father at home. He taught me too much about his precious God so that I was driven to turn away from his evangelicalism. Now that I have stumbled and fallen, I cannot turn to God to pick me up.

Another drop of whisky has warmed me to the gills. A fresh candle is brought to my chair. I am ready to follow my pen on its journey through my melancholy past. Perhaps, after setting it all down, I will better understand all that has happened.

At least I am writing again. Perhaps, one day, I can take these pages and create a world of fiction out of this unhappy world of fact, a feat that the celebrated Mr Dickens has achieved on more than one occasion.

I feel that each Brontë has a story to write. Perhaps this will be mine.

The world of paper and pen is the most important world of all.

I shall set it all down – just as it happened. I will let the words flow: and if I digress and if sometimes I only imagine, I shall not curtail: in truth, I shall not be able to; for this pen appears to have a mind of its own, fuelled as it is by drink.

We Brontës are story tellers. It is the heritage of our Irish father, who told the best stories of all.

But this is my story; and I shall commence telling it here at the Black Bull.

I shall not stop, Dear Journal, nor drink myself to oblivion until all is set down. I shall return to you each waking hour until the story has been told.

When did it begin? It was in January of 1843, during the sixth year of our young Queen Victoria's reign. The narrow road that twisted through the Yorkshire countryside was leading me away from the only place where I felt warm and protected: Haworth and the parsonage where my father tended to souls and where now my sister Emily tended to him and the care of his household.

As winter frost descended upon the moors with the solemnity of one of my father's sermons, I pictured all my sisters in the familiar parlour, sitting close to the warm fire. I imagined Charlotte and Emily scratching feverishly into their composition books: I stole into the kitchen to sample the meal prepared by our beloved housekeeper, Tabitha: I informed father that dinner was ready for the eating. I scratched our dog, Keeper's, fur and allowed our cat, Tiger, to nestle on my lap. It was almost as if I was still safe at home rather than facing the unknown.

Sitting beside me in the crowded post-chaise, was the handsome Reverend William Weightman, my father's assistant, who had kindly consented to accompany me upon this journey to the unknown; to this new position; to this new opportunity that I knew my father and sisters felt was my last chance to make something of myself. I wonder now if I was a greater disappointment to them or myself.

I feared what awaited me at Thorp Green: the position of tutor to the young master where my youngest sister, Anne, was already governess to his older sisters. I had already failed as tutor to a family at Broughton-in-Furness in the Lake District; as a portrait painter in Bradford; and as a railway clerk at Luddenden Foot. I wanted desperately for the coachman to turn his team of obedient horses around and take me quickly home to the safe bosom of my family. I seemed fit for nothing except to be favoured by my father and nursed by my sisters, the latter growing dissatisfied with my lack of progress and my susceptibility to wine and spirits at our neighbouring inn, the Black Bull – a short but familiar walk from our parsonage – where I am presently sitting.

I feigned to the young Reverend that it was the jostling of the coach, its perpetual motion pressing my body against his, that was making me ill; and not the fear of this new venture to which I had attached such great importance. Soon I poked my head outside the window so that I could vomit into the road; much to the disgust of the female passengers, two of the women covering their faces with their lace handkerchiefs, and turning away to stare out of the opposite window.

Upon regaining my equilibrium, I sank back into my seat and welcomed the warmth of the Reverend's body against mine; a barrier against the nipping cold that frosted our breaths.

The Reverend William Weightman was as handsome in appearance as I was ordinary; as tall in stature as I was short. His wavy dark hair and black mutton-chops, his long eyelashes and dramatic brows, his perfect nose, his deep blue eyes and gentle mouth, were irresistible to young women; especially to the Sisters Brontë: for each in her own particular way cherished him. He had been the first to send 'valentines' to the parsonage; and no doubt Anne kept hers in a special place hidden among her belongings at Thorp Green. This cold evening in January, I basked in the warmth of the Reverend's companionship, wishing that the carriage could take us all the way to Scarborough and the sea, where a ship would carry us away to my imaginary world of Glasstown where we could be friends for life.

Even my older and wiser sister, Charlotte, confided to me in a letter from Brussels, where she was studying to become a teacher, that during holiday when she was alone in the great dormitory, with no other company than a number of beds with white curtains, her mind retreated as fanatically as ever to the old ideas and the old faces and the old scenes in the far-off world that we named Glasstown and that she now prefers to call Angria.

It was a cold and wintery dusk when we were deposited at the Wayfarer's Tavern in the small village of Little Ouseburn, from which we were to make our way on foot to Thorp Green, the source of my new employment. The coach would proceed no farther this day; the horses were sequestered for the night; as were some of the passengers who would continue upon their journey on the morrow.

The curate assisted me from the coach; for I had grown weak in the knees and my head swum with dizziness. 'Was ever a face as white as yours!' he commented: for I was known, even at my worst, for the ruddiness of my complexion, set off by the red of my hair, both passed on to me from my father and his Irish heritage; for, in truth, he came from County Down beneath the Mountains of Mourne in the north of Ireland. 'Is it the motion sickness?' he questioned.

I nodded my head feebly; although, in truth, my illness had nothing to do with the coach, but was due to my fear of my new employment at the estate that lay somewhere beyond; my last chance, it seemed, at making something of myself.

'We're taking a room for the night,' Mr Weightman assured me, steadying me by placing a protective arm around my shaking shoulders. 'I shall not have you reporting to work in a condition such as this.'

I nodded my consent. Being taken care of was what I desperately desired. It was something my sisters had done too well.

We watched the assistant coachman lower the bags from the top of the post-chaise. Mine was tattered and frayed, for it had been used by more than one member of the Brontë family; especially my sister, Emily, who carried it all the way to Brussels. Weightman's was a simple small valise, because he had intended to return early on the morrow.

Fortunately, he had already written to book a room for himself, for the inn was filled with many wayfarers. Since there was no other available, I would have to share not only the Reverend's chamber, but his bed as well. He accepted this with equanimity; while I, secretly, relished the thought of the closeness of his company.

'We must get some food into you,' he advised as I fell weakly and fully clothed onto the bed.

'No,' I moaned: for the thought was repellent to me. It was in my stomach my fears always centred, churning and twisting into painful contortions. It was stomach trouble that had recently taken the life of my Aunt Branwell, my late mother's devoted sister. She had raised my sisters and me, and I missed her more than I would have realised. I feared that stomach trouble was a family trait.

'Some soup,' he insisted. 'It will help settle what ails you,' for he knew that I was afraid.

I made no protest as he left the chamber and soon returned with a steaming bowl of beef and barley which he spoon-fed to my mouth. In truth, the broth did warm and soothe the depths of my bowels: but this was due more to the minister than the brew. When he placed his gentle hand upon my forehead to ascertain for fever, I welcomed his solicitous touch. 'You look and feel that much better,' he smiled, pleased with his ministration.

I lay back on the pillow and squeezed his hand. 'A minister not only to a man's soul but to his stomach as well.'

He donned his dark wool over-coat and fastened the many buttons that ran from neck to waist and also secured the wide collar about his throat. 'You are going out?' I questioned, for I did not relish being left alone.

'They are expecting you this evening at Thorp Green. I must walk the distance and tell them they will not see you until the morrow.'

'But it is bitter cold out.'

'The Brontë Family has been good to me. I am delighted to provide any service I can as a repayment of their kindness.'

Indeed he had been good to me. I had had few faithful friends such as this.

'Could this also be because it will afford you an opportunity to visit my sister?' I could not resist asking.

Mr Weightman chose not to reply; but smiled in return. It was such a handsome, hopeful smile, exposing white teeth and lighting up a face that was already radiant with a special illumination.

The Journal of Branwell Brontë

14th September 1845

I am on foot to-day. It is a glorious fall that only Yorkshire can provide. The air is crisp but not cold. I longed to be outdoors and have walked the entire distance to the refreshing falls beyond Haworth so that I can breathe deeply of the salubrious air and feel the sunshine as I continue with my retelling of the events at Thorp Green that weigh upon me like persistent clouds. The sun warms my fingers as they skim across the page. I feel at one with nature and my creativity abounds.

Does a journal become something else entirely when one is recording what one did not actually witness? Are you no longer a journal but simply a tool of a writer's imagination?

Is not a writer's tool his imagination?

I shall put my own to use in surmising scenes I did not actually witness but I am certain happened. Often an imagined scene is more vivid than one that actually transpired, and are not we Brontës, after all, writers?

And in the tradition of such distinguished novelists as the great Charles Dickens, I shall commence to make use of special headings to indicate special portions of my story, such as:

In Which the Author Takes Poetic Licence

I can actually see the handsome Mr Weightman as he appropriated a small lantern from the tavern and made his way along the dark lane that ultimately leads to Thorp

Green. A description of the edifice awaits my own arrival in the morning, but I can well imagine how Mrs Fitzpatrick, the Irish housekeeper, appeared as she opened the massive door, a candle bathing her rotund features in a rosy glow. She was not unlike our own housekeeper, Tabitha, in her devotion to a family and her lips often pressed together in the same look of disapproval that Tabitha often lavished, especially upon me. Her glasses were narrow circles around searching brown eyes, her grey hair a halo of small curls that she often tucked beneath a swatch of delicate lace. She was still wearing her flowered cotton house dress that billowed over muslin petticoats, and her grey shawl against a house that was often a stranger to warmth.

'Are you the Mr Brontë who is expected?' Mrs Fitzpatrick demanded suspiciously in her acerbic voice tinged with a pronounced brogue.

'I am the Reverend William Weightman, his travelling companion.'

Perhaps Mrs Fitzpatrick was even disappointed that the handsome figure standing before her, his regular features enhanced by his lamp-light, was not the tutor who would reside within the walls of the dwelling.

'And where might Mr Brontë be?'

'I feel the journey took longer than we expected,' Weightman replied simply. 'Mr Brontë was taken ill and we thought it best that he remain at the inn rather than walk the distance this evening.'

'Is he that delicate then?'

'Perhaps the excitement of this new appointment had something to do with his condition. I came myself because I feared there might be worry at Thorp Green concerning his whereabouts.'

'Aye, that there was,' Mrs Fitzpatrick concurred. 'Especially from his dear sister, who was making her own self sick with worry.'

‘Has she retired then?’ I can well imagine the hope in his voice that she had not.

‘She often stays up that late reading or writing by candle-light, claiming it is the only time she has to herself.’

The Reverend hesitated, still standing in the doorway, for Mrs Fitzpatrick had not invited him in. ‘I was hoping that ... I am expected back in Haworth to-morrow and...’

Who could resist the pleading look in Mr Weightman’s gentle blue eyes? Not even the formidable Mrs Fitzpatrick. ‘Perhaps she has not retired. The expectation of her brother’s arrival has no doubt kept her awake. Step in here out of the cold and I’ll see if I can rouse her. She’ll be that glad to see somebody from her village. You would think it was County Mayo the way she goes on about it.’

I can well imagine the immediate flush that coloured my sister Anne’s pale cheeks as Mrs Fitzpatrick announced the presence of her beloved William. No doubt she wore the plain black dress with the round lace collar and lace cuffs that had become her uniform. She must have glanced quickly in the glass to smooth down her auburn hair that was parted in the middle and fell into ringlets at either side of her head; and pinched her cheeks for colour as well. ‘Where shall I receive him?’ she questioned unsurely, her soft voice trembling with excitement.

‘Perhaps the kitchen, dearie. Cook’s gone to bed and fire isn’t out yet and you will be warm.’

How my delicate younger sister and the imposing William Weightman must have looked at each other as they stood face to face in the kitchen, their features burning in the glow of the firelight. He must have removed his heavy travelling coat and surely Anne admired the sturdy figure within the clerical suit.

What delight I take even now in imagining what they must have said to each other. It is more pleasurable to me than describing what I have actually witnessed. It is fervid imagination that makes writers of us all, is it not?

'I can safely assume that tutoring agrees with you, Miss Anne.'

How my sister must have looked to him: as delicately beautiful as ever, her grey-blue eyes as trusting as when he last saw her at our parsonage.

'Firelight can be deceiving,' she replied quickly, nervous in his presence: 'for two more difficult charges a governess has never encountered. As for the boy, that's a horse of a different colour.'

Mr Weightman could never tear his eyes away from Anne. There was so little time actually to view her that he must not have squandered even one second. 'I have every confidence that in the bright sun of day, the light would be even more flattering to you, and if these so called charges had been yours from the cradle, they would now be two delightful angels.'

How she always thrilled at the sound of his passionate voice; but she could seldom bear the gentle scrutiny of his penetrating eyes. She glanced into the fire instead. 'And Branwell?' she questioned, to change the subject. 'Why is my brother not with you, sir? Young Master Tom was so anxious to make his acquaintance.'

'I fear his apprehension at the thought of this new employment has reduced him to a state of apoplexy. He has made himself ill and to-night was not fit to begin his employment.'

Anne shook her head slowly: her soft curls vibrated with the motion. 'My poor darling Branwell.'

'I have left him at the inn where a warming bowl of broth is calming both his nerves and his stomach. Rest assured, that to-morrow your brother will present himself at Thorp Green as fearless as Don Quixote and as diligent as your father.'

Anne smiled, her pale eyes lighting up like candles.

'You've been more than a friend to Branwell,' she pointed out. 'You've been a brother as well.'

'Yes,' he concurred, 'and I have acquired three charming sisters into the bargain.'

I can well imagine the smile that brought sunshine to Anne's often serious face. 'I hope that I have not over-praised my brother here at Thorp Green,' she remarked, the corners of her mouth now turning down. 'The Reverend Mr Thornton is impossible to please; but his son is at the age where he needs the companionship of a man. Mr Thornton is no more father to the boy than he is to his oldest daughter.'

William attempted to assuage her fears. 'Branwell is determined to make a success of this endeavour.'

Anne accepted this hopefully. 'It will be so good to have him here with me. I've missed my family so. It is only weeks since I came home for Christmas, and already I am desolate.'

'Miss Emily sends her love. Your father is in robust health: still she watches over him as if she is his nurse.'

Anne beamed at mention of her sister. 'It is her letters and the ones from Charlotte that sustain me.'

The curate hesitated: he could not resist the temptation to ask. 'Are Miss Charlotte's letters still filled with such glowing reports of her Belgian Professor Heger?'

Anne was obviously taken aback that he should so allude to her sister's affection for the married professor who had hired Charlotte to teach English to his Brussels charges. Weightman, detecting her discomfort, plunged ahead quickly. 'It was Miss Emily who...' He did not quite know how to phrase it. 'She does not seem to share your sister's enthusiasm for the professor.' In truth, Emily had studied under the professor as well, but did not return to Brussels after travelling home in the wake of Aunt Branwell's untimely death.

Anne spoke quickly to deflect his inquiry. 'Charlotte is

in Brussels to add Italian to her knowledge of French and German. She will be most proficient when we open our own school in Haworth.'

'And what of theology?' He now wished to steer the conversation away from Anne's oldest sister.

'I'm afraid, sir, that father would insist upon the right of teaching that subject himself.'

Mr Weightman could abide Anne addressing him so formally for one more instant. 'Must you persist, Miss Anne, in calling me "sir", as if you were a disinterested member of your father's church?'

Anne was obviously flustered. 'Since you are assisting my father, what else could I call you?'

'There is William, Willie, Bill – even "Billy" if you like; or perhaps the nickname you have concocted for me.'

' "Celia Amelia"?' Anne blurted it out inadvertently.

'Why did you name me that?'

'It wasn't I,' Anne protested. 'It was Charlotte.'

'What does it mean?' the Reverend insisted.

'It is Italian. It means ... I think...' She struggled to continue. 'It is so difficult to translate from one language to another. Especially when I do not speak Italian.'

'Try.'

Anne took a deep breath; but she could not look him in the eye. 'Well ... "Celia", I believe means a sort of joke one plays on another. An Italian joke, I suppose.'

'And "Amelia"?'

'I believe it just rhymes with "Celia", although...'

'Yes?' The curate was determined to ferret it out.

'It would seem to me that "Amelia" means "loved one".'

He was pleased; a blush coloured his features. 'Why do you think your sister named me that?'

Anne continued to stare at the glowing embers. 'The "Celia" because you made us happy. You brought laughter into the parsonage.'

'And the "Amelia"?'

Again Anne struggled to find the words. 'I believe it is because...' But she was unable to continue. 'You will have to ask my sister, sir.'

' "Sir"?'

'William,' she replied finally.

'That is better,' he smiled. 'And I shall ask your sister when she returns from Brussels.'

Anne gazed back into his eyes. They stood transfixed a moment until she felt compelled to break the silence. 'At what hour should we expect Branwell in the morning?'

'Shortly after breakfast, I presume. I shall see that he eats a proper meal before sending him on his way.'

'I am so grateful to you for bringing him to us.'

They stood a moment in anxious silence. 'Is it to be "Good night" then?' he said sadly, not wanting to leave the pleasure of her presence and the warmth of the kitchen.

'I fear it must. Mrs Fitzpatrick will be about until I retire.'

He took her hand and held it longer than necessary. 'Good night, then.'

Anne made no attempt to pull her hand free from his delicious grasp. 'Good night, "Celia Amelia".'

Finally she extracted her fingers and lifted her candle to lead the way out of the cavernous kitchen. 'Anne!' he shouted, still standing by the fire, the ruddy glow from the embers bathing him in an inviting warmth.

She turned back, her flickering candle adding lustre to her questioning eyes. Mr Weightman could contain himself no longer; he blurted it all out in one desperate breath. 'How I've missed sitting next to you at service! Hearing you sing the familiar hymns! Since you left Haworth it is as if an angel's voice has departed your father's choir!'

No doubt William expressed these sentiments better than I!

Anne felt herself caught up in the fever of his frenzy.

'After you came to Haworth to assist father, I looked forward to service all week! I longed for it!'

He moved closer to her so that her candle-light captured both eager faces in one circle of light. 'Dearest Anne, could you ever love me as much as I love you?'

'More, I think.' She breathed the words softly, but they fell like thunder on his eager ears.

He could no longer contain himself. 'To hear this from your lips; from lips I must kiss this very instant, or die from hunger.'

'I will not have you die.' She set down the candle so that this man she loved could engulf her in his arms.

How sweet his kisses! How eager her response! I can well imagine.

They could not savour enough of each other: propriety made them stop.

William was the first to speak. 'The moment I return to Haworth, I will ask your father for your hand.'

'No! You must not!' Anne looked beseechingly into his delirious eyes.

'If I am to have your hand in marriage...'

'I want to be your bride more than anything else on this earth, William!' Anne professed. 'But father ... after losing my two oldest sisters and then mother... He wants so desperately to hold on to us. He senses our attraction for each other. That is why he was only too happy for me to accept this position at Thorp Green.'

'But...'

'No, William, you must not say a word until I am home and Charlotte has returned from Brussels to pacify him. Only she has a way with him that...'

'But I cannot wait so long; not after holding you in my arms like this.' Again he pulled her to him.

Anne kissed him once more before speaking. 'If you ask father now, he will simply dismiss you. We must wait:

meanwhile you must make yourself as indispensable to him as possible.'

Weightman accepted this plan with alacrity. 'He will not be able to breathe without me!'

'Nor I!'

He would kiss her again, but she retrieved her candle and led him out of the kitchen and to the grand entrance where she watched from the doorway as his lantern made a path through the cold darkness. 'I shall write faithfully!' Anne called after him.

'As will I!' he called back.

'It was I who named you "Amelia",' she whispered loudly; but I am not sure he heard.

Soon his light was not even visible. The road twisting away from Thorp Green suddenly veered into the woods so that all was darkness once again; still, a pen can capture what was once a bright moment in what is to be such a sad history.

I now leave this attempt at literary fancy and once again resume a description of the facts as I actually witnessed them; but in many ways it is more pleasurable simply to imagine. It was my cherished Wordsworth who said, 'We poets begin in gladness and end in madness.' And I am indeed a poet, if not of his greatness, and perhaps a little mad.

I feigned sleep when William carried a candle into our room at the tavern. He stood a long moment at the window, staring into the direction of Thorp Green and his beloved Anne. I had undressed myself and was in my nightshirt but had been unable to sleep. Soon he poured cold water from the pitcher into the basin and stripped off his clothing so that he could refresh himself. I had never observed a man totally naked before – not even my own father – for I never attended a boys' school, as did others of my ilk. However, there is one exception that I will soon confide to this journal.

I marvelled at the sight of the man's healthy, sturdy body. I had always been dangerously thin; my pale skin pressed too tightly against my bones. When he reached his hands into the air to pull his nightshirt over his head I delighted in this feeling of intimacy; to see this kindly and good man standing before me as naked and exposed as the day he was born.

When William extinguished the candle and crawled into the bed beside me I listened to his breathing, content to lie in his presence, smelling his manliness; but finally, I could not resist speaking. 'Did you see Anne?'

'So you are awake,' he stated. I suspected that he knew all along that I was.

'Were they understanding?' 'They' were still the fearful unknown to me: my employers who had hired me at my sister's recommendation.

'I only saw Anne and the housekeeper. They expect you on the morrow.'

'To-morrow,' I sighed. 'I wish it would never come. Could not we just lie here forever?'

'Anne is well,' he said, ignoring my plea, 'but she is lonely for family and is looking forward to your presence.'

'At least I will have one ally in this new endeavour.'

'No-one else besides your sister?'

'Who?' I turned my head to face him in the dark.

'I was thinking of God.'

'Oh yes, God,' I whispered. 'He has never been the comfort to me that he is to you; or my father.'

It is always difficult for me to ascertain where God leaves off and my father begins. God is my father and my father is God. I am never totally comfortable with either. 'Sometimes I think we should have been born Catholic,' I responded finally. 'Then I could simply confess to a priest and everything would be all right again.'

'Perhaps you would like to confess to me.'

'If only I had the nerve...' But I quickly changed the

subject. 'Did you and my sister come to any sort of ... understanding?'

'Understanding?'

' "Celia Amelia".'

William paused a moment, considering how much he should reveal. 'Your sister has sworn me to secrecy: at least as far as your father is concerned.'

'I am not my father.'

'But he loves you the most of all.'

'Too much,' I sighed. 'He has put all his hopes into his only son. It is his daughters who are more deserving.'

'Your sister and I are betrothed. One day soon you and I will be brothers-in-law!'

I was so happy for the news I turned in bed and drew the Reverend to me and enveloped him in my arms. 'Bill, it is the best news I have ever had!' Only I called him Bill, and he appeared to relish it.

He permitted me to hold him a moment before pulling free. 'You must not say a word to anybody. Anne fears your father will dismiss me if he finds out.'

'He will not give her away easily,' I concurred.

'Anne feels that when Charlotte returns from Brussels she will be able to persuade him.'

'She has a way with him: there is no doubt about that.'

'This is the happiest night of my life!' he sighed contentedly.

'You love her so much, then?'

'More than I can convey.'

'I think we all love you, Bill; each in our own way.'

He accepted this in silence. We breathed together until he finally spoke. 'And what if I were a Catholic priest? What would you confess to me, Branwell?'

'Something that I fear would disgust even you.'

He hesitated a moment before speaking. 'You are my friend, Branwell; my future brother-in-law. Whatever you have done I will always understand.'

I wanted to speak; to unburden my soul: but I was afraid that he would not understand, but be repulsed: still, he persisted. 'Does this concern what happened to you on your trip to London?'

I was surprised. 'How have you ascertained that?'

'Because you have never spoken of it.'

I no longer looked at him but faced the darkness of the ceiling. 'Maybe because we are in the dark together; because you cannot see my face: perhaps I could tell you what I have never told a living soul.'

He waited in silence for me to continue. Finally I drew a breath and spoke.

I shall set down on these pages everything that I revealed to him that evening. It will be exactly as I confessed it; under the cover of that darkness, rather than now, in the pale glow of candle-light.

In Which I Make a Startling Confession

'I have always been afraid of London,' I whispered to him in the silence of our room. 'A visit to neighbouring Bradford is more than enough city for me. Our little world of Haworth is the only world I have ever wanted, with my father and sisters to love and shelter me, even though I continually disappoint them.'

'I think you are too hard with yourself,' William replied kindly. I wanted to embrace him once more, but resisted. I was determined to succeed.

'Be that as it may,' I continued, 'when my painting teacher, William Robinson, plied me with letters of introduction and strongly suggested that I depart for London to study at the Royal Academy, and my late Aunt Branwell provided me with the money, how could I refuse? All my family's hopes were centred on their dream of the only son becoming a celebrated portrait painter: their own Sir Thomas Lawrence – though I scarcely possess his talent.'

'But I have seen examples of your work, Branwell,' he interjected. 'Your portrait of your sisters, for instance. You most certainly are gifted.'

'There is *gifted* and there is *blessed*,' I replied. He was referring to what was possibly my best work because it was painted with such love for Charlotte, Emily and Anne. I turned my head on the pillow towards him. 'And do you know why I painted myself out of this portrait?'

'I've often wondered,' he replied, facing me as well.

'I could not capture myself properly because I have no idea who I really am. My sisters are as clear and pure as spring water; whereas I am always murky. When I look in the mirror I do not comprehend what I see there.

He touched me in a way that reassured me and allowed me to continue.

'You have observed how the thought of Thorp Green has affected me. Can you imagine my condition on the coach to London, a city that frightened me as much as the thought of everlasting Hell? The farther we drew away from Haworth, the more apprehensive and the sicker I became. I felt that if I did not leave the coach in Holborn, and have a whisky to bolster my courage, my heart would beat beyond my chest.'

'There was an inn?' he questioned.

'It is run by the celebrated pugilist, Tom Spring, who was only too happy to provide a room and spirits so that for a week I enjoyed his rough companions and squandered my money with plans to depart for London on each morrow; although it was usually late afternoon before I rose, in desperate need of another round of spirits.'

'You never proceeded further?'

'At the end of the week, during the busiest night in the inn, a ravishing young gipsy girl came to dance for the customers. I was reminded of Esmeralda in *The Hunchback of Notre Dame*. She had flashing eyes and dark curls that cascaded from her head like Medusa's serpents. She appeared to dance only for me. A young man, as darkly handsome as she, played the violin to which she danced: the melody haunts me still. I think I loved them both. He smiled at me with his dark eyes in a way that made me want to follow.'

'Did you – follow the gipsy?' William questioned; for I had ceased my story, unsure whether to proceed.

'After she had finished her dance and saw that there was more money in my pocket than I had dropped into her tambourine, she sent the young man to entice me to accompany them to their camp. He spoke in a lilting Romanian accent, and promised me that a fortune-teller there would tell me wonderful things that he was certain were in store for me; and when he held my hand to study my palm, there was fire in his touch as he foretold that I was already on a great journey.'

I could once again envisage their swarthy, hypnotic faces as I described them to William. My heart actually beats faster in memory of them. 'I accompanied them outside the inn and he played his violin and she danced before me under the moonlight. The music was stronger than the siren call that sought to seduce Ulysses. There was no turning back. Perhaps if I had been sober I could have resisted; but I had been drowning in spirits for almost a week. I had no control of my senses.

'Soon there was a fire and gipsy wagons and an old gnarled woman who had a clouded crystal ball in which she said she saw me surrounded by three women who would achieve great and lasting fame. When I questioned her about myself she said that I was obscured by clouds; that she could not yet see me clearly; but still she was sure that one day my destiny would be achieved.

'Then there was laughter and more dancing and a sweet

drink that was passed around and the beautiful gipsy led me into her wagon and undressed me. I had never been with a woman before; but it was something I had dreamed about for longer than I care to confess. The smell of her strong perfume was overpowering. When she shed her skirts and blouse and stood before me so proudly in her nakedness, more beautiful than any Renaissance painting, I was ready for her. It made no matter what I had been drinking; I had waited too long for a moment such as this to let any spirits despoil it.'

William's breathing increased noticeably. Certainly he had never heard such a story before: nor have these pages.

'Such acts as we performed together I had scarcely ever imagined. I was too exhilarated to be ashamed. Somehow, I must have fallen asleep; for when I awakened, the young man was lying naked beside me and the girl had gone. In his own way he was as beautiful as she. His skin was the colour of mahogany in the lantern light and there were dark places about his body that drew me to him. He kissed me about my neck and when he came to my mouth I could not resist him. He possessed me as she had possessed me. I felt no disgust at what we were doing, my lust and desire for him were as overwhelming as they had been for her.'

I looked at William, scarcely visible in the dark beside me. 'Have I disgusted you? Should I not continue?'

And I wonder now if I should continue here; if I should cease confessing to these pages. If someone should ever see...

'You must not stop now,' he responded finally.

I turned away from him and spoke once again to the ceiling. 'The next morning,' I concluded, 'I awakened to find myself naked and abandoned along the side of the road. My money, my clothing, my letters of introduction had all been stolen. The gipsies had broken camp and I was left to walk naked in the woods and bang pitifully at the door of the inn where my remaining clothes were thrown down to me. I had not a cent left to my name. I walked all the way home to Haworth, going days without a thing to eat as penance for my transgressions.'

I waited for some response; for some sort of reply. Finally, Mr Weightman spoke. 'It is forbidden for us to entertain necromancy and superstition; but perhaps you should believe what the gipsy fortune-teller told you.'

'And what was that?'

'That one day your destiny will be achieved.'

'And what is my destiny, Bill?'

'Whatever it is, it lies in the future, Branwell. Sometimes we have to forget the past, or it will destroy us.'

'Would you hold me in your arms and shut out the world just for to-night? Perhaps some of your strength will pass through to me.'

He turned and held me tightly, the warmth of his masculinity as comforting to me as a blanket must be to a baby. I closed my eyes with my head upon his shoulder and now was not afraid to sleep.

In the early morning, when I awakened, the curate had already dressed. I waved good-bye to him sadly as the coach conveyed him back to Haworth. Then I faced the long walk to Thorp Green, beads of perspiration starting on my forehead, even though it was bitterly cold.

If this were indeed a novel and not simply a recollection of the most recent events in my life, I would say that this is where the story truly begins, when I am about to meet the woman who would irrevocably change my life.

Perhaps, one day, when I have a better hold over my emotions and a greater distance from the events described, I will revisit these journal entries and make them the stuff of good fiction. No doubt, my story will begin here.

The Story Truly Begins

The road to Thorp Green is long and sinuous. On this day in January, the weather was cold and grey. I delayed my departure from the inn as long as possible and did not set eyes upon my new abode until well after lunch. Perhaps I should have summoned a carriage from Thorp Green; but that would have heralded an arrival of importance, not that of a servant – which essentially I was to be. Instead, I left my sister Emily's valise in the ostler's care for fetching later.

I passed through a wood and did not actually glimpse the imposing edifice until the road opened onto a clearing. Thorp Green was a small baronial castle that had been in the Thornton family for generations. A gentleman's manor house, it was not a nobleman's seat, although it bore a castellated roof, which battlements gave it a formidable aspect, with three storeys of blackened bricks, two turrets and, at either side, additional wings that I learned had been added by more recent generations, the whole surrounded by sloping green lawns. It was a large estate with woods and farms, its own dairy and brew-house and stabling for fourteen horses. It seemed cold and overpowering as I trembled in front of the large door, wanting desperately to return to Haworth but forcing myself to pull the bell and await my fate.

The butler, who opened the door, was tall and elderly and regarded me with suspicion. 'Is it Mr Brontë, finally?' he demanded, looking down at me. 'Young master was impatient to meet you.' The voice was rich with age but the pronunciation was clipped and there was nothing of Yorkshire in his speech or manner.

'It is not a short distance from the inn,' I offered as feeble explanation.

'The Master does not like to send the horses out during

the winter unless it is absolutely necessary,' he offered as explanation. 'Miss Brontë was hoping that you would be joining her for lunch.'

'I fear I was long on the road.'

The butler had not yet invited me into the house. I longed for the warmth of an inviting fire and a chance to sit down and rest my weary legs. 'The family have departed for the christening of the first grandson of Mr Thornton's most prosperous tenant. They are at church.'

'And how far away is church?' I questioned, for I had passed none during my long morning's journey.

'Some distance beyond,' he said, pointing vaguely. 'Indeed Thorp Green is much more than merely this estate. Thorp means "village" and "farm" and Mr Thornton is master of them all. For generations the Thorntons have been masters here and my father served the Thorntons before me. I am Berwick,' he said, not offering his hand.

I hoped that I appeared impressed, but, in truth, I was blue with cold and my nose would not stop running.

'You may come inside now,' he relented. 'Perhaps cook has saved something for you. I will tell Mrs Fitzpatrick that you have arrived.' He turned to give me one last look. 'I see little resemblance to your sister; other than your lack of height.' For, in truth, only Emily had achieved the stature of my father.

I was ushered into the large entrance hall, two storeys high, whence there arose an oppressively grand mahogany staircase hung with portraits of former generations of Thorntons. This was a palace compared to our cramped quarters at the Haworth Parsonage; yet how I longed for the latter!

Berwick turned me over to Mrs Fitzpatrick, who hustled me into the kitchen, her grey skirt swaying from side to side along the floor as we hurried through one large room after the other and down a circular staircase to the basement kitchen where the inviting aroma of baking bread beckoned to me.

Frieda, the middle-aged Viennese cook, was a testament to her cuisine. She was as round as a pumpkin and proud of her prowess at the stove; at her happiest when someone was eating. 'He needs to be fattened up, just like his sister,' she observed in her pronounced Austrian accent, as she eyed the travelling clothes that hung too loosely on my thin body. She placed a steaming meat pie beneath my nose and commanded me to partake immediately, although I needed no encouragement; for, after my stomach upset of the day previous, I was beginning to feel hungry.

Mrs Fitzpatrick had summoned my sister. Her soft curls bounced as she hurried towards me across the kitchen floor. Her delicate mouth was opened in a smile and there was a flush upon her cheeks I had seldom seen. I supposed the Reverend Mr Weightman's proposal had much to do with it. 'I approve wholeheartedly,' I whispered in her ear, as we fell into each other's arms. Anne pulled back and put her finger to her lips to indicate that nothing more must be uttered. I nodded and pulled out a chair for her at the kitchen table so that she could badger me with questions of Emily and father and share her most recent letter from Charlotte in Brussels.

Soon, after a dessert of Viennese pastry, of which Frieda was justly proud, Anne showed me to my chamber. We ascended a back stairway to the second floor where, in a special niche of the original structure, the servants' rooms were situated. In comparison to my room at the parsonage the chamber was spacious and afforded me a view of the rear of Thorp Green, a mossy green patchwork descending to the stone stable and carriage house. 'What a grand edifice!' I exclaimed.

'A grand house does not a grand family make,' Anne replied somewhat sadly, 'though our own seems scarce the same with the passing of Aunt Branwell, the loss of Tabitha, and Charlotte so long in Brussels.'

'I think it is more than her interest in foreign language that keeps her there,' I replied forthrightly.

'So Emily has hinted.' Her gentle features suddenly tightened at the mention of it. 'I refuse even to consider such speculation,' she added; 'for the Belgian Professor is a married man.'

I did not want to distress my sister, and so quickly changed the subject. 'How envious Emily and Charlotte will be of your news; for they, too, were enamoured of your Mr Weightman. I am that fond of him myself.'

'Not a word, Branwell; you promise. Charlotte must be the next to know – but not until she returns.'

'To think the youngest would be the first to marry!' I marvelled.

'Charlotte's interests are now elsewhere; but I do hope that Emily is not too distressed, for she takes things more seriously than the rest of us.'

'Emily will be delighted for you.'

'Not a word, Branny,' my sister repeated. 'Especially not to the Thorntons. My two young charges would never let me hear the end of it.'

'Are they that difficult then?'

'You shall see soon enough,' she responded glumly. 'Since the death of the baby daughter, Georgiana Jane, a heavy sorrow has hung over this house. We are no longer in mourning; but the Mistress continues to wear black and still visits the family plot daily to place fresh flowers on the grave.'

'Is this house so troubled then? You said little of this before.'

She chose not to elaborate. 'We shall all be at dinner tonight and you shall soon see for yourself.' She pulled the curtains across my window and moved to the door. 'Now you must rest, Branwell, for I see this journey has taken its toll on you.' She held me once more in her arms. 'How glad I am that you have come! I no longer feel abandoned.'

'Perhaps you will name the first boy Branwell after his uncle,' I slyly suggested.

Anne blushed, a rosier colour warming her cheeks, but she put her finger to her lips once more. 'I shall have Berwick send for your valise.'

In Which I Introduce the Heroine

My hands actually shake as I approach this portion of my journal, for I am about to describe my first encounter with the lady, who, as Byron said of his love, '...walked in beauty, like the night'.

I am trembling in my morning bed as outside the autumn wind hurls leaves against my window. Is it the thought of the woman I am about to describe, or the fact that last night I drank entirely too much in the back room at the Black Bull Inn and crave another whisky now rather than the tea that Emily is bringing me? I am positive it is the former, for I feel the same about this extraordinary woman now as I did then.

My case soon arrived and I unpacked my clothing and the lesson books I had chosen for this new venture. I meant to retire for only a moment, but it was already dark when I was summoned by my sister to descend to dinner. Anne helped me slip into my tan waist-coat and matching jacket and made a bow of my black satin cravat beneath my high white collar – a service she had performed since we were children. I glanced in the mirror over the dresser to smooth down the reddish hair that fell in curls about my forehead and to pull at the whiskers that helped to camouflage the narrowness of my face. Except for Emily, we Brontës are not tall enough to be imposing. I will never be a Lord Byron, neither in figure nor poetry. I am not considered handsome, although there is a ruddy colour to my complexion, a blueness to my eyes, and, while my lips are not full, they possess a natural redness; how much this is due to drink, I do not know. At least the few kisses I have bestowed in life have not been rejected.

Anne led the way downstairs. Soon we were in the cavernous dining-room where the Thorntons were already seated. A long rosewood dining-table was flanked by matching, high-backed chairs: sideboards and tall-boys hugged the walls. Dark paintings depicting the hunting of the fox hovered above us. My sister was quick to introduce me: each member of the family eyed me curiously. 'Well, well,' Mr Thornton announced in a booming voice, more interested in the carving of a leg of lamb than in my appearance. 'The tutor finally cometh.'

I had been informed previously by my sister, that, unlike my saintly father, this was a 'Reverend' in name only; one who never deigned to visit his parish, nor ever conducted a service.

'It is a long walk from the inn,' I offered: 'but I am sorry if my tardiness inconvenienced you.'

'Not at all,' Mrs Thornton replied sweetly. 'We had no plans for lessons to-day for we had a christening to attend.' She smiled such a sad little smile and regarded me with such interest and curiosity that I fear my cheeks burned as red as my hair under her careful scrutiny.

Mrs Thornton required neither rouge nor padding to add to her charms. She was a winter maiden with skin as white as snow and hair as dark as midnight and eyes as blue as spring iris. Her nose was straight and narrow and her mouth a lovely rosebud. Her jetty hair, parted in the centre, fell over each ear and was fastened by a sprig of faux flowers. Delicate white shoulders were bare and the cut of her black evening dress was low enough to render me self-conscious whenever I gazed on her.

How strange that I can still remember every frock she

wore in my presence. Is it my artist's eye that memorizes every detail? I know now, in Mrs Thornton's case, it was more.

Mr Thornton was dark of eye and complexion, with brooding, angry, handsome features: his height and naturally imposing stature were qualities of which he was very proud.

Young Master Edmund, a lanky, sensitive-looking lad of almost sixteen, was courteous enough to rise to his feet, to bow to me slightly and to offer his hand in introduction. The boy was a perfect physical combination of his disparate parents. He was as dark and soon would be as tall as the father; yet his eyes were as blue as his mother's and his features almost as delicate. 'I look forward to our lessons together,' he replied in a soft voice, sitting timidly back down in his place.

'Tell Mr Brontë why we need his services here at all,' Mr Thornton demanded gruffly of his son.

The young man hesitated. 'I was sent down from Harrow,' he responded finally.

'You were sent *for*, darling,' his mother corrected.

'I was ill,' the boy offered as explanation.

'Bloody homesick!' the father volunteered. I was shocked that he should speak so in the presence of the ladies.

'I could not eat; I could not sleep,' Edmund offered as further explanation.

'Bloody homesick for his mother!' his father reiterated.

Mrs Thornton spoke softly, almost as if she did not want to say the words at all. 'When we lost … after the loss of our baby girl, I needed Edmund here with me.'

'I was so desperately unhappy at school,' Edmund added so softly that I could barely hear.

'Nobody is supposed to be happy at school!' his father roared. 'Hated it myself when I was your age; but I bloody well stuck it out, even though I had no interest whatsoever in the study of divinity!' He fixed his dark gaze upon me.

'Now, against my better judgement, young master is to be instructed here, at home.'

'There is something to be said for private instruction,' I replied, taken aback again by his use of profanity in front of his family. 'I learned at home at my father's knee and hope that I am none the worse for it.'

'And where did your father matriculate?'

'Cambridge, sir.'

'We are Oxford here; but there's something to be said for Cambridge.'

'Our father served as a tutor himself while he attended that university,' observed my sister, proud of our father's achievement, 'for he held a sizarship.'

Mr Thornton looked from Brontë sister to brother. 'Your recommendation stems mostly from your sister,' he said, as if this was no recommendation at all.

'With whom we are well pleased,' his wife was prompt to add.

'Except I am too old to have a governess now,' complained young Lydia Thornton, who, though christened after her mother, was called by her middle name of Alice to avoid confusion. She was as beautiful as her mother, but with straight blonde hair that fell down her back and was tied with a bright blue ribbon. 'I am just eighteen.'

'We will tell you when you are too old to have a governess,' her mother responded with a sympathetic glance at Anne, who was forced daily to contend with her daughter's constant rebellion.

'And we will not have what happened to Elizabeth happen to you!' the father snorted, broaching a subject that was obviously disturbing to his wife.

I knew better than to question the whereabouts of the missing Elizabeth. Only later, in private conversation with my sister, did I learn that Elizabeth Thornton, who was a year younger than Alice, had fallen deliriously in love with an impecunious Mr Milner and had written him compromising letters, even though Mr Thornton refused to allow her to marry the young man. Mr Milner threatened to publish Elizabeth's letters in the York Press and sue her for breach of promise. It had cost over £150 to silence the conniving young man. Young Elizabeth, who, my sister declared, did not possess the beauty of her mother or her eldest sister, was shipped off to a convent school for young ladies in Paris. Since the Thorntons were decidedly Protestant, this was severe punishment indeed to consign the young lady to the influence of 'devious' Roman Catholic sisters.

Mr Thornton, unhappy with cutting the mutton, dropped the carving knife loudly onto the serving plate. Berwick, formidable in his evening uniform, stepped forward. 'Is there something amiss, sir?'

Mr Thornton looked at his wife as if it were her fault rather than the cook's. 'It is quite over-done. Can you not see that all the goodness is roasted out of it? Can you not see that all the nice red gravy is completely dried away? Is this the Austrian way to destroy a fine side of lamb?'

Mrs Thornton seemed less perturbed than I would have imagined; which led me to believe that her husband's dissatisfaction with the food was a common occurrence in the household. 'Perhaps you would prefer the beef, Mr Thornton? It is left over from last evening.'

How fortunate that they had a choice! One denied to the family of an impecunious clergyman such as my father.

Mr Thornton turned his attention to his fourteen-year-old daughter. 'When did we slaughter this sheep, Mary?'

'Why, just this week, papa. You should have seen it, mother. The blood spurted everywhere.'

Mrs Thornton's pale skin grew even whiter. 'Really, Mary, how can you talk about such things at table?'

'It was a sight to behold!' she insisted.

'I am sure we do not need to discuss this at the dinner

table, Mary,' her mother reprimanded before turning again to regard her husband. 'Now, would you prefer the beef, Mr Thornton?'

'Of course I would prefer the beef!'

The beautiful other daughter screwed up her features in a look of disgust. 'Who would not? After what Mary just told us.'

'You hold your tongue, young lady!' her father snarled back; then glanced severely at my sister. 'Sometimes I wonder what I am paying you for, Miss Brontë.'

'Berwick, would you kindly bring us the beef?' Mrs Thornton interjected quickly.

'And it had better be rare!' Mr Thornton admonished as Berwick departed for the kitchen.

I had expected my sister to bear her employer's reprimand in silence, and was surprised when she spoke up. 'Perhaps if I were given more authority to discipline the children, sir.'

'Children?' young Alice protested. 'Well, I like that!'

'Enough out of you, young lady!' Mr Thornton retorted before directing his ire at Anne. 'And as far as authority goes, I will not have you usurping what is the right of myself and Mrs Thornton.'

'But you know I am not successful with it,' his wife protested. 'I fear I love my children far too much for their own good.'

'Edmund, you mean,' the youngest daughter spoke with a vehemence.

'That is not fair, Mary,' her mother replied, a tinge of colour warming her cheeks so that she appeared roseate in the flickering candle-light.

To my surprise, Mr Thornton appeared to take his daughter's side; he fastened his fierce eyes upon me. 'This is what we have engaged you for, Mr Brontë: to make a man of this son of mine who still hides behind his mother's skirts.'

'I shall make young Edmund as much a man as I,' I

responded unconvincingly. Indeed, I am no more sure of my own manhood now than I was as a young lad.

'I hope that is enough.' It was the Master's last word on the subject, for he was hungry. 'Now where is my beef?!' he called out, so loudly that, even though the kitchen was a floor beneath, I am certain he was heard.

Soon Berwick appeared carrying a silver serving tray brimming with cold slices of beef. Cook, in white apron, bustled after. 'I must protest that the lamb was cooked to madam's instructions.'

Mrs Thornton came to her own defence, her cheeks growing as pink as her husband liked his mutton. 'I thought if, just once, Mr Thornton, we could have our dinner without blood running about the plate! Certainly Miss Brontë does not like her meat uncooked in this fashion. I assumed her brother would feel likewise.'

'You assumed correctly,' I corroborated; for indeed, like all good Englishmen, I preferred my mutton well-done.

'Berwick, will serve you the beef and then can we have done with it?' Mrs Thornton pleaded a trifle impatiently, nodding at Berwick to proceed.

Berwick set a small piece of beef onto a fresh plate for Mr Thornton, who angrily shoved it aside. 'What is the matter with the beef, Mr Thornton?' his wife questioned perplexed. 'I'm sure I thought it was very nice.'

'And so it was very nice; a nicer joint could not be!' He snorted, gathering momentum. 'But now it is quite spoiled!'

'How so?' Mrs Thornton asked, examining the beef herself. It certainly appeared fine to me.

'How so?!' her husband thundered back. 'Why, don't you see how it is cut? Dear, dear,' he shook his head quite vehemently. 'It is quite shocking.'

'Then cook must have cut it wrongly in the kitchen,' she defended, 'for I saw you carve it quite properly at supper yesterday.'

'There is no doubt that cook cut it wrong in the kitchen!'

'But, sir!' cook protested, her chef's hat bobbing from side to side as her head shook angrily. 'I did not think that you would desire more beef this evening. I was preparing it for the shepherd's pie.'

Mr Thornton would not be appeased. 'Did you ever see such a fine piece of beef so completely ruined?' He turned to glare up at the perturbed cook. 'Henceforward, when a decent dish leaves this table, you shall not touch it until I give specific permission. Is that understood?'

The cook's head bobbed up and down. 'Yes, sir.'

'What shall you eat then?' Mrs Thornton ventured timidly.

Her husband reluctantly served himself more beef; making such a face, one would have thought he was dropping offal onto his plate. 'We shall simply have to make do.'

He began to chew his meat and to stuff his mouth with potato and green vegetable as well. The rest of us contented ourselves with munching on the delicious mutton which cook now sliced at the sideboard and Berwick heaped onto our plates.

'And what will we be having for supper to-morrow?' Mr Thornton demanded of the cook whose round figure was scurrying in retreat towards the door.

'Madam has not yet specified,' she replied, turning in the doorway and shouting so that she could be heard.

Mr Thornton turned to address his wife. 'And what will we be having for dinner to-morrow?'

'I ... perhaps some fish, but...'

'What kind of fish?' he wanted to know immediately.

'I do not know.'

'You don't know?!'

'When I ask cook to procure some fish, I do not particularise what kind.'

'A lady professes to keep house, and doesn't even know what kind of fish is for dinner,' her husband thundered.

'Tells cook to purchase fish and does not specify what kind!'

Mrs Thornton could tolerate no more abuse. She rose indignantly to her feet, her eyes filling with tears. I wanted nothing more than to comfort her in her humiliation and embarrassment. 'Perhaps, Mr Thornton,' she managed to stammer, 'you will order dinner yourself in the future.'

She hurried from the table. A light died in the dining-room with her departure: I was no longer hungry. Young Master Edmund leapt up to run after his mother, but his father prevented him.

'Sit back down, young man! You've got a grown man to watch over you now. No more hiding behind your mother's skirts.' Then, as young Edmund sank back into his chair, 'Is that not right, Mr Brontë?'

'I will do my best.'

'I shall hope it will not be "like sister like brother".'

My sister again surprised me by responding to this charge. 'Mr Thornton, with regard to your daughter, Mary, for instance, you allow her to traverse this estate with you in men's trousers, to engage in activities that, I dare say, would repulse a tenant farmer, and then chastise me for not raising her to be a proper young lady.'

Now Mary was determined to have her say. 'If becoming a proper young lady means that I am to be like my older sister in any way, I will have little or none of it.'

The older sister made a point of laughing. 'As if you could!'

'I see very few Yorkshire men beating a path to *your* door,' Mary replied.

'I have had more marriage proposals than any other girl in this county.'

'If you mean poor curates and organ players who wish to elevate themselves by grabbing onto father's money.'

The father drowned his glass of claret before interjecting.

'Now, Mary,' he pointed out to his youngest daughter, 'young Lord Leslie has expressed an interest in our Alice.'

'Well, I have not the slightest bit of interest in him,' the oldest daughter responded loudly. 'A duller, more unappetising man I have yet to encounter!'

'You had better commence discovering an interest,' her father replied threateningly, 'for I expect he will be asking me for your hand at the next hunt ball.'

'He shall never have it!'

'He shall have what I say he is going to have!'

Now Alice leapt to her feet. 'Not as long as I have a breath left in my body to say "no". I had rather be an old maid governess like Miss Brontë than...' But she could continue no longer; the thought of the arranged marriage was too daunting: she fled the dining-room.

'Come back here, young lady,' shouted the patriarch, 'or you shall be packed off to France like your disgraceful sister.'

'Do you wish me to retrieve her?' Anne asked, clearly not wishing to do so.

'Finish your mutton.'

'With difficulty,' Anne muttered, under her breath.

Mr Thornton poured another glass of claret. 'How pleasurable it would be to have a wife who knew how to run a household and a governess who knew how to raise children. Instead, I have an eldest daughter who dares to defy her father, a middle one who has disgraced the entire family and must be hidden away in France, a son who chooses to believe he was immaculately conceived... It is only my Mary who knows how to behave like a daughter.' He half-smiled at his youngest girl. 'If only you could have been my son.'

Edmund leapt to his feet in protest: his father would have none of it. 'Sit back down, young man!'

Edmund obeyed immediately. We ate a moment in silence.

Anne and I shared glances across the long table, not unlike the glances we had shared as children across the parsonage table when our father was displeased with one or all of us. Finally, after devouring his meal, Mr Thornton dropped his fork with disgust upon his plate. 'Enough!'

'Cook has prepared a special pastry,' Berwick advised.

'This family has put me off my food!' he grumbled, getting to his feet. 'Mary, what if we were to plan grouse for dinner? Shall we shoot some on the morrow?'

'With pleasure, papa!'

The father drained the last of his claret, got to his feet and stared down at his son. 'You will accompany us.'

The boy whitened with revulsion. 'But...'

'You shall have the first shot.'

'But...'

'You shall have the first shot!' He advanced between his son and daughter. 'Shall we see to our guns?'

The father put his arm around his daughter's shoulder and led her out of the dining-room. 'Come, Edmund!'

The boy shared a dismayed look with me, then followed obediently. Anne and I spoke volumes with our eyes as Berwick stepped to the table. 'Cook will be disappointed if no-one samples her pastry.'

'Very well, Berwick,' my sister acquiesced.

Berwick took his leave of the dining-room. Anne looked across at me and shook her head sadly. 'Welcome to Thorp Green.'

I understood now why she so relished her vacations at home. I was already longing for the security of my father's parsonage myself.

The Journal of Branwell Brontë

29th September, 1845

I have been neglecting you, My Dear Journal, as of late. When I venture outside to clear my mind and the cold wind races across the moors to tousle my hair and pull at my scarf, I suddenly need the ministrations of a hot toddy and find my steps leading to the warmth of the Black Bull Inn. My sisters persist in being disgusted with me; Emily alone occasionally accompanies me on a walk, and I make no mention of my journal. If nothing else, we Brontës are very private people.

How do writers like Charles Dickens or William Thackeray return to their desks each day to continue their sagas even when they may feel no inclination? I ponder this as I sit, warm and comfortable, in my special chair at the Black Bull and force myself to pick up where I have left off, to tell the story of what transpired at Thorp Green and write until the tale is completed. I must not falter or the story will never be told or understood. I begin again.

My Life as a Tutor

I am still astonished how quickly one slips into the established routine of a new household. It was thus when I was tutor at Broughton House in Broughton-in-Furness as well, even though I did not then reside on the premises. Mr Thornton and Mary often enjoyed an early breakfast in the dining-room before setting off on a morning ride about the estate.

Mrs Thornton, Alice and Edmund usually had their breakfast brought to their chambers; while Anne and I ate in the kitchen; this was our special time together during which we would often exchange whispered observations on the Thornton family: for we Brontës are keen observers of the human condition as letters from my sisters always attest.

After breakfast I would sit down with young Master Edmund and conduct our lessons until lunch, a meal from which Mr Thornton was often thankfully absent.

Master Edmund Thornton's chambers were at the south end of Thorp Green, while his sisters resided in the north. His mother had furnished his sitting-room with bookcases and a circular oak table at which I would teach. Edmund had brought all his school-books home from Harrow; and with what I had packed into my valise there was more than enough to fill his hours of study.

Edmund had an aptitude for Greek and Latin, both of which I had learned well from my father. We also delved into French, which he had difficulty in parsing, and worked on ciphers, which he detested. It was the English language he truly relished, especially the novels of Sir Walter Scott, the poetry of Lord Byron and the plays of Mr William Shakespeare.

During the afternoons, Edmund and I would set aside our language study for a foray into Geography and History, two subjects which also pleased him; or I would school him in the art of painting, as I had been schooled by Mr William Robinson of Keighley who had studied under the great Sir Thomas Lawrence in London.

Assuredly, it was these afternoon sessions that young Edmund enjoyed the most, even if he showed little aptitude for painting. It was the relaxed conversations we shared while toiling over our canvasses that he most cherished. This was a young man as desperate for a male companion as I was at his age; for my father was too frequently called away on parish duties.

Late in the afternoon, Anne would take Edmund away for a piano lesson: and in mastering the keyboard, a skill which his father considered frivolous and something only a young lady should acquire, he showed considerable aptitude. In the playing of Mr Chopin's works he especially excelled: in fact bested his sisters in each piece he attempted.

On a spring-like afternoon in mid-March Edmund struggled to conclude his daily translation of the *Gallic Wars*, his pen scratching slowly, his dark hair, parted in the middle, falling to either side of his pensive face. Slowly he put down his pen and looked at me beseechingly with blue eyes that were mirrors to a hungry soul, unhappy that his Latin had extended into the afternoon. 'If Caesar had to fight these boring wars, why couldn't he have fought them in English, especially since he ended up conquering our sceptred isle?

'Why must we learn this boring Latin?' he persisted. 'Nobody speaks it, except the Catholics at their mass. We are certainly not Catholic even if my sister, Elizabeth, is at one of those peculiar convents.'

'A young man destined for Oxford is expected to have knowledge of it.'

'Why must I go there?' There was almost a whine in his voice; yet there was already the hint of a deeper tone to his speech.

'Because your father did, I daresay.'

'I cannot see that it has done him any good. If your father went to Cambridge, then why didn't you go after him?'

'I went to London to study art instead.'

'And did you?'

'I . . . turned back before I arrived.'

'Why?'

'Because I am like you and prefer to be home with my family.'

Indeed, there is some truth to that.

'Yes, I think that we are alike in many ways,' he said, looking at me shyly. 'I would rather be like you than my father any day of the week.'

'Why?'

'Because ... because I think you make people happy. I don't think that father makes anybody happy, except perhaps Mary, his chosen favourite.'

'And whom do I make happy?'

'Your sister, for one. She is very happy to have you here.' He studied me before continuing. 'And my mother.' My heart leapt at the mention of her. I hoped my young charge did not notice my involuntary intake of breath. 'Mrs Thornton?' I questioned in as calm a demeanour as I could muster. 'What has she said to lead you to believe that?'

'That she finds you most agreeable.'

He could only guess at how pleased I was by his statement. 'I am certainly not as agreeable as she.'

'And you make me happy,' he continued: 'even if I don't like Caesar's boring *Wars*.'

'Would you like to forget them for the remainder of the afternoon?'

'May we, please?'

'I think I hate them as much as you,' I admitted; 'though my father never let me desist until a chapter was completed.'

Edmund willingly dropped his pen and moved around the table to put his arms gratefully about me. He squeezed tightly and moved his head so that it was touching mine. 'I think I should love you, Mr Brontë.'

'And I should love you, young man,' I responded with perhaps not quite the same sincerity, pulling gently free of his embrace. 'Now what shall we do for our afternoon session?'

'Anything but Latin,' he volunteered.

'Would you like to write a story?'

'What kind of story?' Edmund responded eagerly.

'Anything of your choosing.'

'Perhaps you could suggest something.'

'My older sister and I used to write stories together.' I smiled in fond memory of it. 'We called it our Glasstown Saga. We created a world in Africa where our heroes and heroines could be anything we wanted. Everything was possible in Glasstown.'

Edmund was immediately charmed by the idea. 'Anything?'

'Edmund, if anything in the world were possible for you, what would it be? What would you choose to write about?'

'I should like to travel.'

'Where?'

'Everywhere. And in my story you shall be my travelling companion. I shall write that father has sent us all over the world so that I can broaden my education. Perhaps I will be captured by pirates and you shall rescue me.'

'Where shall we venture first?' I could see how excited he was by this prospect of creating a world where anything was possible. Perhaps his true talent lay in literature. 'You must decide so that I can illustrate our story as I did for our Glasstown Saga.'

'I think we shall set sail from Plymouth,' he decided. 'We shall share a cabin and be the curiosity of the other passengers because we will not reveal the purpose of our voyage.'

'And what is our purpose?'

'A secret mission instigated by the Queen herself.'

'I see.'

'Immediately an adventure shall befall us,' he continued excitedly.

'You must begin the story,' I advised, 'while I sketch our ship. It will be a large schooner.' I retrieved sketch pad and pen. 'And what shall we call your story?'

He thought a moment before replying excitedly. ' "In the Service of Her Majesty the Queen".'

‘Yes, I like that.’

‘“The Adventures of Branwell and Edmund”.’ He took his place at the table and regarded me hopefully. ‘I have wanted to call you Branwell, Mr Brontë. Is it not all right if I call you Branwell? It makes me feel ever so much closer to you.’

‘When we are alone,’ I smiled, ‘you may call me anything you wish.’

He repeated the title: ‘“In the Service of Her Majesty the Queen: The Adventures of Branwell and Edmund”.’ Soon he began to write. I studied him, and then slowly began to sketch: first the great ship, from illustrations I remembered, and then Edmund and me standing proudly on the prow, the wind sweeping through our hair, side by side, but not of equal height – for the lad was already taller than I – the whiteness of his handsome face in contrast to his dark hair and cloak.

I felt the same bond with Edmund as I had done with my sisters, especially Charlotte, the eldest, when we created together around our parlour table. Although I loved my sisters as much as ever, I feared that Charlotte now loved me less. I had disappointed her most of all in not realising the promise she had held for me; and through the fact that I had often, as I have now again, succumbed to drink, and – yes, I am ashamed to admit – opium. But now young Master Edmund needed me as much as I needed my sisters. I was determined not to disappoint him.

As he wrote and I sketched in silence, Mrs Thornton burst upon our lesson, something which she had never done previously: a vision glided through the doorway; an apparition that brought both of us immediately to our feet. Her gown was still the black of mourning, but it was offset by silver cuffs and a wide silver satin collar that ended in a V below her bodice and was pinned with a cameo portrait of her lost baby daughter. Her raven hair was parted in the middle and fell into perfect ringlets at either side of her head. There appeared to be more colour in her cheek and a spring to her step that I had not hitherto observed. An electricity seemed to fill the chamber: both Edmund and I were newly energised.

'Have I interrupted Homer or Horace or some other such sage?' she questioned, her voice as airy as her appearance.

'Oh, mother,' Edmund beamed proudly, 'I am writing a story.'

She glided around the table where I had been sitting. 'And what are you sketching, Mr Brontë?' She lifted the sketch and examined it carefully.

'It is an illustration for Master Edmund's story.'

'But you have captured him perfectly!' she exclaimed with delight. She continued to study my illustration. 'But this is more of a caricature of yourself, Mr Brontë; for you are far more handsome than this.'

I could only smile in response, delighted with her compliment, but at a loss for words, as I often was in the presence of beauty. She moved to examine other examples of my work that had been stacked against the wall. 'How beautifully you have captured the Monks' House!' she exclaimed, holding up my ink drawing of what was also known as The Old Hall, a small seventeenth-century country house that had once been inhabited by one of the many worker families employed on the estate. 'How very talented you are,' she continued, studying other examples of my work with genuine interest.

'Mr Brontë is a portrait painter,' declared Edmund proudly, as if he himself was responsible for any skill I may have possessed.

'I should like to see his portraits.'

'I fear I have none here to show,' I responded. 'Most are in the possession of those I have painted. Perhaps on a return to Haworth I will fetch one I have done of my sisters.'

'You must,' Mrs Thornton demanded, moving to examine her son's example of burgeoning skill with a brush.

'I am afraid, mother,' Edmund apologised, 'that I have not yet attained any skill.'

She examined his attempts at watercolour, but did not appear dismayed. 'A promising beginning,' she encouraged. 'Even Mr Rembrandt began somewhere. Indeed, I detect a genuine feeling for colour here.'

The boy beamed – as did I – at his mother's approval. 'You must school my daughters as well.' I agreed – and, indeed, I endeavoured to do so; but neither girl evinced much talent with a paint brush. We waited as she set aside his work, wondering what she would require next as proof of our labours.

'I have intruded,' she announced gaily, 'on account of our unseasonal weather. The gardener has shown me the first crocus and I wish to place it on Georgiana Jane's grave. Would you both accompany me?'

'Oh, mother, yes!'

'I shall be honoured,' was my reply. Indeed, I was.

Although the sun was actually shining, it was not warm enough to venture outside without our respective cloaks; shadows were already spreading across Thorp Green like long black fingers still clutching the remnants of winter. Mrs Thornton wore a dark pelisse that framed her face in a manner suggestive of an ivory cameo, like the one of her baby daughter. She took Edmund's willing hand and I stepped to the other side of her; the three of us descending the sloping hill away from the manor house towards the greenhouse that was nestled at the ends of beds of dormant flowers.

Here the dedicated head gardener, Robert Pottage, was waiting with the sole crocus, which he had lifted and placed in a pot at Mrs Thornton's behest, its vibrant violet hue not unlike that of her vivacious eyes.

'Georgiana, at such a young age, already appreciated our flowers. I think she will especially cherish this first crocus.'

The Thornton graveyard was situated not at the Holy Trinity Church of Little Ouseburn, but atop a green knoll that overlooked a small lake fringed by bare oaks and elms. The Thorntons had been buried there for over a century, but the cruel Yorkshire winters had already obliterated many of the names and dates upon the weathered stones. However, the small granite stone dedicated to the youngest Thornton was as fresh as the flower her mother laid gently upon her grave:

Georgiana Jane Thornton
Beloved Daughter
Born July 14, 1838
Died March 15, 1841

Mrs Thornton fell on her knees and prayed silently, her delicate hands clasped together in supplication. Her son also knelt. I stood waiting, not wishing to intrude upon their sorrow.

'You were not with us long enough, my precious little one,' she said, 'but to-day I feel that you are as bright and happy as this flower, that God spared you from all the unhappiness life can bring because he wanted you to be with him in heaven before anyone could hurt you here on earth.'

'Are you that unhappy, mother?' a troubled Edmund questioned, helping her to her feet.

'Not to-day, my darling,' she replied; 'for last night I dreamed of Georgiana. She was with the angels, protecting little girls just like herself.'

'What a wonderful dream, mother!'

Mrs Thornton turned to her son and pulled him to her. 'What day is it to-day, Edmund?'

'It is the first anniversary of Georgiana Jane's death, but I did not want to remind you.'

She appeared pleased by this statement. 'I fear your father and sisters have forgotten; but I knew that you would remember.'

'I had planned to walk down here on my own accord, after our afternoon lesson,' Edmund informed his mother. 'I was going to have Mr Brontë accompany me.'

'And so I have.'

Mrs Thornton smiled at me with her extraordinary eyes, a look of sudden resolve strengthening her features. She glanced down at the dark dress beneath her cloak. 'I have worn nothing but black for over a year now,' she said, more to herself than to either of us. 'If a crocus can bloom in March, I can don the colours of spring as well, even though we are still weeks away from a true verdancy.'

'Oh, mother, to see you once more in your finery!' her son exclaimed excitedly.

'And so you shall.'

The Journal of Branwell Brontë

6th October, 1845

I have neglected you again, Dear Journal. I worked so feverously over my past entries upon your pages that I made myself ill and was compelled to take to my bed with an attack of ague. I was too feverish to continue my history in a coherent and literary manner. Instead, I lay in bed and permitted my sisters, Emily and Anne, to minister to me. My older sister, Charlotte, scarcely ventured into my room. She continues to be dismayed with me over the events that transpired at Thorp Green. Perhaps one day, when she reads my account of those happenings, she will forgive and understand.

Now my health has improved and I have returned to the back room at the Black Bull Inn where I feel not only comfortable but creative. How comfortable I feel writing here in my special chair away from the prying eyes of my family and where fellow customers leave me alone when I am writing and are willing to share a mug of ale with me when I am too weary to continue and wish to be distracted by conviviality.

Where did I leave off?

Perhaps another title in the manner of Mr Dickens will enable me to pick up the thread. Ah, yes, now I remember.

In Which Spring Withholds her Favours

It seemed the sun was only teasing us after all; for very quickly it retreated and refused to break through perpetual clouds and endless rain.

A crackling fire burned constantly in Edmund's study so that we felt safe and secure against the elements: two shipwrecked souls that had come together on the same small island – or so it seemed, not only in Edmund's story, but in reality as well. We delighted in each other's company. The teacher was learning as much as his pupil: each, with only sisters around him, now finding a brother to love. Perhaps we loved each other too much.

A day free from rain seemed like a special gift, even if the wind continued to howl and black clouds crowded together with threats of more precipitation. On such occasions, Mrs Thornton would don her pelisse and seek us out for a walk across the estate, for it was massive and a trip to the village a journey in itself.

Since the anniversary of her baby daughter's death, Mrs Thornton had retained a healthier demeanour. She had discarded black and, with the wearing of colourful clothes, had bloomed like the violet petals of the winter crocus she had placed on her baby's grave. Now it was only Mr Thornton's offensive behaviour that temporarily dampened her spirits.

How I longed to comfort her on such occasions. A sympathetic look was all I could muster – something which she willingly received.

During an early April day, when a storm did not appear imminent, my sister joined us. How this reminded Anne and me of home and made us both long for our Haworth walk beyond the parsonage. Occasionally young Alice would join us as well, but this day she was in low spirits; while Mary was usually scampering off on her own. We spied her as we neared the stables with her gun trained on a helpless spaniel pup, one of a litter sired by one of the hunting dogs of the estate. Mary was dressed in rough clothing and could have been mistaken for a man were it not for her tangle of hair cascading in dark curls about her head. As she was about to pull the trigger, Anne raced to her and shoved the weapon aside so that the ammunition was discharged into the skies. 'How dare you!' Anne demanded angrily, for she had always loved animals and we had had many pets at the parsonage.

'You have wasted my shot!' Mary protested, as surprised as Anne was angry.

'Mary, how could you do such a thing?' her mother demanded as Mary prepared once again to take aim.

'Father has instructed me,' the girl replied. But Anne had run ahead and scooped the young dog into her arms.

'Whatever for?' her mother persisted.

'We have been hunting this morning, mother. The pup is gun shy. The others took to the fray with relish, but this one would do nothing but hide and run away and cover its face.'

'And who can blame him?' Edmund muttered, more to himself, although we all heard.

'Now set her back down, Miss Brontë,' Mary instructed, 'and let me be about my business.'

Anne clutched the spaniel even tighter, the black and white dog shivering uncontrollably, its little tongue seeking her out with eager licks to her chin. 'I will not have you take pleasure in this animal's demise,' my sister declared in a tone of voice that I had never before heard, for in all our family, Anne was the most reticent. 'Not in a million years, Miss Mary.'

'She's gun shy!' Mary insisted. 'Useless and a bad example to the others.'

'Certainly you are not gun shy, Miss Mary!' my sister retorted. 'Nor never will be!' She hugged the grateful pup even closer to her bosom. 'Look at the poor thing, shaking in its boots.'

'She'll soon be out of her misery!' Mary stated.

'You will have to shoot me first!' My sister held her ground.

'Don't think I haven't thought about it!'

'Mary!' her mother exclaimed.

'Mother, make Miss Brontë put her down!'

'I most certainly will not!' her mother retorted.

'She's worthless!' Mary persisted. 'Her brothers and sisters were that eager to retrieve and relished the sound of papa's gun, while this one ran away and cowered inside the barn.'

'And who can blame her?' Now I was voicing an opinion.

It appeared to be four against one, but Mary was not deterred. 'A pup like this is not worth the food she eats. Every animal at Thorp Green must earn its keep. You've heard papa say so yourself.'

Anne continued to assuage the dog's fears with the gentle touch of her precious hand. 'Then this little one shall survive from morsels from my own plate!'

Mary knew that she had been temporarily thwarted. She glared at each one of us then started off. 'I shall see what papa has to say about this.'

She shouldered her gun and stalked off in the direction of the stables. A clap of thunder punctuated her departure. 'I fear that rain will soon be upon us,' Mrs Thornton prophesied, clutching her hood about her fair head. 'I suggest we depart for the manor house.'

Anne allowed the spaniel to snuggle within her arm, smiling down at the puppy as it whimpered, and gently stroking its sleek fur. 'No harm will come to you, my pet. I will see to that. There, there, that's a good little puppy,' she added as the spaniel quieted. 'Such nice soft fur. Just like floss. So silky and fine. I think I must love you already.'

Edmund was next to succumb to the appeal of the spaniel; he began to pet the dog as well. His mother smiled at this demonstration of her son's tenderness, then took my arm, the touch of her gloved hand against my cloak as thrilling as if it were her bare skin against my own. 'If we don't depart now we shall soon be drenched.'

No sooner had we begun our ascent to Thorp Green Manor than Mary, still clutching her shot-gun, came running after. 'Papa is coming,' she threatened. 'He will see to this.'

Anne whirled around and clutched the puppy close to her. I had never seen her so determined: a ferocious mother protecting her baby. The auburn hair that poked beneath the white lace fringe of her black bonnet was buffeted by the wind. Her dark cloak was blown about her and she looked as formidable as Lady Macbeth. 'Not one hair will Mr Thornton touch of this pup.'

'We'll see about that,' Mary retorted.

The Reverend Francis Thornton was upon us. He, too, carried his fowling-piece; one of many in his collection of gleaming guns. He was wearing his brown tweed hunting jacket with matching breeches, an Irish cap stuffed in his coat pocket and tan riding boots – his customary uniform. 'I am sorry, Miss Brontë,' he thundered, 'that you think it is necessary to interfere with Miss Mary's amusements.' His dark eyes were flashing, his dusky hair blowing about his large head, as dramatic as the weather.

Anne did not cower, so firm was she in her determination to save the cowering pup. 'When Miss Mary's amusement consists of injuring a helpless creature, I will always find it necessary to interfere.'

Mr Thornton eyed the shivering puppy. 'Why should you concern yourself with the life of this worthless creature?'

'Among other reasons, because a young lady should not be encouraged to develop such pernicious habits.'

'I am afraid I must concur with Miss Brontë, Mr Thornton,' his wife interjected.

Mr Thornton ignored her. 'A puppy, Miss Brontë, must earn its way at Thorp Green – as must you yourself.'

'And so Flossy shall,' Anne triumphed.

'You have already named her?' This from an astonished Mary.

'And how shall Flossy make her way at Thorp Green?' Mr Thornton demanded, somewhat taken aback by my sister's determination.

Anne did not need a moment to think before launching into a declaration of all the uses Flossy would be to her: 'First she will provide me with companionship during the hours when I am not actively involved in the monumental task of providing education and guidance for two young ladies who have not the slightest interest in either. Flossy will also accompany me and be a protection to Miss Alice and myself during our walks to and from the church and the village. Your eldest daughter has blossomed into quite a fetching lady, Mr Thornton; such beauty has not passed unnoticed by the young men of the village, nor by our new young curate.'

I marvelled at Anne's quick reasoning and stubborn defiance in the face of the lord of the manor. I had never realised before how overshadowed young Anne had been by her older sisters, especially Charlotte, who was determined to dominate one and all and to whom Anne always submitted. Perhaps it was her secret engagement that was giving her courage.

'Miss Alice will be seen in the company of young Lord Broughton and none other!' Mr Thornton exclaimed at mention of the penurious curate.

Anne smiled down at the dog that eagerly licked her protective hand.

'I will instruct Flossy in such particulars.'

I loved my younger sister in that moment more than I ever had previously. I wanted to sweep her into my arms and kiss her proudly on the brow; decorum prohibited.

'And what will this puppy of yours eat?'

'Portions of food are so generous at Thorp Green, sir, that often I must leave almost a full plate behind me at the table, for, in truth, we eat much less at my father's parsonage.'

'I will not have that worthless pup at my table.' He was adamant, his voice as loud as the thunder that threatened us overhead.

'Then I shall absent myself from table and eat with cook and the other servants in the kitchen.'

No doubt Anne relished the opportunity to do so.

'And so you shall,' the master agreed with alacrity. 'And you can take your brother into the blasted kitchen with you.'

'Francis!' Mrs Thornton exclaimed involuntarily, her hand flying to her mouth, her eyes seeking me out. I hoped this meant that she would deplore my absence.

'I have never approved of servants dining with us in the first place.'

'Edmund will be bereft,' Mary stated gleefully.

'Edmund will learn to converse with his father at supper on any subject of my choosing.' This appeared to be the end of the conversation, for Mr Thornton turned abruptly on his heel.

'Then you are permitting Miss Brontë to have her own way, are you not, father?' Mary called after him.

The master swung round and shouted loud enough for each of us to hear. 'On occasion I enjoy such obstinacy – even when it is directed at myself!'

With that he strode rapidly away. His daughter watched the departing figure, then moved to Anne and, to my surprise, reached out to pet the puppy. 'I really didn't want to shoot her, Miss Brontë,' she confided. 'It was father who insisted. I felt if I refused, he would think me as cowardly as my brother.'

Edmund bore this insult in silence.

'It does my heart good to hear it,' Anne replied. As we started up the green slope to the manor house, Anne lagged behind and whispered so that only I could hear, 'William shall love this precious pup as much as I.'

Suddenly, the ominous clouds overflowed with rain. I took Mrs Thornton's fragile arm and quickened our step so that we might reach shelter before we were drenched. Nevertheless, when we reached the manor house our cloaks were soaked and we all shivered in search of a fire. Flossy was happiest of all, to be inside with a promise of warmth. Mrs Thornton, Edmund and Mary ascended the large stairway while Anne and I turned towards the kitchen. Edmund looked down at us sadly. 'I shall sorely miss your company at dinner.'

'And I yours.' But, in truth, it was his mother I would miss most of all.

The Journal of Branwell Brontë

27th October, 1845

A fire burns in the hearth here at the Black Bull Inn. It is night. Outside it feels as if winter is here already. How warm and safe I feel at my writing chair here by the fire, a tankard of ale at my side. I return to you, Dear Journal, my one true friend, as I continue not only the saga of my own burgeoning love but begin the story of another romance about to bloom like the spring roses at Thorp Green.

Again I title a section in the spirit of Mr Dickens. In truth, such a device will enable me to find my way through these pages on later perusal. I shall always be in the great author's debt. I christen this section:

In Which Miss Alice Thornton Loses her Heart

The handsome young man had been sent to Thorp Green from a neighbouring estate where he had already performed to great acclaim. He was an itinerant actor who specialised in declaiming the glorious works of Mr William Shakespeare.

Henry Roxby was not tall, but sturdy as a tree trunk, the taut muscles of his legs boldly defined in the black tights he wore beneath the dark tunic that suggested young Hamlet, for the actor was as blond as I imagined the melancholy Dane to have been. His features were symmetrical: the straightness of his nose, the sensuousness of his full lips, the intense green of his almond-shaped eyes, were all complemented by a powerful physique: yet the way his feet turned slightly inward suggested there was still something of the boy.

We were assembled in the great hall, the Thornton family seated in chairs while the servants stood attentively behind them, each of us riveted by the stirring performance of Mr Roxby. He paced in front of a roaring fire in the massive fireplace, speaking in a voice sometimes as powerful as a military call to arms, at other times as soft as a milkmaid's. He was concluding the famous wooing scene from *Henry V*. As the last sentences tumbled from his lips, he moved before young Alice and addressed the final words to her, his voice caressing each syllable; the ardour of his passion astonishingly real:

> 'Put off your maiden blushes; avouch the thoughts of your heart with the looks of an empress; take me by the hand, and say "Harry of England, I am thine:" which word thou shalt no sooner bless mine ear withal, but I will tell thee aloud – "England is thine, Ireland is thine, France is thine, and Henry Plantagenet is thine;" who, though I speak it before his face, if he be not fellow with the best king, thou shalt find the best king of good fellows. Come, your answer in broken music; for thy voice is music, and thy English broken; therefore, queen of all, Katharine, break thy mind to me in broken English: wilt thou have me?'

'Oh, yes! Yes, I will!' Miss Alice exclaimed before she could stop herself.

We laughed at this; even Mr Thornton, although there was a hint of disapproval behind his mirth. 'Well, well, very nicely done, young laddie,' he quickly interjected. 'Now if you will retire to the kitchen, I am sure that cook will...'

'No!' Miss Alice interrupted. 'More, father. We must

have more!' We applauded this; for indeed we had all been enjoying his extraordinary performance and none of us wished it to end.

'Very well,' her father agreed reluctantly. 'But it is getting past time to retire and I am sure our young actor is weary.'

'To-night I am inspired!' Roxby exclaimed. 'I feel that I could declaim forever!'

'One more, Mr Thornton, please,' his wife cajoled; for she was as mesmerised as her daughter.

'Very well,' he acquiesced. 'Just one more.'

The performer considered. 'We have done with Romeo and Hamlet and Orlando and Henry... A sonnet by the Bard, perhaps?'

'Oh yes!' Alice exclaimed.

'*One* sonnet,' Mr Thornton insisted.

The dynamic young man once again addressed his performance to Alice, which only served to give the words of Mr Shakespeare greater passion and poignancy:

'As an unperfect actor on the stage
Who with his fear is put besides his part,
Or some fierce thing replete with too much rage,
Whose strength's abundance weakens his own heart;
So I, for fear of trust, forget to say
The perfect ceremony of love's rite,
And in mine own love's strength seem to decay,
O'ercharged with burthen of mine own love's might.
O, let my books be then the eloquence
And dumb presagers of my speaking breast;
Who plead for love, and look for recompense,
More than that tongue that more hath more express'd.
O, learn to read what silent love hath writ!
To hear with eyes belongs to love's fine wit.'

Miss Alice burst into applause. The rest of us followed

suit, with the exception of Mr Thornton, who had clearly heard enough. 'I scarcely understood a word of that,' Miss Mary whispered to my sister.

Anne, in contrast to Mary, had been most taken by the piece – no doubt thinking of the Reverend William Weightman. Flossy, at her feet, must have agreed with Mary, however, for the spaniel, enjoying the warmth of the fire, slept through the entire performance.

'Another! Another!' Miss Alice demanded, her hands applauding wildly.

'We've had quite enough,' her father declared, rising from his chair. 'It's off to bed for all of you!' He took a sizable amount of coins from his pocket and dropped them into the young actor's eager hand. 'Here you go, laddie. Now off to the kitchen with you.'

'I thank you, sir,' the actor responded, bowing profusely.

Mrs Fitzpatrick, who had not completely enjoyed the performance, whispering to Berwick that the speeches were 'too fancy', took the actor by the arm. 'Come along, young man; it's that hungry you must be, speaking all those long words.'

'Acting was never as pleasurable as it was to-night,' said Henry Roxby, smiling in the direction of Miss Alice.

'To bed! To bed!' Mr Thornton shouted, not relishing the attraction Shakespeare seemed to have for his daughter.

Mrs Fitzpatrick handed Roxby over to cook who led him towards the kitchen. 'We've got a lamb stew that should fill your belly; and a berry pie as well.'

The company began to retire.

'I must have fallen asleep three times,' Mary moaned, to annoy her older sister, who was clearly transported, not only by the performance, but by the actor.

'I shall not sleep a wink all night.'

'How he makes me long for the entire play,' Mrs Thornton remarked to her husband as he took her arm. 'Perhaps one day if we were to journey to London…'

'London is London,' Mr Thornton interrupted, 'and Yorkshire is Yorkshire.'

Suddenly Alice stopped on the stairway and turned as if to hurry back downstairs. 'I must have some hot chocolate from the kitchen!' she exclaimed.

'To bed!' her father thundered, impervious to this ruse whereby she might join the itinerant actor.

'But...' then Alice turned back reluctantly. 'Yes, father.'

Mr and Mrs Thornton and their daughters moved along the upper hallway towards their bedrooms, candle-light creating shadows on the ancestral portraits that glanced down at them. Anne and I and young Master Edmund tarried a moment at the head of the stairs; for we, also, had been affected by the magic poetry of England's finest poet. 'Truly Shakespeare needs to be heard to be appreciated,' Anne sighed. 'Merely reading him does not provide the same pleasure.'

'I half expected Miss Alice to speak Juliet's part,' I observed with a smile.

'I think now that I will be able to interest her more in the study of the Bard,' Anne added hopefully, drawing close to me and kissing me on the cheek. 'Good night, dearest brother.'

'Good night, Anne.'

'How Emily would have loved Mr Roxby's performance.'

'I think Charlotte, as well.'

'Emily is our true romantic.'

'Emily?'

'Someday she will find an outlet for the secrets she shares only with the moors.' She turned to address my young charge. 'Good night, Master Edmund.'

'Good night, Miss Anne.'

Anne left us, taking more than her light with her – taking a beatific serenity, an expectation of happiness, that made me almost as joyous as she. I waited until she turned the corner of the hallway before moving with Edmund into the south wing. 'It seems your oldest sister has made a conquest of this handsome actor,' I remarked as we walked along the dark hallway.

He glanced shyly in my direction. 'How well Shakespeare expresses what we all are feeling.'

I put my arm across Edmund's shoulders and drew him to me. He succumbed to the warmth in my arm as Anne's puppy did to her. 'Should we set aside our Greek and Latin and take a respite with Mr Shakespeare?' I suggested.

'Could we, Branwell?'

'With what play would you like to commence?'

He considered this a moment, pursing his sensitive lips, continuing to shelter himself in the warmth of my body. 'Since I am the age of Romeo, perhaps that would be a proper place to commence.'

'A Romeo who has not yet found his Juliet?'

'Even so, Branwell,' he replied, his innocent eyes glistening in the candle-light. 'I can still understand why one should wish to die for love.'

I released my hold of him, for we were standing in front of the doorway to his bedroom. 'Would you like to come inside, Branwell? Could you help me to prepare for bed?'

'I must prepare myself,' I replied softly, seeing the disappointment in his eyes. In truth I would have taken pleasure in tucking him in, but I feared the child was hungry for something more. 'Good night, sweet prince; and flights of angels sing thee to thy rest.' I hugged him for a moment then pulled quickly free.

'Is that *Romeo*?'

'No, it is *Hamlet*.'

'Perhaps I identify with him as well.'

The Journal of Branwell Brontë

28th October, 1845

It is the following morning. I am writing in bed, alone in my room, my bedclothes keeping me warm and safe against the rain that beats like pebbles against my window.

Rain figures in my narrative as well, as another title in the style of Mr Dickens will reveal.

A Rendezvous in the Rain

Dear Journal, I will attempt once more to describe an incident which took place at Thorp Green and which, though I did not actually witness, I was informed of soon afterwards. Of what use is a writer if he cannot utilise his own imagination and skills in depicting that which has only been reported to him but upon which he has later elaborated?

This incident occurred during the April downpour, which was scarcely different from the torrent that had already buffeted us in March. Miss Alice had yet to settle down after the fervid presentation of William Shakespeare by Henry Roxby. On the first day free from rain, she encouraged my sister to take Flossy on a walk that drew them to Little Ouseburn.

In front of a small tea-shop which somehow managed to survive on the thirst of the local citizenry, Alice feigned weariness, and Flossy, who had grown considerably, was glad to stop and rest her tired paws as well.

'Miss Brontë,' Alice exclaimed, 'I must fortify myself

with a cup of tea or I will not have the strength to trek the long way home. I am that cold, besides,' she added as my sister hesitated.

Anne's eyes looked heavenward, for the late afternoon sky was turning dark and the increasing wind was bending the branches of trees beginning to produce new leaves. 'It appears about to rain, and I have never known you to lack the least bit of strength or energy.'

Alice was instant. 'But it would be ever so nice, Miss Brontë. We could have tea and cakes and what is left over you could feed to Flossy.'

'I doubt if they would appreciate a dog on the premises, even one as well-behaved as this.'

Alice would not be deterred. 'I am a Thornton, am I not? They will welcome your Flossy.'

Anne bent low to pet her spaniel. 'I suppose for Flossy's sake. She does love her cakes.' But Anne remembered that she had ventured out without her reticule. 'I have not brought any money, Miss Alice.'

'I have brought more than enough.' Indeed the pocket of Alice's pelisse jangled with coins.

Warm embers burned in the fireplace of Miss Varden's cosy tea-shop, which was known more for her cakes that even cook had admired. Flossy moved as close as possible to the flames for warmth. The shop was decorated with Miss Varden's colourful needlepoint and a large framed lithograph depicting the coronation of the young Queen Victoria, Lord Melbourne, her Prime Minister, standing at her side, burdened with the heavy sword of state. There were small tables about, each flanked with needlepoint cushioned chairs. Miss Varden obviously enjoyed her own scones, for she was round of figure and her cheeks were as plump and red as pippins. There was no-one else in the shop and Miss Varden was delighted to see two customers in the shape of my sister and Miss Alice; she even extended her welcome to the floppy-eared spaniel. 'Miss Thornton and Miss Brontë!' she exclaimed. 'Welcome to my shoppe. And with a delightful puppy!' she added, stooping to ruffle Flossy's fur as the dog settled contentedly before the fire.

'I hesitated to bring her in with us,' Anne apologised, 'but Miss Alice…'

'Nonsense!' Miss Varden interrupted. 'The dog is as welcome as my tabby, Lady Caroline, who at this very moment is taking her afternoon nap above the oven, a spot which she cherishes.' She led Anne and Alice to a table. 'And is life progressing at Thorp Green?'

'Nothing ever progresses at Thorp Green,' was Alice's quick reply.

'Miss Alice!' Anne reprimanded.

Miss Varden plunged ahead, desiring her customers to be contented and happy. 'It is not the most pleasant day to be out and about, is it?'

'In Haworth, on such a day as this, my sisters and I would be walking the moors.'

'I fear I have never been to Haworth,' Miss Varden responded. Like most country people of her class, she seldom strayed beyond her own bailiwick.

'I am sure that it is as dreary as it is here,' Alice interjected.

'Miss Alice!'

Miss Varden was sympathetic. 'Perhaps I had similar feelings when I was Miss Thornton's age, but now I wouldn't leave Little Ouseburn for the world.'

She stopped herself from proceeding further. 'Now with the tea we have fresh scones, butter cakes and cobblers as well.'

'The butter cakes would be nice,' Alice responded immediately.

'I think I shall have scones,' Anne decided. 'I shall share them with Flossy.'

Miss Varden smiled. 'Just the thing for you to share with that pup.' She retreated to the kitchen. 'I'll just be fetching your tea.'

My sister and her charge sat a moment in silence, grateful for the warmth of the fire. Alice continually glanced towards the doorway until my sister was prompted to demand, 'Are you expecting someone, Miss?'

'Certainly not!'

Almost immediately Miss Varden returned to set a steaming pot of tea upon their table. 'I'll just be getting your cakes.' She hurried off again.

Anne poured the tea, adding lumps of sugar and cream, while Alice continued to glance anxiously back at the doorway, finally giving this up to sip the bracing hot liquid. 'Now aren't you glad we stopped, Miss Brontë? Isn't tea just the thing on such a cold, windy day?'

'It most certainly is,' Anne smiled, 'but you must permit me to pay you for my part upon our return.'

'You will do no such thing!' Miss Alice protested.

Henry Roxby suddenly opened the door, startlingly handsome in his navy-blue cloak and matching top hat, the wind kicking up behind him, the blond hair beneath his hat falling over his forehead. 'Why, Mr Roxby!' Alice exclaimed in feigned surprise; for she was already skilled in such pretence. 'What a pleasant surprise!'

'Miss Thornton!' He had already demonstrated his Thespian skill. 'What brings you out on such a blustery day?'

'I wonder,' my sister mused aloud, for the deception was transparent.

Alice beamed as if the sun had suddenly broken through. 'Mr Roxby, you remember Miss Brontë. She was as impressed as I with your performance.'

He smiled warmly at my sister. 'Of course I remember Miss Brontë. She was a most attentive audience.' He moved to the fireplace and bent low to stroke the reclining Flossy.

'Have you ever read what Mr Edward Jenner has written about the faithful spaniel?'

'Oh, do tell us!' Alice exclaimed.

Roxby stood beside their table to recite the poetry.

> 'The hollow winds begin to blow;
> The clouds look black, the glass is low:
> The soot falls down, the spaniels sleep,
> And spiders from their cobwebs peep.
> 'Twill surely rain; I see with sorrow
> Our jaunt must be put off to-morrow.'

'Then it is going to rain, you believe?' Alice questioned anxiously.

Roxby moved back to the dog. 'If this spaniel is any indication.'

Anne protested: 'But Flossy is not really asleep like the spaniel in your poem.'

Alice leapt to her feet. 'If this poem is true we must hurry home before we get caught in a downpour. Mr Roxby, while Miss Brontë has her tea and Flossy shares her cakes, perhaps you will be kind enough to escort me home.'

'With the greatest pleasure,' he responded enthusiastically.

Anne immediately rose. 'I forbid it!'

'But we have only one umbrella and that I shall have to leave with you!' Alice protested. 'You know, Miss Brontë, how susceptible I am to colds, so I mustn't tarry!'

'The healthiest girl I have ever seen,' Anne protested. 'If we Brontës had half your strength...' Alice hurried to the doorway and glanced outside.

'We mustn't tarry, Mr Roxby, the clouds look ready to burst.' She quickly deposited some coins on the table. 'This will pay for everything.'

Before Anne could stop them, Alice and Roxby had fled the shop. 'Miss Alice, I forbid it!' fell on deaf ears.

Miss Varden returned from the kitchen carrying cakes and scones. 'Now where has Miss Thornton gone off to?'

'I fear to her destruction, as well as my own,' Anne lamented. 'Forgive our hasty departure, Miss Varden; but Flossy and I must set off in pursuit.'

'But your cakes!' Miss Varden took great pride in her skill as a baker.

'If you would wrap them up, please,' my sister responded. She pulled Flossy's leash and prepared for her departure. 'For catching up with Miss Alice,' she promised the spaniel, 'you may have all you can eat!'

Alice and Henry Roxby had disappeared before Anne and Flossy could get out of the shop. Rather then sniffing them out, the spaniel insisted on pulling Anne home to the warmth of Thorp Green for, indeed, the threatening rain manifested itself, drenching my poor sister and her puppy.

And now, as in my Glasstown stories of yore, I shall write a scene of love; this one as pure and innocent as these two who had sought shelter in an abandoned barn, the deluge descending on the slate roof. Longing to kiss each other, they nevertheless kept a respectful distance at first, simply delighting in each other's company. 'Have you memorised the piece as I instructed, Miss Alice?'

'Oh yes!' she responded breathlessly. 'I have studied it ever so diligently.'

'May I hear?'

She hesitated. 'You must turn your back while I perform it.'

'But I must observe you as Romeo observes you,' Henry insisted. However, he moved behind a dilapidated hay wagon, saying, 'But I shall observe you unobserved, as Romeo does Juliet in Shakespeare's play.'

Alice took a deep and nervous breath before plunging into the celebrated words:

> ' 'Tis but thy name that is my enemy:
> Thou art thyself, though not a Montague.
> What's Montague? It is nor hand, nor foot,
> Nor arm, nor face, nor any other part
> Belonging to a man.'

And so she continued, her recitation at first unsteady and unsure, but when Henry spoke his first line to her:

> 'I take thee at they word:
> Call me but love, and I'll be new baptis'd;
> Henceforth I never will be Romeo.'

Suddenly Alice responded as if indeed she were actually Juliet. The intensity between the two grew until with Henry's line, 'And what love can do, that dares love attempt,' they fell into each other's arms and kissed until young Miss Alice, fearing she would no longer be able to breathe, pulled away. 'Yes! Yes!' Henry cried. 'You are my Juliet.'

'There was nobody to drill me on it,' Alice bubbled, excited with her success. 'If anybody found out. If Miss Brontë were to tell my father that...'

'Not only my Juliet, but you could be my Rosalind, my Ophelia and my Katharine as well!' Roxby interrupted.

Alice was momentarily speechless. 'Do you truly believe...?'

Henry nodded enthusiastically. 'Yes! Yes! With work and practice, we could...' And here another kiss. 'And soon they would be asking for us even in London.'

'London?!' The name of the city was thrilling to her. 'Oh, Henry, to get away from here – as far away from Thorp Green as possible.'

The young man had made up his mind. 'I shall speak to your father to-night. I will demand your hand!'

Alice froze as if it were she who had been trapped in

the rain and not my sister. 'You mustn't! You mustn't! Father would lock me away forever, and I don't know what he would do to you – kill you, I suspect.'

'I am not afraid.' And indeed the young man was not; for, unlike myself, he had been independent since he was a youth.

'We must not be hasty,' Alice cautioned. 'You must not come near Thorp Green. I shall get word to you somehow. I will hide a message in the church prayer book as usual.'

He took her hands. 'I shall treasure that book forever because of the notes I have discovered there.'

She wanted to go on holding him, but there was little time for pleasures such as this. 'Henry, you must stay in the village until I get another message to you. I shall insist that Miss Brontë accompany me to church to-morrow for a special visit. By night-fall there should be word for you.' How dearly she loved the intrigue of scheming to find a way to be with the young man with whom she believed she had fallen truly in love. Indeed, they were like Romeo and Juliet, although she hoped their ending would be far less tragic.

'The Queen herself could not command me to do otherwise.'

'I love you!' she whispered.

'And I you!'

Again they embraced, until Alice reluctantly compelled herself to pull free. 'I must hurry. If Miss Brontë were to arrive home first and tell father ... although I doubt she will tell him anything she does not have to.'

'Parting is such sweet sorrow...'

How the sound of his rich voice thrilled her. '...that I shall say good night till it be morrow,' she concluded, before turning and hurrying out of the barn. 'Now I must flee!'

'Sleep dwell upon thine eyes, peace in thy breast!'

When Alice, soaking from the continuing downpour, sneaked back into Thorp Green, the fading colour of late afternoon dusk had turned as black as the merciless sky. She discovered my sister and Flossy seeking warmth in front of the kitchen fireplace where I, also, was sipping tea and waiting for supper, cook and her assistant busy with the preparation thereof. Anne turned to glare at Miss Alice, hurt and anger in her eyes. She conducted her out of hearing of the others. 'As soon as your father returns from Lord Broughton's I shall demand an interview with him.'

'But ... I simply hoped to escape the rain.'

'And did you?' my sister questioned suspiciously, for Alice was clearly wet.

'We took refuge in the barn, but then I knew you would be worrying.'

'How thoughtful of you.'

'Please, Miss Brontë,' Alice pleaded softly, for she did not want the others to overhear, 'you must not say anything to father. I shall make this up to you somehow, I promise.'

'How?'

'I shall think of something. Perhaps you will accompany me on a visit to church to-morrow so that I can beg God's forgiveness.'

'Your father has sent word ahead that young Lord Broughton is coming to dine this evening. He asks that you be dressed in your best clothes.'

'I feel that I have caught a cold. I shall go directly to bed and have supper in my room,' Alice responded defiantly.

'You shall do no such thing!' my sister retorted. 'I have had specific instructions. Mrs Thornton has already selected what you are to wear.'

'I shall stay in my room!'

'You stubborn girl!' Anne remonstrated.

'Unless...' A small smile turned up the corners of Alice's delectable lips.

'Unless what?' Anne demanded.

'If you promise to say nothing to father of this afternoon, we shall go upstairs and you shall help me make myself most presentable, even though I believe that Leslie Broughton is the dullest, most unattractive man in all of Yorkshire.'

'You drive a hard bargain, miss,' my sister responded.

'Well, what is it to be?'

Anne sighed reluctantly and shared a look of dismay with me as she rose to her feet. 'Come, Flossy.'

The dog trotted obediently behind them as the ladies wound up the twisting stairs. Indeed, my heart went out to Miss Alice, for I had had occasion to observe Lord Broughton myself. There was certainly nothing handsome about the tall, angular man with a large nose and uncontrollable hair. His love for horticulture had turned him into a complete bore. He talked of nothing but flowers and his hope one day to name a new rose after the fair Alice. The gardens of Broughton Manor were known throughout Yorkshire for their singular beauty as Miss Alice was known for hers; though she had hitherto expressed no interest in becoming mistress of his estate, nor in having a flower named after her.

I Meet a Young Lord

Leslie Broughton's father had the misfortune to die at a young age so that the son, scarcely out of his teens, had already assumed the title and all that it entailed. Although neither Anne nor I were included in this special supper for young Lord Broughton, nonetheless, we were later asked to witness both young Alice and Mary perform piano pieces taught to them by my sister, who had the true gift and ear for music in my family. Afterwards young Edmund was called upon to deliver a speech that we had worked on from Shakespeare; Mark Antony's famous oration over the body of Caesar. Although he had performed it splendidly in my presence, the stern judgmental face of his father appeared to unnerve him. However, half-way through he got hold of the speech and suddenly it seemed as if the citizens of Rome were actually at his feet. 'Bravo!' his mother shouted proudly as we all applauded, the angular Lord Broughton fulsome in his praise. 'It appears we have a young actor in our midst,' he observed.

Young Edmund, beaming under such praise, shared his look of triumph with me. He was exceedingly handsome in his stylishly-cut, blue velvet jacket that accented the leanness of his figure. A matching blue cravat, highlighted against the white of his high collar, brought out the similar colour of his eyes. He had recently turned sixteen and was now indeed a young man.

'I would rather he become a highwayman!' Mr Thornton asserted, reminding me momentarily of my father. In truth, he did have the voice for the pulpit, but chose to brow-beat his family rather than his parishioners.

'Acting is a noble profession, papa,' young Alice protested. Her long blonde hair had been twisted into red-ribboned plaits that fell evenly to either side of her adorable head. Her evening gown of pink silk was embroidered with small red roses that bloomed with the colour of her complexion.

'Most of them are pickpockets,' her father persisted.

'We had such a fine actor who performed for us here, Lord Broughton,' Alice said. 'To think what he would have done with the speech!'

Edmund's face fell; his eyes met mine until his mother came to her son's rescue. 'Edmund performed it most admirably.' Mrs Thornton turned as if to congratulate me as well and our eyes met in a way that made my heart momentarily skip. She was even more beautiful than her daughter – her shoulders the colour of ivory, the contours of her exposed bosom a seductive suggestion of what was concealed by her elegant blue frock.

'Now it is your turn to do something, Leslie!' Alice cajoled the dinner guest.

'But I have no such talent, except in the greenhouse.' He was flustered, and in love with Miss Alice, for his eyes seldom strayed from her, except to admire the early spring flowers from Thorp Green, which Mrs Thornton had placed about the great parlour.

'Then we shall all sing together,' Alice declared, taking the young Lord's hand and leading him to the piano. To her parents' delight she had been flirting all evening with Leslie Broughton. Her mother and father shared looks of approval while Anne and I traded glances of suspicion. 'Come, Miss Brontë,' young Alice demanded. 'Play something that we can all sing together. I am sure that Lord Broughton has a very fine voice.'

'But I do not sing at all,' he protested. 'I'd much rather hear you sing.'

'Nonsense! Everyone to the piano!' she insisted.

I had never seen her so radiant. I had no doubt that she could have made even the austere John Wesley fall in love with her that evening. Anne set aside her needlepoint, moved to the piano and took her seat on the bench. Even though her frock was a simple black affair with white tucker and matching cuffs, she was as pretty to me as any of the other women in the parlour, except perhaps Mrs Thornton who radiated beauty in a very special way.

'What shall we sing, Miss Brontë?' Alice questioned.

My sister hesitated, then smiled shyly at me as I took my place beside the others. 'Perhaps the song which is our father's favourite,' she suggested, looking now at the Thornton children. 'I have taught it to all of you.'

I knew immediately to what song my sister was referring. It had become my favourite as well. When she began to play *The Last Rose of Summer* I could picture Charlotte, Emily, Anne and me around the parsonage piano. How happy we were in our youth before the world intruded upon us in the odious, but necessary, guise of employment. Oh to be born with money and a silver spoon in one's mouth!

The Last Rose of Summer was from my father's treasured copy of *Irish Melodies*, consisting of the poetry which the Dublin-born Thomas Moore wrote to traditional tunes. Patrick Brontë had never truly shaken the soil of County Down from his feet.

'Tis the last rose of summer, left blooming alone:
All her lovely companions are faded and gone.
No flower of her kindred, no rosebud is nigh,
To reflect back her blushes, or give sigh for sigh.

Perhaps my voice was louder, because I knew the song so well, but soon Mr Thornton was joining in and drowning even me out. I saw our reflections in the large parlour window, and I could not help but notice how handsome we all appeared, our flushed faces rosy in the candle-light; even young Mary was aglow in her yellow frock, her natural curls festooned with matching ribbons: even I in my best dark evening coat, the curls of my red hair flaming; the lights of the girandole appearing like individual dots of fire on the window glass. For a fleeting instant I thought the reflections of the young Thornton girls were those of Charlotte and Emily, but a blink of the eye took them away from me and I was back at Thorp Green, with little notion of the great upheaval and tragedy that was in store for us all.

If only I had proffered my resignation and left Thorp Green then and there. How different, perhaps even happy, my life would now be.

The Journal of Branwell Brontë

3rd November 1845

Will snow soon arrive at the Brontë Parsonage? It is so cold that I have not ventured outside and sit here in the parlour at the same table where my sisters have transcribed their secret books. Perhaps I will one day share with them what I am writing. Will they be intrigued by the title which I bestow upon this portion of my history? Indeed, they share my love of literature, about which I am about to write.

A Journey to York

I bless my father for providing me with a love of literature. Fortunately, Mr Thornton and his wife were avid readers, as were my sister and I – and, through us, their children. Books were not to be procured locally, but in York, a distance from Thorp Green. Previously, one of the servants had been dispatched to fetch reading material from Mr Henry Bellerby's Library at Number 13, Stonegate. Now I happily volunteered to drive the buggy this distance, so that I could personally select reading material for both parents and children. Master Edmund was eager to accompany me on this excursion to York.

We set forth during the first week of a glorious May. Edmund sat with me in the driver's seat of the black buggy, pressing close to me – he said, 'for warmth'. The sky was as blue as a milkmaid's bonnet, and Barley, the cream coloured mare, carefully groomed by William Allison, was obedient to my touch, for I was not an experienced driver. We Brontës had never owned a horse, much less any form of equipage. We made our journeys on foot.

The sun was shining in the special way it does in spring: with the promise of stronger rays for summer. Along the dusty road to York vegetation was maturing with vigour. Great ash, oak and elm skeletons were restored to majestic life; woodland plants had sprung up profusely; the hedgerows were aglow with wild primroses, their pale gold gleam spreading sunshine across the horizon. When we paused at a gently-flowing beck so that Barley could drink, numerous varieties of moss filled the hollows of its banks and golden kingcups fringed its boggy margins. 'Rough winds do shake the darling buds of May,' young Edmund quoted, for he was basking in the bucolic beauty, '...but not to-day!'

We stood on the edge of the beck as Barley drank eagerly, the gentle flow of bubbling water over slippery rocks a music that only spring can comprehend. 'And summer's lease hath all too short a date.' I completed the Shakespeare quote.

Edmund breathed deeply of the pure sylvan air. 'A perfect day like this should never come to an end. At Thorp Green there are always shadows – the largest being that of my father.'

'We shan't think of Thorp Green to-day, Edmund,' I responded gently, and then tousled his raven hair which had fallen carelessly to either side of his noble brow. Edmund had removed his tall black chapeau and his reflection in the clear water was arresting; the ripples lengthening his striped breeches, twisting the twill of the ochre-coloured jacket that matched his waist-coat. He took my hand as I removed it from his head and held it tightly, then turned and looked at me hungrily, the intense blue of his eyes expressing such love and need, that for a moment I could not escape their penetration. 'I love you, Branwell Brontë,' he said simply.

'And I love you, Edmund,' I responded, too quickly; for in truth, I wanted to shelter the trusting boy in my eager arms and protect him from the world and all the painful pangs of growing up that I had endured – but such behaviour would have been unseemly. Who knows where it might have led? We would be crossing the Rubicon: there would be no turning back.

Fortunately, at that moment, a colony of rooks burst so suddenly from the neighbouring oaks, I would have thought a farmer had fired a decisive shot. The birds flew upward in great profusion, their croaking caws as doom-laden as Cassandra's warning to Troy.

Edmund and I laughed. The seductive spell had been broken. We had returned to surer footing. It was once again simply a glorious spring day. Barley, unmindful of the rooks, continued to drink, and was not pleased when I pulled him away from the water. 'You are not a camel,' I admonished the animal; 'and Mr Allison has warned us that you tend to drink more than is necessary.'

'I think that applies to Mr Thornton, as well,' Edmund smiled, making light of his father's fondness for spirits.

'To-day is enough drink for me!' I exclaimed, breathing deeply of the delicious air. Edmund had no inkling that I myself had too often succumbed to the wiles of John Barleycorn, disgracing myself on more than one occasion.

'When we reach York, I shall be hungry, Branwell.' He breathed deeply, his blue eyes as alive as the clear sky.

'And so shall I!'

I am not comfortable in any township larger than my beloved Haworth. Bradford, where I studied portrait painting under the tutelage of William Robinson, was intimidating; but York, although certainly larger than my native Haworth, was less so. The citizens were a friendly sort, and the streets hummed with leisurely activity. Edmund and I dined on leg of lamb and browned potatoes at a crowded establishment, before seeking out Mr Henry Bellerby's Library.

I liked Mr Bellerby at first sight. He looked as warm and inviting as his lending library, book shop and stationery store, a cosy niche from which the enterprising young man also published the local *Yorkshire Gazette*. He reminded me of the celebrated illustrations of Charles Dickens' Mr Pickwick, though he certainly had more hair – a mass of brown curls that fell to his forehead – and his features were less pointed and more inviting; but his spectacles were as narrow and his face so animated that each expression reminded me of that famous character.

'Welcome to Bellerby's!' he smiled at us, looking up from his writing desk and pushing his glasses to the top of his head where they became submerged in his sea of curls. 'Is this young Master Thornton I see?'

'Yes, Mr Bellerby. I've come with Mr Brontë, my tutor, to fetch some books.'

'Mr Thornton is one of my most valued customers,' Mr Bellerby exclaimed delightedly, arising from his stool to shake my hand. 'Henry Bellerby. I am pleased to meet you, Mr Brontë.' He shook my hand vigorously, surveying me intently until he decided he liked me almost as immediately as I liked him. 'And is Master Thornton mastering Greek and Latin, as every young man must to make his way in the academic world?'

'He is a most apt pupil.'

'Mr Branwell is teaching me how to write as well, Mr Bellerby,' Edmund enthused. 'We are writing a novel together that will rival Mr Scott!'

'Indeed!' Mr Bellerby exclaimed. 'Perhaps one day I will carry it for my readers.'

I did not want to dampen young Edmund's enthusiasm, so I remained mute on the likelihood of such an event ever occurring. I quickly changed the subject as I surveyed the shelves of books stretching to the ceiling and the newer editions for sale displayed on a long table. 'How my sisters would dote on such a wonderful shop such as this. I fear we have nothing like it in Haworth.'

'Haworth,' Mr Bellerby repeated, and then, turning to Edmund, 'Did not a Miss Brontë accompany the fair Miss Alice here on one occasion?'

'My sister, Anne,' I interjected. 'She is one of my three sisters and we have relished books since we were able to spell our names. Indeed we have written for almost as long.'

'And have you been published?' the bookseller asked eagerly.

'More than one of my poems has appeared in the *Bradford Herald*,' I said proudly. Indeed, many of my efforts had graced that newspaper.

Mr Bellerby led me to the rear of his shop where his newspaper was both written and printed. 'I publish my own newspaper,' he said, his voice forceful and hearty as if he read the news aloud to the townspeople.

'Perhaps Mr Bellerby can publish your poems in the *Yorkshire Gazette*,' Edmund suggested hopefully.

I would have liked nothing better, but a warning sounded somewhere deep within me that the Reverend Mr Thornton would not appreciate such a display from anyone in his employ. Indeed, I had only shared a few of my efforts with Edmund in an attempt to encourage him to write poetry himself, a skill for which he was displaying genuine talent. 'At the moment we have books to buy and borrow and will look forward to your recommendations, Mr Bellerby.'

'I trust I know everyone's taste at Thorp Green. I have a serialised Dickens now published under single cover, and a new Walter Scott as well.'

'He is my father's favourite,' I exclaimed, remembering how my father treasured books. 'When he received the customary four pounds for obtaining his degree at St John's College, Cambridge, he immediately bought a copy of *The Lay of the Last Minstrel* – quite an extravagance for one who was usually so careful with money.'

'We have *Quentin Durward.*'

'I shall read it immediately!' Edmund exclaimed, grabbing a copy and poring over it eagerly.

'And what is the Dickens?' I asked curiously. I was taken with the author, while my older sister found him ostentatious.

Mr Bellerby fetched a copy from his display table. '*The Old Curiosity Shop.*'

I fingered the books as if they were pieces of fine china. In Haworth we were seldom able to read the serialised versions of Charles Dickens in such publications as the *Monthly Magazine*; instead we had to wait for the book to be printed in its entirety, which was perhaps the proper way to read the great story-teller – in one voracious gulp.

'And what of the ladies of Thorp Green?' Mr Bellerby questioned, delighted to be sharing the new literature with us. 'Have they no preference?'

'Jane Austen,' I volunteered.

'I believe they have not yet read *Northanger Abbey*,' Mr Bellerby advised.

'What happy hours before us!' I exclaimed, for I could scarcely wait to dip into both Dickens and Scott so that I could be transported to places where only novels such as these could safely carry me. 'And for the Reverend Mr Thornton, I have Balzac,' Mr Bellerby added.

Later, in the sudden chill of afternoon which cautioned us that spring could quickly withdraw its warmer promise, Mr Bellerby loaded our buggy with volumes of eagerly anticipated books before pulling me aside and shaking my hand warmly one last time. 'Are you permitted any free time away from the manor house?' he whispered in a voice low enough for Edmund not to hear.

'My Sundays are free. Many nights I am not required,' I replied.

'Of almost any evening, you will find me at the George Inn on Coney Street. Betsy Waller serves up a fine supper and the ale is there for the tasting. Such an inn is the best place to gather news, I can assure you. Perhaps one night you will chance by with one or two of your poems and we shall see if my readers take to them.'

'I shall most certainly do so,' I whispered back; then Mr Henry Bellerby released my hand and sent us on our way.

A week later, on an afternoon when Master Edmund was compelled to ride about Thorp Green with his father to collect outstanding payments from farming tenants, I stole away on Daphne, a gentle steed, selected and saddled by William Allison, who promised me the mare had often made the trip to York. Copies of my poems that had already been published in the *Bradford Herald* were folded in my coat pocket. What a luxury it was to ride and not be dependent on one's own feet. There is something to be said for owning a horse.

Henry Bellerby, the industrious publisher, was a man of his word: he was indeed ensconced at a window table at the George Inn. Betsy Waller's meat pies were as hearty as she, truly something to savour, as was the ale that slid down my throat so quickly that I was inebriated before ever I intended; but not so much that I could not still read my poems aloud to the receptive listener, who immediately agreed to publish *Blackcomb*, and, one of my particular favourites, *The Shepherd's Chief Mourner*, in which I depict a faithful sheep-dog watching alone by his master's grave. Perhaps it was merely the excess of ale, but my carefully written words brought tears not only to the reciter's eyes, but to the listener's as well.

'We must not publish under my actual name,' I was still sober enough to advise. 'I fear my employer would not appreciate such.'

Mr Bellerby nodded that he understood. 'And what shall we call our fine new young poet?'

'Northangerland,' I replied immediately.

'Northangerland?'

'It is a name from the world my sister and I created in our stories. It is after Alexander Percy, the Earl of Northangerland,' I explained. 'He is the revolutionary hero of Glasstown, which my sister now calls Angria.'

'And where is Glasstown?' Mr Bellerby questioned curiously.

'It is somewhere in the interior of Africa: a world of knights and ladies, intrigue and gallantry, that I fear exists only in our imagination.'

'Northangerland it shall be!' he exclaimed, raising his glass. 'Betsy,' he called out loudly, 'a fresh round of ale! Mr Brontë and I are celebrating.'

I had found a new friend that evening, one to whom I could occasionally sneak away, with whom I could imbibe and discuss the words of Byron, Shelley and Keats – and especially Wordsworth – to whom I once sent an example of my poetry, but who never responded. But I could forgive silence from such a genius.

Fortunately, whenever there had been an evening of entirely too much talk and spirits Daphne knew her own way home, for to stay atop the beast was all that I could muster.

It felt good to be drinking again, if only occasionally. I felt at home at the George Inn, where everybody appeared to be your friend and nobody disapproved.

It reminded me of the Black Bull where I write these pages now. Even though it is next door to my father's parsonage, it seems a world away. How strange it is to be about to describe the advent of summer when winter has descended on Haworth with a vengeance, but I shall turn my mind back to those days of warmth.

The Journal of Branwell Brontë

18th November 1845

How strange to be writing of a summer at Thorp Green as winter descends, an uninvited visitor, upon the Brontë Parsonage.

Can one ever predict when the summer will begin? I think it has nothing to do with the solstice – at least not in Yorkshire, where the weather has a mind of its own. It was in early June that summer truly spread her warmth across the countryside at Thorp Green.

The Summer Begins

Lessons did not entirely cease, but interest waned until, in early July, I promised Edmund that we would set aside Greek and Latin and concentrate only on the things that pleased us until the leaves began to turn.

Summer was for horse-riding, for rowing on the small lake, for long walks to unexplored corners of Thorp Green, for cook to prepare a hamper, and for Mrs Thornton to spread our picnic atop a knoll where the Yorkshire countryside stretched beneath us in all its blooming glory.

Summer was for bright beds of iris, paeony, rose and poppy to bloom in such myriad profusion, that the baskets in which Mrs Thornton collected them overflowed with their beauty; delicate flowers with which she strewed her baby daughter's grave; and Mrs Lydia Thornton was the most beautiful flower of them all, moving as gracefully across her estate as Wordsworth's daffodils swaying gently in the wind, her straw bonnet sheltering eyes as blue as any gentian, her skin as white as any lily that floated along the shores of the pond, her lips as pink as the most delicate rose in her garden, her hair as raven as the rich depths of a summer night.

These picnics were occasions which even Mrs Thornton's recalcitrant daughters appeared to enjoy. Anne and I would drag sketchbooks along and instruct the Thornton children in their attempts to portray the glorious views, while Flossy ate the remainder of our feast.

Young Master Edmund brought new imagination to his depiction of the Thorp Green countryside; but it was Mary who demonstrated the most skill. Although she preferred to be off hunting with her father, she nevertheless took pride in her skill with water-colours.

Occasionally Anne and I were left alone to work on our own sketching; she would find an excuse to colour her beloved Flossy while I concentrated on the abundant beauty around Thorp Green. My favourite water-colour of the spaniel was actually painted by my sister, Emily: it depicts Flossy running eagerly after a bird in flight, the expression on the face of the partridge as delicious as that of the dog. I regret now that few examples of this period of our lives survive, but there is one ink drawing in our possession that carries me back to that glorious summer at Thorp Green before everything went so desperately wrong. It is titled 'The Old Hall, Thorp Green', a depiction of a seventeenth-century country house on the outskirts of the estate also known as Monks' House. I think it was the twisted trees surrounding the stone edifice that caught my imagination. I hope that I have done them justice. It is a delicious reminder of a halcyon time in my life, although it was this very dwelling that would precipitate my downfall.

Even a humble tutor and governess are granted two weeks

of summer vacation, a treasured respite; although my task of schooling Master Edmund was a pleasant one.

The Thorntons were in the habit of spending the month of August in Scarborough, a fashionable watering place on the North Sea. Anne had accompanied them previously and described vividly the picturesque view from their Georgian house overlooking the bay. Mr Thornton's mother and sister, who invariably joined them there, were occasional visitors at Thorp Green.

Edmund was heart-sick because Anne and I would not be going with them, but Mr Thornton had determined that the month of August was to be his time with his son. 'And you, Mrs Thornton, can see to your daughters without the aid of Miss Brontë,' he declared.

That lady, although she said little, also appeared perturbed that Anne and I would be absent. It was during a last visit to her child's grave that she took one pale rose from the bouquet she had placed against the small head-stone and handed it to me. 'Perhaps you will keep this as a reminder of Edmund and me until September,' she said softly.

'I shall miss you so,' Edmund stammered. He put his arm around me as I looked into Mrs Thornton's searching eyes and pressed the rose to my lips. Its petals are still preserved between the worn pages of my copy of Wordsworth's *Ode on the Intimations of Immortality*; they are a constant reminder of this happier time.

Soon all was packed and departure begun for the station. Berwick, Mrs Fitzpatrick, cook, her assistant and two personal maids were to accompany the Thorntons.

Anne and I waved them off and watched as the carriages wound around the driveway and grew smaller until they slowly disappeared into the woods. 'How I would love to return to Scarborough,' my sister confessed, 'but not as a governess and not with the Thorntons! It is such a delightful town; the air is bracing and the sea as blue as India ink.

Someday we must all vacation there, we Brontës, away from father's church and the demands of his parishioners.'

'Perhaps you and William could honeymoon there,' I volunteered.

Anne smiled a private smile of anticipation. 'I shall return to Scarborough one way or the other.' She bent to scoop Flossy up into her arms and kissed the eager dog on its furry head. And you shall run and scamper along the beach and dart in and out of the waves.'

The Journal of Branwell Brontë

20th November, 1845

In this winter of 1845 we are battening down the hatches against a month so cold I often have to warm my fingers at the fire before I can write.

My Return Home

As the post-chaise neared Haworth, my sister and I glanced expectantly out of the window and breathed more deeply of the familiar summer air, fragrant with August heather, the heath's shades of brown, green and grey flecked with burgeoning purple, stretching in endless abundance beneath us. From this vantage point at the crest of the hill all of Haworth basked below: our precious valley, protected by sinuous hills that stretched to the horizon; our small village, a twisting of flag-stone streets and houses, the tower of our father's church at Changegate Road and, far below, at the bottom of our valley, Ebor and Bridgehouse Woollen Mills, not only supporting our economy, but providing parishioners for father's church as well.

Soon the post-chaise came to a stop at the top of Main Street, where it widens into West Lane and Changegate. This is our small coach-station, little more than a stable where the horses are refreshed and fed before they proceed to Keighley and then beyond to Bradford and Leeds.

When Anne, with Flossy in her arms, alighted from the post-chaise and spied the Reverend William Weightman, his handsome face as excited as hers, she almost stumbled before catching her breath and hastening anxiously to where he was waiting. She was wearing her black satin summer travelling cloak, and her black bonnet trimmed with lace and purple satin tied with a ribbon beneath her long neck. Much of her auburn hair was visible, parted as it was at the middle and falling almost to her eyes, which, like her bonnet ribbon, were violet too. How excited William was at first sight of her! How handsome he appeared in his black clerical suit! What a beautiful couple they made – as perfectly matched as our Queen Victoria and her beloved Albert!

If ever two people were fated to love and marry, it was my sister and William Weightman! How happy I was to see the two of them together: Anne setting Flossy down beside her and taking his hands, each lost momentarily in the other's love-filled eyes.

'How good of you to meet us, Bill!'

He released Anne's delicate hands to shake my own. 'Your father insisted.' He glanced back at Anne. 'Although it certainly required no urging.'

'It is so good to be home!' Anne enthused, bending to scoop Flossy back up into her arms. 'I wish you to meet someone who has become very near and dear to me, William.' She held out the spaniel's paw to the curate. 'This is my darling Flossy.'

'Ah, the famous spaniel you have written me so much about!' he exclaimed, taking the extended paw gently in his own hand. 'How do you do, Miss Flossy?'

The dog barked her greeting and attempted to lick Bill on the face. The curate laughed delightedly. 'I think we shall be fast friends.'

'So you shall,' Anne asserted. 'Flossy has very good taste in whom she chooses to conquer. She completely ignores our employer.'

'I shall see to the bags,' I said, hoping to give them a moment of privacy, but William, always the gentleman, came to my assistance.

The descent to the parsonage along Changegate is not far. Anne and I grew happier each step we took along the flagstone street. We were home. This was our village. It is as much a part of us as our own hearts that beat faster as we neared the parsonage.

How familiar was our father's stone church, blending into its square tower! How many members of our family had already been laid to rest in the cold chancel beneath the church: first our beloved mother, still a young woman when insidious disease stole her from us; then our oldest sisters: Maria at eleven and Elizabeth at nine, starved and half-frozen at the Clergy Daughters' School at Cowan Bridge in Lancashire. Is it any wonder that consumption claimed them both? Fortunately, my father removed Charlotte and Emily from the same school before the sickness could claim them as well. And only last year, my formidable Aunt Elizabeth Branwell, who raised us after our mother's death, was laid to rest in the vault beside the sister whose maternal duties she had so faithfully assumed.

Between the church and the parsonage is the graveyard, a small sea of stone slabs, box tombs and head-stones, each etched with the names of faithful souls who have died – some centuries before. What a strange place for four young children to run and play and hide, as often we had done in our youth, much to the displeasure of our father, who did not approve of our playing on hallowed ground. How often we were reminded of death when it lay just outside our window! How often it had stolen its way into our very own house!

We faced the parsonage now, our faded brick home with large windows fronting the small garden. Waiting in the doorway was my sister, Emily. She hurried down the walk and flew into her sister's arms.

As always, her vigilant hound, Keeper, was at her side. A formidable mix of labrador and mastiff, this sandy-coloured mongrel protected the Brontë Parsonage with such ferocity that he had already become legendary in Haworth.

Keeper sniffed at Flossy suspiciously and I feared the worst. Flossy, however, wished only to be friendly and wagged her tail, shook her floppy ears and licked the larger canine. Perhaps because Flossy was the female to Keeper's sturdy male, the mastiff accepted the younger spaniel and grudgingly licked her back.

Emily and Anne held each other so tightly that they did not notice the immediate interaction between their respective dogs. My younger sisters were similar in both feature and demeanour. It was Charlotte, our eldest, with her darker hair and eyes and determinedly set features, who differed from her siblings. Soon Emily was in my arms and holding me tightly as well. 'Oh, Branwell, how I have missed you!' she exclaimed softly in that gentle voice which I have seldom heard raised in anger.

'And I, you!' I responded, delighting in the sweet smell and warmth of her.

'If only Charlotte were here,' she lamented, 'then we would all be together again!'

'I fear we have lost her to Brussels,' I replied.

'Do not even think such a thing, Branwell.' A startled Emily pulled back to look me in the eye. 'When she has completed her studies she will return to Haworth and we Brontë sisters shall open our very own school.'

'And what fine teachers you will make!' I declared. 'Especially Charlotte, who has always told all of us what to do.'

'How happy I will be to leave Thorp Green!' rejoined Anne.

'Is this your precious spaniel?' Emily questioned delightedly. 'And look how Keeper has accepted her!' Anne scooped up Flossy and placed the dog in Emily's arms where the spaniel licked my sister excitedly.

'This is Flossy,' Anne introduced proudly, 'a new addition to the Brontë family.'

'Oh, Flossy, how delighted I am to meet you!' Emily laughed at the spaniel's unbridled affection. Meanwhile Anne and I petted Keeper, who was delighted to see us both and demanded our attention.

I glanced at the doorway of the familiar home half-expecting to see the reassuring form of Tabitha Aykroyd, our beloved retainer, who had helped raise us since we were children. But Tabitha had been forced to leave us because of a broken leg which had refused to heal properly, so that she had become lame. Instead, it was the small frame of the fifteen-year-old Martha Brown, daughter of our sexton, who greeted us shyly. It was she who assisted Emily in running the household. Meanwhile Emily had set Flossy back down and the two dogs were playing.

Soon father was upon us, leaning on his gnarled walking stick, a habit that had begun in his youth; for he had been nicknamed 'Old Staff' by his clerical companions when he was still a young curate at Hartshead. He was sixty-six years old and looked every year of it: the loss of wife and children had lined his features with sorrow. His hair was as white as the sewing-silk scarf he wore around his neck to protect the throat of a man who must deliver a weekly sermon; the lines on his forehead and about his eyes were as deep as the furrows in his bony cheeks. His pointed nose had enlarged with age and his lips had been pressed together too long in a permanent grimace at the profligate ways of mankind – especially those of his son. His sight was failing, something that he refused to accept, though obvious to us all. It was only when father smiled that a touch of 'blarney' twinkled behind the heavy spectacles covering his blue eyes. It was just such a smile that parted his lips as he approached us now, a tear in his eye as well, though he refused to acknowledge it. In the depths of my heart I knew that my father loved his only son best of all and I flew to him and engulfed him in my arms, for I loved and respected him in return. He held me tightly and patted my back with his stick. 'Has the Prodigal Son returned?'

Anne broke free from her sister to embrace him. 'The Thorntons are most pleased with Branwell, papa. He has made quite a conquest of young Edmund, who looks up to him like a colt to his mother.'

'Well, well,' replied my father, now taking Anne into his arms. 'This is my beloved son in whom I am well pleased.' Somehow old age was softening my father.

How happy we all were to be together: Anne, Emily, father and I holding on to each other in a way that would have been unthinkable in our youth! I think the loss of our mother, older sisters, aunt and the departure of Tabitha had forced us to embrace what remained behind. Even the sight of young Martha Brown was a tonic.

'I have prepared a special supper for this evening,' Emily announced. 'And I have set a place for William Weightman, as well.'

Bill glanced from sister to sister and nodded happily that he would be delighted to share our supper with us.

The dogs followed as we stepped inside the house. The indefinable air of a place revisited; the familiar smell of something cooking in the kitchen; the lingering aroma of father's pipe; the memory of my sisters and I sitting before the fire in the parlour and scratching into our notebooks: all overwhelmed me. I had stepped back into a comfortable womb, one that would always call me home no matter how high I had risen or how low I had fallen. This occasion was a proper homecoming, for as yet I had done nothing at Thorp Green for which I needed to feel ashamed – although disgrace would soon follow.

Night had not quite fallen when we sat in the crimson chairs and took our places around the mahogany dining-table in the comfortable parlour, a table which Emily and Martha Brown had happily lengthened to accommodate our return. 'It has been just father and me for too long,' Emily declared as she spread our late mother's very best white lace tablecloth in preparation for our supper. Flossy and Keeper had fallen asleep in front of the fire. I missed the familiar sight of Tiger, asleep in his soft basket, for our beloved tabby had recently expired – pampered into an early grave, I fear. Except for the absent Charlotte, the hearth was almost complete.

As was customary, father said grace and the generous meal was served. Emily, more than Charlotte and Anne, had a genuine skill in the kitchen. The roast was not over-done, the potatoes were golden, the Brussels sprouts were succulent, the Yorkshire pudding was magnificent, and the negus warmed our throats.

As night descended and Emily stood to light the candelabra, William Weightman and Anne exchanged furtive glances that only father did not perceive. Emily, her hair in ringlets about her translucent skin, her pale blue eyes almost grey with the evening, attempted to disguise her distress by busying herself with serving the supper. Throughout the meal, as was his wont, father refrained from discoursing on some theological issue dear to his heart, but asked questions concerning Thorp Green. I responded more often than Anne, who, in attempting to deflect William's adoring gaze, kept her eyes upon our delicious food.

'And what news of Charlotte?' Anne questioned finally, not wanting to speak any further of our employment. 'Branwell and I have not had a letter this month.'

'Our sister writes that she is becoming so proficient in French and German that she will excel in teaching these languages when we open our own clergy daughters' school.'

'I wish we could do so to-morrow,' Anne ventured, 'so that I would never have to return to employment.' She stooped to feed a morsel of beef to the hungry Flossy, who had roused herself from the fire. 'You would like to stay here, would you not, Flossy?' The spaniel appeared to assent.

'And where will this school be?' my father demanded curiously.

'We have not yet decided, papa,' Emily responded, 'but with the little money Aunt Branwell has left us, perhaps some place can be secured.'

'I should think my daughters would make fine teachers, don't you, William?' my father asked of his curate.

'So fine that I should become a student once again.' He looked from Emily to Anne. Could there be any doubt why they both loved him? – so handsome and agreeable that I loved him as well.

'We are all students,' my father replied, his voice as forceful as ever. 'The day Patrick Brontë stops learning, he shall be dead.'

'Let's not talk of death, papa,' Emily interjected quickly.

'And what will I teach at such a school?' I demanded, not wanting to hear any more of death either.

'Branny, we have not considered that you...' but Emily stopped herself from continuing.

'It is to be just a clergy daughters' school,' Anne added.

'Perhaps your little students will need Branwell's expertise in art,' my father volunteered.

'Perhaps,' Emily responded.

'I fear that men will not be welcome at this establishment,' William volunteered, attempting to mitigate my rejection.

'I hope that you are as successful as father in teaching,' I added, not so wounded as one might think, 'for I certainly learned well at his knee.'

'Yes, perhaps father could assist at the school,' Anne suggested.

'Nonsense!' my father retorted. 'I scarcely have the strength for all the funerals and baptisms in this parish. We have not put one in the ground before a new baby arrives. If it was not for William here, I would be severely burdened.'

Emily looked adoringly at father's assistant. 'We are blessed by your presence, Mr Weightman.' She turned to Anne, whose blue eyes glistened with her own love in the candle-light. 'If it was not for Mr Weightman, papa would be inundated.'

'It is my pleasure to assist,' the young curate responded modestly.

'And he has been a help to Martha and me,' Emily added. 'It is William who assists Martha with the shopping and carries the groceries back to our house. Sometimes I think we could not survive without him.'

The hollows of Bill's cheeks flushed as red as his claret. How much easier if he had been my father's only son, rather than myself, for I had never had the slightest inclination to assume the mantle of the ministry so precious to my father. In his defence, though, I must add that papa never attempted to influence me to follow his vocation. I think he must have understood – even in my youth – that I was not cut from the same black cloth as he.

It was Emily who broke the silence she had created with her extravagant praise. She called out to the kitchen where young Martha Brown could be heard washing the supper dishes. 'Martha, we are ready for dessert.'

And what a dessert it was! A warm mincemeat pie accompanied by a tempting hard sauce, a special recipe handed down from mother to daughter. It was time to toast the cook with a post-prandial glass of elderberry wine and for Emily to protest that she had created nothing special.

After dinner Anne and Emily took turns at the piano, playing the songs our father treasured. William Weightman revealed the most pleasing of tenor voices as he blended harmoniously with our father's deeper register as we sang *The Groves of Blarney*, another of Thomas Moore's *Irish Melodies*.

The music floated like incense throughout the house, dispelling all the sorrow that had once pervaded it. When father insisted that we kneel in his usual evening prayer before retiring, I was actually glad to repeat this ritual that I had so often resisted. I was not only at peace with my family, but with myself as well. When father trudged wearily up the stairs and wound the tall grandfather clock on the landing before retiring, an act he had performed since I was a child, I loved him with all my heart.

When Emily, sadly accepting the inevitable, bade Anne accompany Mr Weightman to the door, I took my sad sister in my arms, substituting silence for the words of comfort that somehow stuck in my throat. I think I understood so well because I had developed similar feelings for a woman who was also committed to another: Mrs Lydia Thornton who, indeed, I truly adored from afar.

When Anne, carrying a candle, joined us for our journey upstairs, her cheeks were unmistakably flushed. 'What a wonderful dinner, Emily,' she enthused, her breath excited and short. 'How fortunate father is to have you to care for him.'

'It gives me pleasure,' she replied simply.

'One day we shall all be home again,' Anne hoped, her voice tremulous as she ascended the stairway.

'Perhaps not all,' Emily said almost accusingly. She turned to look down at her sister, her face ghostly white in the flickering candle-light.

'I shall always put my family above all else,' Anne promised. She stepped up to her sister and put her arm around Emily's waist. 'I cannot bear to be away from you.' Emily, who felt things more deeply than the rest of us, said nothing, because she was the most private.

I used to envy my sisters as they tramped across the moors that rose slowly behind the parsonage, their arms locked around each other's waist. Many in Haworth considered them eccentric: the clergyman's daughters, who braved the foul weather, the way a mariner braves the ocean, their dark cloaks gliding across the terrain like ships across the sea.

It was Emily whose love for the countryside was fiercest. She was taller than her sisters, her lithesome graceful figure beautiful to behold as she stepped blithely through the pathway behind the parsonage that led to the moors. Her light brown hair was the colour of the Yorkshire soil and it danced wildly in the wind that buffeted us, for there was always wind in Haworth, even on the calmest of days. Her summer cloak was swept behind her like a whirling cape. It was all I could do to keep pace with her, although Keeper and Flossy somehow managed.

Anne had remained home to dote on our father and accompany William on visits to the sick of the parish. A vicar's work is seldom completed. Is it any wonder that I never desired any part of it?

Soon the moors were stretching like purple mist before us, the violet of their summer flowers dazzling beneath the morning sun, their delicate fragrance tickling our lungs. Emily stepped across the fields with the sure foot of a mountain goat. Even a munching herd of sheep raised their heads to marvel at her as she skipped across a beck.

It was three miles to the waterfall that was our destination. When we were children, we used to call this mystical place 'The Meeting of the Waters', our special oasis where few others ventured. We crossed the long stones that served as a bridge across the beck beneath the falls where Emily turned to wait for me. The two dogs panted contentedly, glad for a respite and a drink. The water gurgled and snorted beside us. 'It's hardly a waterfall now,' she surmised, her accent as Yorkshire as the moors themselves. 'I love it most in early spring, when the snow has melted and the water rushes down and slaps like thunder against the rocks; or when the purple heather is in bloom and the moss is Irish green.'

'There's a wildness in you, Emily,' I declared, 'that manifests itself only when you are here above Haworth. At home you are often deceptively quiet.'

'And there is a wildness in you as well, Branwell,' she retorted, 'but it is not here that it manifests itself but indoors when you have been soused with spirits.'

'I hope those days are behind me.'

'So do we all, Branny,' she responded; then snatched a sprig of heather from above the beck and forced it through my lapel. 'Even if they are not, Branny, I will love you nonetheless.'

'We are alike, you and I, Emily.'

'In some ways, yes.'

I studied her curiously.

'Is it William that troubles your heart?' I questioned finally, lifting her lovely face so that the sorrowful eyes could not escape me; yet she refused to respond. 'He has captured all of your hearts, hasn't he? First Charlotte, then you and now Anne.'

'Am I that transparent, Branny?' she finally replied.

'To your brother, yes.'

'Charlotte has recovered nicely in Brussels.' There had been hints that my oldest sister had become infatuated with her married professor, the Belgian Constantin Heger, but the subject was too troubling for Emily to continue. She turned away from me. When she finally spoke, there was a trace of bitterness in her voice. 'One had only to see them together last night to know that Anne is the one William favours.' She shook her head ruefully, her wild tresses falling like troubled leaves across her brow.

‘They mean to marry,’ I revealed. I felt that she ought to know.

Emily sat down on a large rock and trailed a small tree branch through water. I was reminded how she, as a child, used to stir the tadpoles in the water and study them with great interest. ‘At least he will be a member of the family. I’d rather have William marry my sister than never see him at all.’ These words were uttered with great difficulty.

‘Nothing must be said until Charlotte returns. She will know how to deal with father.’

‘I wonder if he will ever let go of any of us,’ Emily sighed, her chameleon eyes now reflecting the purple of the heather. ‘In truth, Branwell, I would never be happy anywhere else. I was miserable in Brussels and wanted only to come home.’

She surveyed the abundant moors stretching in waves beyond us, her own private domain. She breathed deeply of the scented air and spoke so fiercely that her voice echoed around us. ‘This is my husband,’ she announced determinedly. ‘I am married to the moors!’

Emily took my hand and squeezed it with a frenzy that startled me. ‘Let us return by way of Top Withens!’ She pulled me with her, beyond the waterfall, the dogs following. The heather gave way to beds of angry rocks and barren stretches of soil until finally Top Withens, a deserted stone manor house appeared forebodingly above us. The sun suddenly passed behind a cloud so that the neglected estate looked even more ominous and lonely, only a few gaunt trees remaining to shelter it from the elements.

Emily looked up at it, the wind whipping her hair and raising her cloak. ‘I often wonder what happened here.’

‘One can only imagine.’

She quoted four lines of her poetry. They are from Gondal. I have copied them down since.

What have these lonely mountains worth revealing?
More glory and more grief than I can tell:
The earth that wakes one *human heart to feeling*
Can centre both the worlds of Heaven and Hell.

She bent low to gather strands of purple heather. 'Oh, Branwell,' she said, handing some to me. 'Do you and Anne *have* to return to Thorp Green? We are so lonely without you. Even with William Weightman...' but she trailed off.

'Emily, you are alone even when we are all here with you.'

How I used to dread the advent of Sunday! The children of Patrick Brontë were expected to assume their seats at the foot of their father's pulpit and set an example by listening attentively as his mellifluous voice wafted through the austere church. He was an Evangelical. My father relied almost exclusively on the Bible, and the New Testament in particular. He laboured assiduously to wrap each and every sinner in the forgiving arms of his Saviour. '*Resurgam!*' he would often declare. 'We shall rise again in paradise!'

The only theatricals in my father's parish were provided by these sermons, always extempore. Without writing anything out before-hand, the Reverend Patrick Brontë found the perfect phrase, the exact word, to inspire his parishioners to practise greater denial and self-sacrifice. He was well known in Haworth for his oratorical skill. Parishioners flocked to his church, especially the woollen-mill workers who appeared the most eager to devote their one day of rest to my father and his Saviour.

On the Sundays after I had had too much of John Barleycorn of a Saturday night at the Black Bull Inn and could not be cajoled out of bed, my father would shun me for the remainder of the day. Only at supper – if I chose to attend – would he reiterate his sermon and declare that I, of all Haworth, needed the mercy of his God the most.

On this particular Sunday, on the occasion of our holiday from Thorp Green, I was happy to attend my father's sermon, and sit solemnly between my two sisters in our familiar pew against the east wall, close to the altar, beneath the organ loft. Unfortunately, this meant that we had to face many of the parishioners, a circumstance that Charlotte vehemently detested. She would insist on sitting in the corner seat, which meant her back would be to the pulpit; but at least she did not have to pretend excess piety under the scrutiny of her father's flock.

These parishioners were often restless during prayers, fidgeting in their seats and gazing at the tree beyond the large window, for there was little of stained glass in our severe place of worship. When my father ascended the high wooden pulpit, eyes would become focused and there was an immediate change of attitude. His flock hungered for each of my father's words. They would sit attentively for at least an hour, which was the usual duration of Mr Brontë's sermon, the musical lilt of his voice singing like opera throughout the church.

My father's favourite saint was Paul. The subject of the sermon on that particular Sunday was the saint's conversion to Christ. He constantly invoked St Paul as the most potent example of a sinner – a persecutor even – being miraculously touched by God's infinite grace.

As our father invoked other climactic examples of the conversion of sinners to Christianity, I shared a look with Emily and we smiled a secret smile, something in our eyes revealing that we would rather be back on the moors, that it was the rugged nature of our beloved valley that was our true church and not this stone edifice. Anne, however, sat in pious attention, her eyes riveted on our father declaiming above us. Of all the Brontës she was the most religious, deriving a simple solace from his sermons which did not touch the rest of us.

In the afternoon there would be another service conducted by the Reverend William Weightman. Again my sisters would sit on the hard pews, Anne gazing up at the handsome preacher, but for reasons very different from those which occasioned her attention to my father; but I found it difficult to sit through more than one service. I chose rather to walk the streets of Haworth and reminisce with companions of my youth, who were only too willing to invite me in to enjoy a cup of spirits. Somehow I managed to avoid the Black Bull Inn on my way home and arrived in time for our late afternoon Sunday supper.

Emily appeared to have graciously accepted her loss of William to her sister and made little attempt at conversation. Anne, too, remained silent, content to gaze rapturously at the object of her affection as the two ministers debated moral principles, a conversation in which I feigned an active interest.

Later, my sisters sat at the piano and played a childhood duet, their heads a cascade of wild curls, their Sunday evening satin dresses shimmering in the glow of the fire-light, while I savoured a salutary glass of delectable port. I felt as warm as the embers in the fire, as content to while away my life in the comfort of a soft chair as our pampered tabby had been. When Flossy attempted to join the music by howling wildly, our laughter – such a welcome sound – filled the parsonage.

It took an intrusive knocking on the front door to sour our perfumed air. Father was often roused at any hour to perform the duties of a curate; but the summons, in the guise of a written message, was for Anne and for me.

The Thorntons' vacation in Scarborough had been terminated at the conclusion of their first week. We were summoned to return to Thorp Green immediately.

I wonder now, if we had ignored this summons and never returned to that place of employment, how different our lives might have been – certainly mine, at least.

I wish desperately that I had remained home and never ventured back to our place of employment: only tragedy came from it. I shall write no more to-day.

21st November, 1845

Thorp Green: We Resume our Employment

On the morrow, as we waited at the top of Main Street for the post-chaise, I distanced myself from Anne and William so that they could have this last moment together. With similar delicacy Emily had absented herself from our departure altogether. Flossy was reluctant to leave the side of her mistress, but I walked the dog far enough away to provide some privacy.

Somehow it seemed as if this was the last day of summer. The morning sun that had risen early at the top of our valley seemed pale in comparison to the yellow orb which had followed us from Thorp Green. Encroaching shadows stretched across the streets of Haworth beneath me and there was a resigned stillness to the valley, an early acceptance of another harsh winter to come.

As the coach made its winding ascent to the top of Main Street, I detected a solitary tear flowing from my sister's eye. How desperately she and William wanted to embrace and kiss each other; but propriety forbade such a public display of affection, especially from the youngest daughter of a clergy-man. It was more proper for me to hold William in my arms and press the comfortable warmth of his body against mine. I would miss the reassurance of his trusting face almost as much as she. Neither of us could deny ourselves a last look at him as he waved us bravely off until we rounded a final corner and he was lost to sight. We continued the ascent to the top of our valley. Soon we would make the crossing to Leeds, an industrial city not to my liking, and then venture across Yorkshire until at last we came to rest at the small village of Little Ouseburn, whence we would walk the distance to Thorp Green.

Dusk was descending when we reached our destination. Imagine my surprise to observe young Master Edmund waiting for us at the inn. Young Mary was in attendance and William Allison had brought the buggy to convey us home.

Edmund hurried over to me and shook my hand vigorously. 'Mr Brontë!' he exclaimed. 'We were afraid that you would not be arriving this afternoon.'

'Is there something dreadfully wrong at Thorp Green?' Anne questioned anxiously, for the obstreperous Mary appeared equally glad to welcome my sister. 'Why did you return from Scarborough so suddenly?'

'We will tell you in the buggy, Miss Brontë, for papa insisted that we return in time for supper whether you had arrived or not.'

'Are you that anxious to resume your studies?'

'There are worse things than learning how to utilise one's mind,' Mary responded.

Flossy appeared as happy to greet the children as they were to see her. She waved her black paws and whined her welcome in excited gasps. 'May I hold her, Miss Brontë?' Mary asked eagerly.

'This creature that you wanted to destroy?' Anne could not resist reminding her.

'I would have missed her on purpose,' Mary protested.

Anne handed the wriggling canine into Mary's arms.

'I'll be getting your valise, Mr Brontë,' William said as bags were lowered from the post-chaise.

I squeezed in beside Edmund and faced my sister and Miss Mary. 'Oh, Mr Brontë,' Edmund asserted, 'I have gone ahead and written a little more of our story. I hope you will approve of our next adventure together.'

Edmund had gained colour during his week in Scarborough. It was becoming to him and complemented the intense blue of his eyes that watched me beneath dark lashes. He appeared to have grown taller in the space of a mere week. The dark beauty of his mother was written in masculine strokes upon his face. I wanted to run my hands through his abundant hair.

Anne turned to Mary sitting next to her. 'Now you must tell us immediately what brought you back so early.'

'Henry Roxby.'

Anne was shocked. 'Was he in Scarborough?'

Mary nodded vigorously. 'Just "happened" to be in the neighbourhood. Father was apoplectic when he discovered a handbill advertising Mr Roxby's appearance with the Hanlons, a travelling Shakespearean troupe ensconced in Scarborough for the month of August. They are related to the famous Hanlon-Lees Acrobatic Troupe. He forbade Alice to attend any of the performances, but she stole away nevertheless. When papa discovered her missing, he called out the constable who found Alice with Roxby in his room at a disreputable hotel. If they had arrived any later they would probably have discovered her in his bed!'

'Miss Mary!' Anne exclaimed, dismayed by such reckless indelicacy.

'When she defied papa and said she would sneak out again at the earliest opportunity, he declared that Henry Roxby had destroyed our holiday and decreed that we should pack and return home immediately. If she made any further attempt to see Mr Roxby, papa vowed to have him thrown in jail.'

'And where is Miss Alice now?' Anne ventured.

'She has been locked in her room until your return.'

'Now I understand why we have been summoned back so quickly.'

'You are to move into Alice's room, Miss Brontë, and she is never to be out of your sight.'

'So I shall be her jailer.'

'I for one, am glad that we have returned early, for we missed you both,' Edmund said with a smile.

'And I missed you,' I replied; but there was more to Thorp Green than its youngest denizen. I missed his mother too.

'If it were not for Mr Roxby, I think that we would have attended all the Shakespeare,' Edmund lamented, 'but he was listed as appearing in each production, and father would have none of it.'

As William Allison lit the lantern attached to the carriage, Anne and I shared a bemused smile. How much simpler our life seemed at the parsonage in Haworth in comparison to these intrigues at Thorp Green.

'No matter how diligently they attempted to keep Juliet away from Romeo,' I observed, 'she found a way.'

'And look what happened to her!' exclaimed Mary.

The Diary of Emily Brontë

7th June, 1844

I resolved never again to commit to my note-book the pain and anguish I so often feel in life.

My older sister thinks nothing of poking through my belongings, violating my hidden places, as if she were my teacher, and commenting upon the style in which I have transcribed my tortured thoughts through poetry.

When I caught her making notes on the margin of one of my most precious poems, I snatched it away from her angrily.

I still love her dearly, but now I am suspicious and must be on my guard.

I have hidden my poetry notebook away where I hope Charlotte will never discover it; and this diary must be destroyed before my sister returns from Brussels; for, indeed, she will ferret it out and I could not bear to be so brutally exposed.

I remember bitterly what Charlotte wrote on the margin of one of my poems:

For the moors, for the moors where the short grass
Like velvet beneath us should lie!
For the moors, for the moors where each high pass
Rose sunny against the clear sky!

She felt that the repetition of 'for the moors' was unnecessary. How dare she! I never sought her opinion of my writing. Nor ever shall!

It is only my brother who understands me. We have a secret knowledge of each other that my sisters cannot fathom.

He spoke the truth at our precious waterfall. He said that I was still alone when everybody was here.

I do feel apart from my sisters – and sometimes from him as well.

There is a part of me that I fear – a part of me that loved William Weightman so fiercely that he would have been repulsed had he ever suspected it.

I wished to be as wild with him as I feel here at Dove Stones Moor, when the sky is such an angry grey, and the wind unsettles my hair and there is only the rustling of heather to heed me.

I loved William Weightman in a way that I am ashamed to admit even to you, my diary.

I desired every inch of him – every lock of his coal hair – the corners of his warm smile – the blue of his gentle eyes. I wanted to explore him as Sir Francis Drake explored the New World. I wanted to tell my secrets to him as a Roman Catholic does in confession.

I believed him to be my salvation.

Now I have not only lost him, but God as well.

For love of William Weightman I would willingly have become a curate's wife. I would have embraced his God as father has compelled me to embrace his.

Through sinful love of man, I would have found my path to God and salvation.

Now there is only the wild, untangled world behind the parsonage that calls to me – that snares me in its crags like a fox caught in a trap.

It is Anne who has triumphed, for she is the true Christian among us all. Even Charlotte cannot compete with the gentle piety of our youngest sister. Anne is the embodiment of everything that is good.

William did well to claim the youngest and fairest of us.

No doubt, one day, Charlotte will find her own clergyman.

It is too late for me.

Could I ever love such unabashed goodness as William Weightman again?

Salvation comes but once.

Let the lightning streak.

Let the thunder roar.

Let the rain fall upon me with such force that my very clothes are torn asunder

Let the moors have me.

I am theirs.

The Journal of Branwell Brontë

29th November, 1845

You possess me now, Journal. You are my new mistress, demanding that I fill your pages. This cold day in November I will not stir from my bed. I shall not even dine till I have described the events which I will title:

The Hunt Ball

At Thorp Green, the October of 1843, scarcely two years ago, autumn was anxious to obliterate the traces of summer and drench us in rusty colours. The leaves had changed from green to reddish-brown in the blink of an eye. The wind could not resist making careless circles of them about the sky before abandoning them to the drenched fields and muddy hedgerows.

The air was as crisp as a butterfly's wings, as invigorating as the first daub of morning water poured from the ewer on my dresser with which I would splash my sleepy face, my blue eyes crusted with slumber, my hair askew about my head.

No matter how early I arose, it seemed that Master Edmund had already breakfasted and was awaiting me in the kitchen.

We were now in the habit of taking an invigorating constitutional before ascending to the classroom. Edmund was now taller than I. He had the long legs, but fortunately not the girth of his father, and stepped with such celerity about the estate I was compelled to quicken my stride to keep pace with him.

On one early morning in late October, preparations for the hunt ball were in progress. The carpets were laid down, the bed-hangings festooned, white counterpanes were spread, toilet tables arranged, furniture rubbed, and vases set to be filled with fresh flowers. The floors were scoured, the steps and banisters of the grand staircase polished to the brightness of brass, and the grand piano tuned to perfection.

Cook was baking special pies in the kitchen; outside, the gardeners were clipping hedges, raking leaves and spreading new gravel along the twisting drive that led to Thorp Green. Wagons were arriving with food-stuffs and decorations for the great hall. Extra servants had been engaged from the village. Guests would arrive from York, Bradford, Leeds, and as far away as London. The air was electric with anticipation. Only Anne and I were detached, uninvolved in the impending festivities, for we would be observers and not participants; the art of observing is one that suits us Brontës well.

As far as Mr and Mrs Thornton were concerned, the highlight of the weekend festivities would be the announcement at the great ball of their daughter Alice's engagement to young Lord Leslie Broughton, for the apprentice horticulturist had finally relinquished his flowers long enough to ask for this beautiful young lady's hand in marriage.

To say that Miss Alice was displeased by the impending nuptials would be an understatement. It took all my sister's saintly patience and forbearance both to appease and police the recalcitrant young lady.

Young Edmund was also disturbed, not by the engagement of his sister, but at the prospect of his compulsory participation in the fox hunt that was to precede it.

On this particular morning in October, when we passed by the estate kennels, the horde of spotted beagles, clamouring already for the hunt, scratched their anxious paws against the wire of their cage and demanded our attention. Edmund knew most by name and we let ourselves inside so that we could pat their smooth pelts.

Soon Mr Parkening, the kennel-master, descended from his horse and approached us, watching Edmund stroke the lively animals. 'They seem awfully hungry, Parkening,' Edmund remarked, observing how eagerly the hounds licked at his fingers.

'Well, they should be, Master Edmund,' the burly man, who was all drooping moustache beneath a soft cap, replied. 'You have to keep them lean and hungry before the hunt, else they'll lose interest in the fox.'

Parkening moved closer to the pen.

'Perhaps you'd like to see the fox, Master Edmund,' he suggested. 'We have just brought him in this morning.'

Edmund hesitated. 'I would rather not.'

Parkening, not deterred by Edmund's refusal, continued: 'It may be the only decent look you get,' he persisted. 'Once those hounds get hold of him, there will not be enough left for a lady's stole. Have you ever seen a fox up close, Mr Brontë?'

'Only at a distance,' I replied.

'Would you like to see it, Mr Brontë?' my pupil questioned.

'Yes, Edmund, I would.'

Parkening led the way. 'We've got her caged in the shed next to the chicken coup. How that little foxie would love to mix in with those chickies! Feathers would be flying!'

How pitiable and small the vulpine creature looked, locked in a small cage, away from familiar babbling becks. Its radiant fur was the colour of my hair, its penetrating eyes were as brown as roasted chestnuts. Although its legs were short and sturdy, its body was long and sleek. In captivity she was helpless and anxious, darting eyes pleading for some plan of escape. 'She should lead you on a merry chase,' Parkening predicted.

'I have a good mind to let her go,' Edmund stated.

'That is not a good notion, young sir,' Parkening admonished, 'for we cannot have a fox hunt without the fox.'

'Should we give it a name?' I ventured.

Edmund shook his head. 'I would rather not name something that is going to be so brutally murdered.'

'Come,' I said, pulling the boy outside, for we were both growing depressed. 'Latin is calling.'

Edmund was only too happy to escape the captive fox and stride back to the manor house. 'Does not Caesar ever finish fighting these wretched wars?'

I shook my head. 'War will always be with us.'

Soon even I became caught up in anticipation of the festive occasion. As guests began to arrive in the afternoon, their carriages winding up the drive-way, my heart began to pound a little faster and my cheeks flushed with excitement.

Edmund, who in contrast to his tutor was more in dread of the frivolities, had been summoned downstairs to help his parents greet the arrivals. I watched alone from the tallest turret, observing the graceful progress of ladies from their carriages; how pleased they appeared to be summoned to Thorp Green, how dashing their husbands.

As I returned to my chamber, Edmund advanced down a corridor towards me, so young and handsome in his maroon jacket and white shirt, bowing to the ladies so that his dark hair fell over his forehead and framed his angelic face. 'Mr Brontë!' he called, then hurried over to me and clasped my arm. 'Mama has sent me to inform you that you and Miss Brontë are requested to attend maestro Liszt's concert this evening.'

I smiled broadly, for I was determined to hear the acclaimed genius play, even if that necessitated my standing outside beneath a window. 'We would be delighted.'

'Mama says you are to stand in the rear of the chamber against the wall, for there are scarcely chairs enough for our guests. Of course, if I had my way, you would be seated right beside me at the feet of the great maestro!'

'I am sure Mr Liszt's music will be glorious no matter where one is positioned.'

Edmund wished to stay and converse, but duty prevented his tarrying.

However, he could not resist turning back once more and smiling. 'I think I should prefer Caesar's Wars to what is required of me this week-end.'

How shall I describe the luxurious repast being prepared in the kitchen? The enormous pig, with a large pippin apple in its mouth, dressed with garden greens and a colourful chutney garnish, was surpassed by the turbot, on a steaming bed of rice, accompanied by succulent vegetables of all sorts.

Mr Liszt was long and narrow with an impressive mane of dark hair. He hovered over the grand piano like a giant eagle determined to subdue his prey and succeeded beyond expectation. The great hall reverberated with the melodious strains and prodigious bravura of his performance.

Anne was as thrilled as I. We hugged the walls and remained as unobtrusive as possible. Edmund, startlingly handsome in a navy-blue velvet suit, turned on more than one occasion to smile at me. The young Miss Alice, a vision in pale pink with matching ribbons adorning the ringlets of her blonde hair, turned to exchange dismayed looks with my sister when Lord Broughton seized an opportunity to hold her hand during a particularly moving passage. Even Miss Mary, lovely in a mauve satin dress that exposed her shoulders and suggested a fount of undiscovered femininity, beamed in our direction. But it was to the radiant Mrs Thornton that my eyes were drawn. I was the moth to her irresistible flame.

How beautifully placid she appeared under the hypnotic spell of Mr Liszt's music; such a contrast to her nervous anticipation during the days preceding this occasion. I feared that she would wilt under the weight of her responsibilities, but now she seemed to thrive on the approval of her guests; for, in truth, it was Mrs Fitzpatrick who had taken matters in hand so that all would run smoothly.

I was mesmerised as much by the beauty of Mrs Thornton as by the audacity of the pianism. If the translucent white of her long graceful neck, her sloping shoulders and exposed bosom were not enough, there were her large blue eyes, as brilliant and sparkling as the sapphire necklace about her neck; and her fine head of hair, raven-black, and so becomingly arranged – a crown of thick plaits behind, and long glossy curls in front. She was dressed in pure white silk: a blue sash hung over her shoulder and across her breast, was tied at the side, and descended in long fringed ends below her knee. She wore a single white flower in her hair, a camellia, the perfect contrast to the jetty mass of her curls. I remember each detail of her extraordinary appearance as if it were yesterday.

In the crescendo of Liszt's rhapsody Lydia Thornton turned to seek me out. For a fleeting instant our eyes met and held each other.

How well I remember that Saturday! Even under the influence of spirits here at the Black Bull, that day is as clear as the sky that welcomed it. It was a perfect morning for the great hunt. Leaves of myriad colours floated like scarves above us touched by the light of a compliant sun. The sky was a friendly shade of blue and the few clouds hovering on the horizon were as pale as lilies.

I lingered over my breakfast, observing the hectic parade of servants to and from the dining hall. Soon I ventured outside to view the assembly around the stables in preparation for the great hunt. I was standing on a rise above the estate so that the riders appeared like bright red streaks in a John Constable landscape, an artist whom I greatly admired. If only I had been gifted with his ability with a brush. I could well imagine how brilliantly he would have depicted the canvas stretching before me: the scarlet jackets and the black hats, the ladies' dark riding gear, the assortment of horses, and the hounds running eagerly under-foot in anticipation of the fox. I fear I will never be more than a promising painter of portraits. To depict such a scene will always be beyond my talents.

My eyes sought out each member of the Thornton family, only the mistress of the house absent, for she neither rode nor enjoyed the hunt. Her husband cut a fine figure atop his black stallion, his hair, falling beneath his cap, as black as the mane of his horse. Mary, who did not usually ride side-saddle, had acquiesced on this occasion and was sitting on her mount, as magnificently as her father, her skirt gathered about her, her whip in readiness to spur the steed. The beautiful blonde young Alice did not appear as anxious as her sister to commence the hunt. Certainly she did not want to be in the lead, for she lagged behind the others so that young Lord Broughton was compelled to turn his horse around and trot back so that he could ride alongside her. Even he, usually a gangling contradiction of elbows and knees, looked dashing in his scarlet and red. But it was young Edmund who cut the most imposing figure. How paradoxical that the one rider who wished to have absolutely nothing to do with the hunt looked the most imposing. What a handsome young man he was!

All was in readiness now. A stirrup-cup was passed, the hunting horn sounded. 'Tallyho!' someone shouted at sight of the fox being released. Horses reared and the hounds barked vociferously: their tails awhirl in excitement until they were permitted to pursue. The hunt was on! Away the riders flew!

Soon only I and the stable-hands remained. When you are the impecunious son of a parsimonious preacher, you are not included in such frivolities. Perhaps if I did paint like John Constable I could have made inroads into this polite society. Even now, as I write this, even after the terrible things that have happened, perhaps one day, as a novelist, I can find acceptance.

Luncheon was to be served to the hungry and thirsty hunters *en plein air*. Tables had been set up alongside the lake, which provided the proper sylvan setting. I had retired to labour over the completion of a poem I hoped suitable for the *Yorkshire Gazette*, but instead spent the time gazing outside my window. Outside the emerald lawns were a hive of activity. Servants carried food the long distance to the lake, then scurried back for more. They resembled lines of worker ants. Mrs Thornton stood with her flowered parasol that matched her beautiful dress. What a contrast she would make to the ladies in their black riding outfits.

Suddenly, on the far horizon, a red-coated rider emerged from the woods far beyond the lake. He was galloping furiously as if he himself were being pursued; and, indeed, another rider immediately emerged from the forest to give chase. As the steeds drew closer, I discerned young Master Edmund fleeing towards the manor house with his father in close pursuit. As the young man reined his horse to a halt and jumped to the ground at the foot of his mother, the look of anguish on his face was so alarming that I hurried out of the room and made a hasty descent to ascertain the cause of his distress. As I ran outside Mr Thornton reined his horse and dismounted. 'Come here, you poltroon!' he bellowed, threatening his son with his whip.

'What has happened?' Mrs Thornton pleaded, her eyes widening in alarm.

Ignoring his wife, he continued to advance upon his retreating son. 'How dare you disgrace me in front of our peers!'

'What has he done?' Mrs Thornton enquired.

Young Edmund's lips were trembling, yet he managed to find the words to defend himself. 'I'm not sorry for what I did. You should not have insisted that I come!'

'You are going to start behaving like a huntsman or...' He brandished his whip. 'Hunt, shoot, and fight: the rest is not worth a fillip!' He raised his whip higher. 'Come here!'

Mrs Thornton stepped bravely between her husband and her son. 'What has he done?' she demanded once again.

'It was the fox!' Edmund struggled to utter the words, for there were hot tears starting down his cheeks. 'When the hounds finally found it, I knew they were going to rip it apart. It was making such pitiful cries! Mr Parkening was there with his shotgun. I pulled it away from him and shot the fox before the dogs could destroy it.' He stared defiantly at his father. 'You insisted I learn how to shoot! Well, there! I made a good shot, didn't I?'

'You little fop!' His father lashed him across the face with his whip. 'This is something I should have done a long time ago!'

His wife attempted to stop him, but he brushed her aside. I could tolerate no more. I stepped between them and tore the whip from Mr Thornton's hand.

'You stay out of this!' he threatened me angrily.

'I forbid you!' I held the whip away from him.

'You forbid me?'

'Our guests are returning for lunch!' Mrs Thornton whispered urgently; for indeed they were riding towards us en masse.

Her husband glanced behind him: a scarlet sea of riders was trotting out of the woods and towards the lake. He glared from me to his son, the vein running from his scalp to his temple so red and pronounced it looked as if it was going to burst. 'I will deal with you later!' he said to me, and snatched the whip from my hand. 'As for you!' he said, turning to his son, 'I don't want to see your mealy-mouthed face outside your room until every one of our guests has departed!'

Mounting his horse with the ease of a much lighter man, he rode off. 'Oh, Edmund,' his mother cried, going to her son and holding him in her arms. 'One day your father will learn to appreciate what a fine son he has in you.'

'When Hell freezes over!' Edmund spat out vehemently, choking back his sobs.

Mrs Thornton pulled free and looked towards the lake. 'Mr Branwell, will you take Edmund inside? I must see to my guests.'

I nodded and our eyes locked a moment before she glided across the lawn, as beautiful as any flower Mr Pottage grew in his greenhouse. I put my arm around Edmund and led him towards the house. He was shaking with humiliation. My heart reached out to him. 'Come, Edmund.'

'Please, Mr Branwell,' he whimpered, 'could we go to your room instead of mine? As soon as she rides back Mary will seek me out to humiliate me as well. I cannot face anyone but you.'

I hugged the young man a little tighter. 'I would be honoured to entertain such a distinguished guest.'

We ascended the stairs slowly and were soon inside my chamber. 'I feel safe here,' Edmund said, drying his eyes.

'And so you shall be.'

'Oh, Branwell,' he sighed, flying into my arms for protection. 'Was it wrong to do what I did?'

'There is a fox in animal heaven who is blessing you this very moment.'

'I feel so safe here in your arms,' he murmured, squeezing me tightly.

I pulled back a little to look at him. There was an angry streak of red across Edmund's handsome face where his father had struck him. 'Does this hurt?' I asked, gently touching the mark.

'Not when you touch it,' he whispered, taking my hand away from his cheek and kissing the tips of my fingers. 'I love you so much, Branwell.'

Before I could stop him, his eager lips found mine. There was such an innocent gentleness about his kiss that I was powerless to resist; but soon, as his lips grew hungrier, I stopped. It was not that I had no desire for this fragile young man, but the figure of his mother loomed before me, stronger than that of the son.

I slipped off his red hunting jacket, led him to my bed and pulled off his boots. 'You must sleep, Edmund. Shakespeare himself says that it is sleep that knits up the ravell'd sleeve of care.'

He was eager to feel the warmth of my blanket. He made himself comfortable and stretched out his arms to me. 'Will you sleep beside me, Branwell? Will you hold me in your arms so that I can feel protected?'

I could not resist.

I moved to my door, locked it and fell onto my bed and into Edmund's warm embrace. How could I refuse to be the shelter from his storm, the retreat from his torment? This was probably the closest I will ever come to being the recipient of unbridled love. This was the unquestioning ardour a dog gives its master.

As young Edmund held me as tightly as his young strength would allow the stirrings of his youthful masculinity were unmistakable. He wanted more from me than simply to be sheltered, but somehow I resisted. I simply engulfed him and held him tightly until he fell asleep, his gentle breath a whisper in my ear.

This was all that transpired. The father did not matter; but if I had gone further I could never have faced the mother, for I knew I loved her as this boy loved me.

How long did Edmund and I sleep in each other's arms? When I awoke the sun was setting. Beyond my doorway I could hear footsteps scurrying along the hallway. Preparations were underway for the great ball. Edmund's arm was across my chest, his sleeping head nestled next to mine. How trusting and innocent and content he appeared, protected, as he was, in the niche of my body. I stroked his abundant hair and kissed him gently on the forehead; he came slowly awake. 'How long have we slept, Branwell?' he questioned.

'All afternoon, I suspect.'

He stretched luxuriously and clasped his arms about me. 'I would choose never to quit your bed.'

'But quit it you must, for to-night is the Great Ball.'

'To which I am no longer invited,' he reminded me.

'Your father may have relented. Everyone will be wondering where you are.'

'With someone I love very much.' How romantic was youth! He was a Romeo with no proper Juliet.

Edmund pulled himself reluctantly from the bed. As he stood over me I was reminded of the dark gipsy boy who had seduced me; but there would be no seduction here, no matter how much he desired it. I watched Edmund pull on his boots and coat. The arresting red of his hunting jacket was in vivid contrast to his dark hair and brows. 'The only thing I like about hunting, Branwell,' he smiled, 'is this costume.'

With that he came back to my bed to embrace and kiss me once more; a gentle peck at the lips was all I permitted. He would have crawled back in beside me to be held all over again, but instead I led him to the door. One last squeeze of my arm and he departed. I was suddenly hungry, for I had not had a bite of lunch, and the enticing aroma of cook's preparations for dinner were wafting to my room.

I dressed quickly in my dark suit of the previous evening and made my way downstairs, anxious to observe from a discreet distance the guests in all their wealthy finery. I managed to find a meal amidst the pandemonium of the kitchen and, returning upstairs, I could already hear the strains of music from the dining-room where guests were being summoned to dinner. The sound of violin, harp and fiddle was intoxicating. My toes were tapping of their own accord. I longed to dance, but I was not invited, and, besides, there was no-one to dance with, except my sister and neither of us had had any practice.

The couples descending the great stairway looked even more elegant than on the previous evening, especially Mrs Thornton, a vision in blue, who spied me observing her from my over-head niche and smiled such a smile of understanding that I trembled at it.

Young Lord Broughton saw me as well, but refused to acknowledge my presence, as did many of the other guests.

The last to make their descent were the Thornton girls, followed by my sister, who accompanied them to the bottom of the stairway. They were elegantly dressed. Anne had supervised their costuming to perfection.

As Anne watched her charges make their imposing entrance into the dining-room, I observed how proud she was with their fine appearance. I applauded from above; my sister looked up startled. 'Branwell!' she exclaimed, starting back upstairs.

'They look radiant this evening,' I told her. 'One would never know what trouble they have been.'

'I have never been more anxious to see two girls married,' Anne smiled, reaching me at the landing where I had been hiding.

'Except, perhaps, yourself.'

'There is truth to that,' she admitted.

The music floated upstairs on clouds of Mozart. 'May I have the honour of this dance, Miss Brontë?'

'We have not had much experience of dancing.'

'All the more reason that we should practise now.'

It was not music to dance to – that would come later in the evening – it was music to dine by; but we attempted to dance nevertheless, forgetting ourselves as we endeavoured to be graceful and light on our feet. 'There is someone else you would rather were holding you in his arms,' I teased.

'I have yet to dance with William,' Anne confessed; 'but I have the strongest suspicion that he will be skillful.'

Edmund stepped out of his doorway to behold us in the act of whirling down the hallway. He had changed into his elegant evening clothes in case he was summoned. 'How handsome you appear!' he exclaimed delightedly.

Anne stopped and flushed with embarrassment, but Edmund immediately stepped up to my sister and bowed to her. 'May I have the honour of this dance, Miss Brontë?'

'You should be downstairs with the others, Master Edmund,' Anne sympathised; for surely all the servants had discussed what had taken place between Edmund and his father. 'I champion what you did. I think your father is being unnecessarily cruel.'

'I would much rather be here with you and Mr Brontë,' he replied, looking happily over at me. Doubtless he wanted to dance with his tutor as well. 'Now, if you please, I would like to have just one dance.'

How could my sister refuse such a gentle offer? She opened her arms to Edmund and he towered over her as he whirled her along the hallway. He was already a skilled dancer.

They had so sooner begun than the music stopped. 'If I know father, he is making his first toast of the evening. At least I am not down there to hear it.' He released Anne and took my arm as well. 'I am very hungry and I hope that both of you will accompany me to the kitchen.'

'I am hungry as well,' my sister confided.

'And I shall observe you both, for I have already dined amidst the great uproar of preparation.'

Edmund greatly enjoyed his repast at the kitchen table.

'Meals are so much more pleasant in here!' he exclaimed, happily sampling one of cook's pastries. 'Perhaps father will consign me to the kitchen forever. He spreads such gloom across our table. He has us all on edge and puts everyone off their food.'

'But not to-night,' Anne responded.

'With guests, he is a different man entirely,' Edmund agreed. 'Especially when a Lord is here for the catching.' He devoured the remainder of his pastry and dabbed his lips with a napkin. 'I shall have to miss the grand announcement of the evening.' He held up his glass. 'To my sister, for gaining our entrance into the House of Lords!'

Anne picked delicately at her food. 'Miss Alice has been so compliant of late, I cannot help but be suspicious that something is afoot. I have scarcely had her out of my sight, and now the fateful evening is upon us; but still...'

'Perhaps she has decided she likes the sound of "Lady" before her name,' Edmund suggested.

'It takes more than a title to make a lady,' Anne responded in a way that reminded me of her eldest sister. Anne had been always so gentle and saintly that I am still surprised at the defiance the Thorntons unearthed in her.

After supper, we donned our great-coats for warmth against the October chill and ventured outside to observe the revellers through one of the large windows in the great hall that was now a ballroom. Men and women waltzed by the window with great abandon and the music became so fervid that we could not help but tap our own toes. Candelabra blazed brightly; the many flowers were visible throughout the hall. Finally, the music ceased. Mr Thornton stepped in front of the musicians with Lord Broughton towering beside him. 'I have a special announcement to make this evening,' he began. 'One that makes my family very proud. Champagne has been poured for one and all for I should like to make a toast. If my eldest daughter will please join us...'

We waited anxiously for the appearance of the beauteous Alice, but it was not forthcoming. 'Has anyone seen my eldest daughter?' He waited anxiously. 'Alice?' he shouted. Then: 'Mrs Thornton, would you kindly fetch your daughter?'

'I fear the worst,' Anne murmured and ran towards the entrance of the manor, Edmund and I hurrying after.

Inside the manor house we beheld Mrs Thornton slowly descending the stairs and clutching a letter that she read until she collapsed on the steps, where her husband, storming out of the great hall, discovered her. 'And where is Alice?' he demanded.

'Here, Mr Thornton, read this for yourself,' his wife whispered as she thrust the epistle at him. 'She has gone – run off with that itinerant actor. They are to be married. She plans to appear with him on the stage.'

'I will see them burn in Hell first!' He turned to see us approaching and lashed out at my sister. 'This is your fault, Miss Brontë. It was your responsibility to be vigilant.'

'And so I was,' she protested, 'until the very moment Miss Alice descended to dinner and was placed under your watchful eye!'

'She slipped away after dinner to attend to her toilette,' her mother recalled. 'Until you began to make your announcement I had no idea she had been missing so long.'

'After them! We must go after them!' he exclaimed. 'I have promised her to another and she will wed him if I have to carry her bound and shackled down the aisle myself!'

'But where would they have gone?' Mrs Thornton wailed.

Mr Thornton turned to my sister. 'Do you know, Miss Brontë?'

Anne bristled at such an insult. 'I have no such knowledge!'

He glared at her. 'You and your brother! Worthless! Both

of you!' Then he noticed his son and became even more agitated. 'You have been confined to your room!'

'You should have confined Alice!' his wife retorted.

'I would not be surprised if you approved of this behaviour!' he countered.

'I do not share the same disgust for acting that you do, Mr Thornton,' his wife responded, pulling herself to her feet. 'But as to our daughter running off in such a manner, I am as distressed as you.'

'What kind of children have you raised in this house? Girls who are no better than whores and a son who is as feeble as a popish nun!'

Mrs Thornton lifted her head, determined to salvage a modicum of decorum from what we had witnessed. 'I suggest, Mr Thornton, that you spend less time in castigating your wife and go after our wayward child before it is too late.'

'By God, I shall,' he threatened. 'And bring her back dead if she dares defy me.' He started off, but, realising he was still wearing evening clothes, turned instead to his son and barked at him. 'You have Allison saddle up Yellow Jacket. Go!' he yelled as Edmund hesitated. 'Show me that you're at least good for something!'

Edmund turned and ran outside while I stood with Anne. 'Oh, Madam,' she began, 'if there is anything that...' but Anne did not really know what more to say.

Mrs Thornton smoothed her dress and arranged her hair. 'There is nothing anyone can do at this moment, Miss Brontë. I know that you have done your very best and do not hold you culpable for my daughter's shameless behaviour.' She somehow found the strength to continue. 'Now there are guests to attend to.' She resumed her graceful descent. 'All we can do is pray for the best. I do not know if I should confide the truth to Lord Broughton or pretend that Alice is indisposed. If she is not retrieved he will be crushed

… but he does have his flowers to comfort him, doesn't he?'

News of the flight of Francis Thornton's daughter spread through the manor house like the keen Yorkshire wind. Servant whispered to servant, who in turn confided in master and mistress until a pall descended over the mansion from which Sunday could not recover. In the morning the skies were as grey as the humour of the guests, who made their departures from Thorp Green rather earlier than anticipated. Soon each and every neighbouring village would have news of Alice's disgrace and now young Lord Broughton would never stoop to marry her, even if Mr Thornton were able to retrieve her from the Thespian clutches of the handsome Roxby. She was ruined. November was truly upon us.

It was William Allison who returned from London with a note from the incensed father. I did not set eyes on it, but its meaning was conveyed eagerly to my ear by Edmund during our morning lesson. Soon the entire household was abuzz with the news. Alice Thornton had married Henry Roxby at Gretna Green shortly after her flight from Yorkshire and was now playing alongside her husband with the same acting troupe with which Roxby had appeared in Scarborough. But now they were at London's Haymarket Theatre.

Edmund could hardly contain himself at the news. 'No amount of coercion on my father's part could persuade Alice to renounce her new husband and return to Thorp Green – not that Lord Broughton would have her now anyway.' He stopped to catch his breath before continuing excitedly. 'Father declares that he has disinherited her and is so disgusted with the way mother has brought us up that he has accepted an invitation to accompany an expedition into Africa. Who knows when we shall see him again? Mother is supervising the packing of his clothing now so that Allison can carry it to him.' He moved around the table to where I was sitting, fell to his knees and clasped his arms about me. 'It is such glorious news that I simply must have a kiss, Branwell.' He pulled my head down to his so that his lips could reach mine. Usually I resisted these kisses, but I did not want to destroy this new happiness. 'If only Mary would be sent off to school; it would just be you, mother and me. Everything would be perfect!'

'But that would mean my sister would have to depart as well.'

'I did not think of that,' he replied, getting to his feet and embracing me from behind. 'For she is as dear to me as you and I would hate to lose either of you!'

'Enough to put up with your sister?'

'One hundred times more than that!' How happy he was! His young body tingled with the excitement a debtor must feel when he is released from prison. The shadow over Thorp Green – the shadow of his father – had passed.

I tousled his hair and sat him down in his own chair. 'Since Miss Alice is now performing Shakespeare, we shall resume our study of *Macbeth*.'

'Oh, Branwell,' Edmund enthused, opening the text, but still too happy to concentrate. 'We must incorporate an African safari into our adventures together. We shall have a character like my father and he will be captured by cannibals and cooked in a big pot.'

'Do you hate your father that much?'

He pondered a moment before responding. 'Not that much, I suppose, but I doubt that absence will make my heart grow fonder.' He studied me curiously as I searched for our place in the play. 'Do you love your father, Branwell?'

'With all my heart.'

'More than you love me?'

'The love of a son for his father is different.'

'Why do you love him?'

'Because, no matter how disappointed or disgusted he might be with me, I know he will always forgive me.'

'Do you think my father loves me, Branwell?'

I would not lie to this young man. 'I am not sure. Perhaps more than we know.'

'What a strange way he has of showing it.'

'That might sometimes be remarked of my own father too.'

The end of November spread an icy mantle of frost across Thorp Green that seldom deigned to melt. At such times as these, when we were reluctant to leave the warmth of the hearth, a letter from home was welcome indeed, especially one from the Reverend William Weightman, or from Charlotte in Brussels.

Anne burst into our classroom, Mary at her heels, so eager to share the news of our oldest sister. 'Charlotte is coming home to stay!'

'In time for Christmas?'

Anne scanned the letter. 'She will be spending her last Christmas in Brussels, but will return so quickly afterwards that she will be home in Haworth to ring in the New Year!' Anne marvelled at the quick passing of the years. '1845! Soon we shall be at half-century.'

'And I shall be all grown and do what I want with my life,' Mary proclaimed.

'And I shall be grown as well,' her brother echoed. 'And Branwell and I shall travel about the world and never come home!'

Anne looked curiously from pupil to teacher. With the departure of Mr Thornton, Edmund's attachment to me had become more pronounced. However, on this morning filled with news of our sister, Anne had other matters to consider. 'What a wonderful New Year it shall be!'

'Not for us,' Edmund stated forlornly, 'for it will be only mother, Mary and me for company.'

'We shall manage,' Mary interjected, for although she was genuinely fond of my sister, she did not care for her strict regimen of lessons.

'Is it Charlotte's way with father that has you so excited by her return?' I teased my sister.

'Whatever do you mean?' she questioned, wide-eyed, yet knowing full well. 'I have missed Charlotte terribly.'

'Perhaps she will be able to influence father in a manner to your liking.'

'What manner?' Mary was quick to question.

'We are speaking of family matters,' Anne said sharply.

'And are we not family now?' Edmund asked.

'Hush!' my sister admonished, wishing desperately to change the subject that had coloured her cheeks so suddenly one would have thought she was in the throes of scarlet fever. She brandished Charlotte's letter and quickly found the passage. 'Here – our sister has actually observed Queen Victoria on her visit to her uncle, Leopold, King of the Belgians.' She narrowed her eyes to read the passage. 'She describes our Queen as "a little, stout, vivacious lady, plainly dressed and not much dignity or pretension about her".'

'It sounds as if I should like her!' Edmund responded with enthusiasm.

'What a fine husband you might make some-day for the Little Princess Royal,' Anne smiled.

'Does he not have to be a prince himself,' Mary wondered.

'It does not matter,' Edmund responded, 'for I shall never marry.'

'Nor I!' Mary rejoined.

Neither Anne nor I echoed these protestations; for she, at least, hoped she would soon be joined in Holy Matrimony with the personable William Weightman, a man whom I would certainly treasure as brother-in-law. 'You shall soon change your minds, both of you,' she responded finally. 'One day you will meet someone you will love and that will make all the difference.'

'And have you met someone you love, Miss Brontë?' Mary enquired curiously.

'We are not speaking of me, but *you*!'

'Then that day will never come!' Mary responded with spirit. But Edmund remained silent, glancing shyly at me.

'At least your older sister has taken the plunge,' I said to draw her attention away from Edmund. At mention of Alice, Anne suddenly reached into the pocket of her black winter dress and produced another letter. 'I had almost forgotten. We have received a letter from Miss Alice as well.'

Mary pulled at the envelope to better read the inscription. ' "We"?' she snorted. 'It is addressed only to you.'

Anne opened the envelope carefully. 'But I am certain that it was meant for all of us.'

'Well, read it, then,' Mary demanded, more anxious for news of her sister than she cared to admit.

' "Dear Miss Brontë",' my sister read aloud, ' "doubtless you will be surprised to hear from me, and to learn that of all at Thorp Green I think I miss you most." '

'Well, I like that!' Mary complained.

'Now, Mary,' my sister soothed. 'You two never really got along.'

'It was just as much her fault as it was mine!'

Anne continued reading: ' "Of course I love mother dearly, but father has forbidden her to receive letters from me and I know that Edmund is her favourite and Mary is father's." '

'She is still jealous of me,' Mary snorted, turning to her brother. 'And of you as well.'

Anne ignored her and continued to read: ' "I am so grateful that after Henry's appearance at Thorp Green you insisted I study Mr Shakespeare. Of course I did not have the slightest idea then that I would actually be performing the Bard for London audiences who seem to delight in my appearance. In fact, I believe that Henry is jealous of the attention I am already receiving. My first appearance has only been in an evening of scenes from Mr Shakespeare's plays, but my

Juliet, with Henry as Romeo, was so well received that Mr Hanlon has insisted I learn the entire part. Also, in our evening of Shakespearean scenes, I have performed Ophelia in Hamlet's wooing scene, and this has also been well-received." '

'How I wish we could see her!' Edmund sighed.

'She was always acting anyway,' Mary declared begrudgingly. 'She might as well be paid for it.'

'Read on, Anne,' I prompted, for I was curious for the remainder of Miss Alice's news.

' "Mr Hanlon has confided in me that his wife is now entirely too old to portray Juliet and Ophelia and other of the leading parts in Mr Shakespeare's comedies; and, having observed her – although she is a fine actress – I can well agree; so I shall be learning many of these rôles." '

'Then my sister is to be a comedienne as well as a tragedienne,' Edmund mused.

'They probably pay her very little. I wonder how they live,' said Mary.

Anne was perhaps dreaming of her own future. 'When you are young and in love, Mary, sometimes that is almost enough.'

Mary pursed her lips. 'What else does Alice say?'

' "Miss Brontë, the Hanlons have a lady dresser who helps them with their costumes and their changes and brews their tea and performs other sundry duties. I would dearly love it, if you would consider coming to London and becoming my own personal lady." '

'The very idea!' Mary exclaimed.

'You would not accept this position, would you, Miss Brontë?' Edmund asked unsurely.

Anne made no reply but read further. ' "It would be wonderful to see you again and to have you with me always. I am sure that you would find the theatrical world most fascinating. If you would please write to me at the enclosed address – a dreary rooming house with scarcely enough heat – and let me know of your decision…" '

'You would not leave us, would you, Miss Brontë?' Mary pleaded.

'Certainly not to become a backstage maid.'

'Good.' Mary sighed with relief, then glanced at the letter. 'Look, there is more.'

Anne found her place and continued. ' "Thank God that father has gone off to Africa. He made a terrible nuisance of himself and Mr Hanlon finally had to summon the police to keep him away from the theatre, which, as it was in Scarborough, is just a tent. Father can keep his old money, although Henry and I could certainly use some now. I must return to learning my new roles, but I shall write again with news of future performances. Please convey my good wishes to Mary, Edmund and Mr Brontë. Affectionately, Alice." '

'Well, at least she mentioned us,' Mary observed to her brother, somewhat satisfied that they had not been entirely neglected.

'Post-script,' my sister added. ' "Do you think Lord Broughton will take back the name of the flower he named after me?" '

Anne folded the stationery. 'I must say that Miss Alice writes a very nice letter.' She glanced pointedly at Mary. 'Our composition exercises have not been in vain.'

'Nor has Mr Shakespeare.'

'Which we shall resume immediately. Since your sister will be portraying Ophelia, we shall delve into *Hamlet*.' She locked her arm with her pupil. 'Come, Miss Mary, the Bard awaits.'

I returned to the table and faced my own student. 'And we shall continue to study the Melancholy Dane as well.'

'Is not Hamlet a student my age?'

'Indeed, almost he is, but the part is not often performed

by one so young, for I assume it takes great experience to portray such a complex character.'

'Perhaps I also shall venture onto the stage some day.'

'Is that before or after our trip around the world?'

Edmund smiled across to me. 'During, I suspect.'

How much easier our lives would have been if we had just run away. I almost wish now that we had done so. If we had run off and I had given in to Edmund's youthful desires, I wonder now if that would have been so terrible after all? Certainly the outcome might have been happier than the tragedy which engulfed us.

The Diary of Emily Brontë

12th October, 1844

Father's eyesight has become so weak that he can scarcely see the nose on his face, let alone read the sorrow on mine.

Perhaps Martha Brown, even at such a young age, suspects my agony of unrequited love, but she keeps her silence.

I attempt to ignore William when he comes to assist father at the parsonage but my resolve melts like spring snow at sight of his welcome face. I wait anxiously to be noticed by him and appreciated. I become the foolish girl I never was in childhood.

Has he yet taken Anne in his arms and whispered love in her ears so that no-one else can hear?

Has he pressed his precious lips against hers as I desire him to press those same lips against mine?

Has she felt the comforting warmth of his compelling body?

Oh, William, must I spend the remainder of my life in your company without ever being able to declare my love for you?

Must I spend my life denying my longing?

Why did you choose Anne when it is I who could love you with such intensity that you would scarce recover from it – even though I know you are too good for me and would be shocked by the depth of my feelings for you?

These feelings erupt like vents of fiery lava and consume me: yet God would forgive such passion if it were tempered in marriage to you and blessed by his Holy Name!

William Weightman – William Weightman – William Weightman!

I take such pleasure in simply writing your name.
Emily Weightman! Would it ever be so?
I shout it to the moors, but it is Anne who will bear your name – not I!
When you first came to the parsonage and discovered that neither my sisters nor I had ever received a 'valentine', you walked all the way to Branford to post your special missives to us, so that no-one else in Haworth would know. The heart you drew for me then captured my own and made me your prisoner.
I doubt that Charlotte still has your 'Valentine'. I suppose Anne has hers. Mine is preserved forever!
We sat in our parlour and created a poem together to send back to you in response. Even then I wanted to create my own. I wish now that I had, so you would know that it is I who love you the most.
What would I have written?
I no longer have the words.
A broken heart is like a broken arm that can no longer hold a pen.
Yet sometimes this pen has a will of its own.

He comes with western winds, with evening's wandering airs,
With that clear dusk of heaven that brings the thickest stars;
Winds take a pensive tone and stars a tender fire
And visions rise and change which kill me with desire –

The Journal of Branwell Brontë

9th December, 1845

How many sentences I have written here, Dear Journal, and still the story is not complete and it will soon be Christmas.

Since all my sisters are at home, I no longer have a room of my own and must share with my father. How disgusted he is with a son who stumbles home at close of the Black Bull Inn and who remains in bed long after his father has risen to minister to the faithful of his parish.

I remain in my morning bed long after everyone has risen, safe beneath my covers, warm against the bitter chill of a cold house where the evening fire has died. Is nothing as cold as a Yorkshire winter?

I uncover my journal and attempt to pick up the pieces where I left off. How strange to tell a tale in which I am the protagonist. I know my sisters have not faced this dilemma. If only it were fiction, I could fabricate a happy ending instead of the bitter truth.

In Which Winter Arrives at Thorp Green

November at Thorp Green. It was a happy time for me despite the cruel weather. With the elopement of young Alice and the departure of her father the tenor of the manor house had changed. Mrs Thornton had retired to her chambers and took her meals in her rooms, but my sister and I and our charges continued as if nothing had changed. Real tragedy had not yet found its way to the Thorntons' door.

Anne and I had no knowledge of events at Haworth. We were content in the seclusion of Thorp Green and warm beside the fires of our rooms.

Why am I not able to continue? I am simply too tired to proceed to-day with you, My Journal. I shall set you aside and rest. To-morrow morning I shall chain myself to my desk and write till my fingers can no longer hold the quill.

The Diary of Emily Brontë

14th November 1844

Dear Diary, I return to you now when all is lost.

When his precious life hung in the balance, hypocrite that I am, I ignored these pages and turned to God. On more than one occasion, I stole into father's empty church to pray that one life at least, would be spared.

I could not bring myself to write on these pages when he lay so ill and I was powerless to save him.

It is the cursed water of Haworth that has taken so many.

It has stolen my beloved William Weightman who can never be replaced in my heart. The water from Head Well is often so green and putrid that even the cattle refuse to drink it. Water is fouled by the overflow from the putrid middensteads. We Brontës are blessed with our own privy; few others in Haworth are. Is it for this reason that we have been spared? Will cholera be a constant threat to us all?

If William had not relieved my weary father from visiting the sick, would my beloved be alive to-day and my father taken instead?

How solicitous William Weightman was in ministering to the ill, with little or no concern for his own well-being.

The epidemic, which began in late August, finally captured him in late September; yet he continued to linger painfully through three short weeks of October before God snuffed out his precious life.

I believe my father was as distraught as I by the illness of his curate. He visited William twice daily in his lodgings.

They would pray together and the saintly curate would whisper to my father that he was prepared to meet his Saviour.

Although father forbade me to risk infection from William's illness, I defied him and stole into his lodgings the day before his death. The air of his small room was thick with malady. No doubt Dr Wheelhouse had done all he could for William, but cholera was an unrelenting scourge that only death could still. As with other victims to the disease, William had become a sickly shadow of his former self. There was little fluid left in his thin body and when I insisted he drink, he was scarcely able to swallow the water I held to his parched lips. When he attempted to smile, I choked back tears at memory of the light that once radiated from his bright eyes.

Still, there was something angelic about his emaciated appearance – a different clarity, as if he were already in sight of paradise.

I took his sweet hand and pressed it to my lips. He watched me curiously. Somehow I think he understood that it was I, Emily Jane Brontë, who loved him most and best of all.

'I have not written Anne of your illness,' I said finally, squeezing his hand, 'because you are going to get well and I do not want to distress her.' I finally released his precious fingers and held the water glass to his lips once more. 'You must drink.'

He tried, but shook his head. 'I have already had a glimpse of our Saviour. He is waiting for me.'

I knew it was the truth. 'Must He be so impatient?'

'I have lived twenty-eight years,' he whispered.

'Your life is just beginning,' I protested. I was thinking of his marriage to my sister. I would rather that he get well and marry Anne than be taken from me entirely.

'I have served our Lord,' he breathed, looking past me. 'Perhaps that is enough.'

'We should have sent for my sister,' I ventured uncertainly.

William managed to shake his head. 'Let Anne remember me as I was. I couldn't speak of it to your father … you will tell her how much I truly loved her.'

'Not as much as *I* love you.'

I am not sorry that I finally said it.

'If only I could have married you all.' He coughed, yet kept his eyes fastened on me. 'I chose Anne because she was best suited to become the wife of a curate, not because I didn't love you and your sister as well.'

'You made the correct decision.'

I kissed him then, a gentle pressing against the wan lips. It was foolhardy, I know. Just once I had to have a taste of him.

William mustered all his feeble strength to push me away. 'You mustn't contaminate yourself!'

'I do not care!'

'Your father has lost two children. That is more than enough.'

He closed his eyes. He shut me out – the world – and went where people go when their bodies are too ill to sustain themselves.

I stole away before anybody should know I had been there.

When my father preached a Sunday afternoon sermon in the memory of his favourite curate, he did something he had never done before. Hitherto he had always preached extempore. This time, in honour of his extraordinary assistant, he had written out his sermon in advance. If his words were perhaps too willing to consign such a young man to his Saviour, they were nevertheless heartfelt. 'A pious youth does not fear to die,' he began. When he concluded, 'We were always like father and son,' tears started down his cheeks.

I had copied out my father's sermon to bring to Branwell

and Anne. There wasn't time to inform them before the service. My father saw no necessity in it, for they could not have arrived in time.

The Journal of Branwell Brontë

15th December, 1845

Dear Journal, I am not a man of my word, for I have neglected you these past days. But now, as December lengthens, I am reminded of another December of a previous year, one that I am eager to transcribe. Without further ado:

December at Thorp Green

Is it only a year since last December? It was a month that began at Thorp Green as any other.

Here at the parsonage the spirit of Christmas, 1845, has yet to descend upon my sisters. Will we Brontës ever recapture our special feeling for this holiday we possessed in our youth?

I shall never forget the year my father gifted us with a box of wooden soldiers, sturdy figures that inspired us to create a history for each and every one of them.

Where are these soldiers now? They have been put away with other childhood things, and our childhood memories.

At Thorp Green, on that first day of December, the house still shrouded in darkness, I awoke to the sound of rain beating against my window. Edmund had crept silently into my bedroom, awakened me with a soft kiss on my forehead and crept in beside me for warmth.

At least, with the advent of rain, there would be no frost; and if the rain lifted, we could stroll about Thorp Green and marvel at how fresh and clean the world looked after an early December bath.

Mrs Thornton was still a stranger to us. We seldom saw her. Once again Anne and I were dining with the children in the cavernous dining-room while the mistress of the house continued to take her meals alone in her room.

On the first afternoon of December, Anne, Edmund, Mary and I tramped energetically about the estate after the rain had ceased. A rainbow arched high above us – surely a sign of hope, though so little was to ensue.

We had stopped in the rose garden to observe a pair of mistle-thrushes splash in the rain-filled bird-bath, their chattering calls filling our ears. The mistletoe berries, from which they derived their name, were already in evidence, and the birds' spotted bellies looked rounded and full.

Mist was rising from the warming soil and everywhere but the rose garden was miasma.

In the distance, towards the trees, where the road opened up from the woods and twisted to the manor house, a figure emerged and glided mysteriously towards us as if indeed it was sailing on water, with nary a foot on ground. This was a hooded apparition, a black cloak billowing behind as if the wraith could fly if it had a mind to.

As the spectre drew closer, Anne's hand flew to her mouth. 'Branwell!' she exclaimed apprehensively. 'Emily!'

In that same instant I recognised my sister's purposeful stride: the determined steps that carried her across Steeton Moor beyond the Haworth parsonage. What could she be doing at Thorp Green? Had father been taken from us?

We ran to her and suddenly she was in our arms, holding Anne the tightest. 'Is it father?' Anne breathed. 'Please, God … not father.'

Emily shook her head, and pushed back her hood so that her wild hair was exposed. I was reminded how beautiful she was. 'Father is well and sends his love and eagerly awaits your return for Christmas.'

'Then what brings you here, Emily?' Anne persisted. 'To make such a journey in the rain?'

Emily clutched Anne's young hand. 'We must speak alone, dear sister.'

I was offended, as I always have been, when my sisters shut me out – a shunning that has increased with the years until now, a year later, I am hardly tolerated. 'Am I not to hear?'

'In due time, Branwell.'

Anne locked her arm in her sister's: 'Come inside, Emily. We shall have tea brought to my room where we can warm ourselves.' She turned to me. 'Branwell, will you remain with the children?'

I nodded obediently and watched my sisters glide together through the rising mist until they disappeared into the house. 'Children!' Mary bristled. 'Well, I like that!'

'Your sister is very comely, Mr Brontë,' Edmund complimented.

'Yes,' I agreed. 'It is only the brother who was not gifted with the family good looks.'

'I think you are most handsome, Mr Brontë,' Edmund responded.

'I would not go that far,' Mary disagreed. 'Especially with those spectacles.'

What had prompted Emily to venture to Thorp Green alone without any sort of escort? I was filled with speculation as I watched my sisters disappear in the house.

The sad tidings would be conveyed to me soon enough.

Dear Journal, I shall be creative once again. I shall depict a scene I did not actually witness, but even now, I can imagine full well what transpired. Is this not the function of prose? Being well acquainted with my younger sisters, I can put the words in their precious mouths that I feel certain were actually spoken. Is this not my prerogative?

I am certain a steaming pot of tea was brought immediately to Anne's room and a warming fire was lit in the grate. Cloaks had been removed and my sisters were seated together on the chintz settee in front of the burning logs, Emily wearing black with a white tatting lapel, and Anne in a russet-brown sacque, the colour of which flattered her light hair.

Emily waited until the tea had been poured; she took a sip before beginning her sad task.

Anne, however, who had a premonition, spoke first. 'It is Mr Weightman, isn't it?'

'I was going to write to you; but then I thought: "How can I put such a thing in a letter?" Somebody should be with you when … of course Branwell is here, but…'

'Has he given his heart to someone else? I have not received a letter from him in weeks. I feared…'

'He could not, Anne,' Emily began gently. 'He was ill … very ill.'

'Is he better now?' Anne asked hopefully.

'We have had an epidemic of cholera in Haworth. Mercifully, father and I were spared. I wrote you that much. Many others were not so fortunate. William insisted on ministering to the sick.'

'But William was strong and healthy – robust. He, of all people could not…'

'Father was with him at the end, Anne.'

'The end?' Anne could not, would not, believe the worst. 'Did he…? Was there no special word for me?'

'He took your secret to the grave.' She handed Anne sheets of paper. 'Here is father's final tribute to him. I copied it out for you.'

Anne was unable to weep, or even to speak. She turned and read the sermon. Emily waited patiently. Finally, Anne spoke: 'The night that William came here and declared his love for me and held me in his arms was the happiest night of my life. Perhaps that is the only true happiness God intended me to know.'

'We all loved him, Anne. You are the fortunate one because he loved you in return.'

'I have his letters.' Anne went to her dresser and, opening a drawer, pressed the epistles to her breast. 'So many lovely thoughts of how our lives would be together. He was already making discreet enquiries about a parish.' She clutched the papers. 'These mean more to me than any sermon.'

Sighing, she sank back down beside her sister. 'Oh, Emily, am I to be a governess for the rest of my life?'

'One day we shall have our own school, Anne. Charlotte will return from Brussels at the end of this month; the plans will be made.'

Anne opened a treasured letter and read it to herself, tears suddenly flowing down her cheeks and sliding onto the paper. 'I can hear his voice and I can see his face,' she wept. 'Am I never to know either again?' She fell into her sister's arms and shed bitter tears onto her shoulder.

Emily, who bore her own weight of grief, wept too. 'You must come home with me now, even though it is weeks before Christmas. We shall await Charlotte's arrival.'

Anne considered the possibility, wanting desperately to return to the parsonage and assuage her grief with both sister and father there to comfort her. 'But to leave so soon?'

'You must have time to grieve properly for the loss of one you loved so dearly. Certainly you can return here after Christmas, if needs be. You have written me that only Mary is left for you to instruct. Could she not survive without you for one month?'

'She would certainly choose to.'

Emily was determined. 'I shall not leave for Haworth unless you accompany me. As I am your older sister, I shall speak to your employer for you.'

'Mrs Thornton has retreated to her chambers since the departure of husband and daughter. I doubt she is ready to assume responsibility.'

'I shall not leave without you,' Emily persisted. 'We shall tramp the moors together, as we used to, even though snow will soon be upon us. We shall leave one Brontë behind. That is sufficient.'

Anne hesitated, pressing the letters to her heart. 'Perhaps Branwell is the one who should return to Haworth for good.'

Emily was puzzled. 'Whatever do you mean?'

Anne shook her head ruefully, unable to express the anxieties that the sight of Edmund's devotion to me had aroused in her. (Is it enough to say here and now that I am innocent of any such impropriety?) 'Our brother, as is his wont, sometimes gives himself over to a new venture too wholeheartedly. He has permitted himself to become the centre of his pupil's universe. He dotes on that boy like a father. They are growing too close. We Brontës should have our own children instead of taking care of others'.' This is how delicately Anne must have stated it. The thought of her own loss overwhelmed her; she could not continue. 'Oh, Emily,' she cried bitterly, 'where have they buried my beloved?'

'He is in Haworth churchyard, close to our own family; for, indeed, father loved him as if he were his own son.'

'How we all loved him!' Anne exclaimed softly. 'How painful love can be.'

Although Emily spoke little of her interview with Mrs Thornton, the outcome was a permission for Anne to leave immediately for Haworth in the company of her sister; whereas I would remain until the week of Christmas. Indeed, Anne's departure was the catalyst that compelled Mrs Thornton to abandon her retreat and become once again a mother to her two youngest children.

We were vouchsafed a carriage to convey my sisters to

the Wayfarer's Inn at Little Ouseburn. William Allison drove the horses while I faced my solemn sisters. Little was said during our short journey; yet how beautiful my sisters looked, even in sorrow. The rain had not returned, but the sky was grey; a chilling wind promised a cruel winter ahead.

Soon we reached our destination. My heart was in my throat as I assisted my sisters from the carriage and into the post-chaise awaiting to convey them away from me. Death comes too easily to the ones we love. I could certainly not bear to lose either of them. 'I loved William too,' I confided to Anne in parting; 'in my own way as much as you. You have no idea how much we all needed him. Father most of all. He was my replacement in father's eyes.'

Anne held my gaze; her blue eyes burrowing deep into my very soul. 'I think we Brontës love too much,' she said, then accepted her sister's arm and stepped up into the coach.

I wish now that I had returned home with them: but with William gone there was no-one outside my family to turn to.

Anne could share her desolation with Emily, who understood her loss of William better than she could imagine. Later, in the winter refuge of my father's parsonage, she poured her sorrow into four lines of exquisite poetry that are etched in my heart to this very day:

And I have felt so full of love,
So strong in spirit then,
As if my heart would never cool,
Or wander back again.

William Allison and I rode home. As we emerged from the dark woods to discover Thorp Green looming before us, I had little inkling of what lay in store.

The snow did not delay in coming: white flakes fell like manna from heaven, bleaching the surrounding countryside.

To walk the milky glades of Thorp Green after such a chilly benison was to feel purified; the sharp air promised to expel each and every demon. Edmund, who strode beside me, had, since his mother's retreat to the confines of her chambers, drawn even closer to me. Is it possible we could have continued together like the characters in his story – teacher and pupil – and sailed off into the blissful sunset on an endless sea?

We had stopped at the graveyard, which was now a silvery knoll, and Edmund, whose young eyes were much keener than mine, was the first to spy the figure as it emerged from the distance. 'It is mother!' Edmund exclaimed.

I was as astonished as he.

Mrs Thornton was clad in grey, her hooped skirt dancing, as if of its own accord, across the snow, her woollen surtout providing winter warmth and a soft contrast to her jetty hair and the luminous white of her skin. In her gloved hands she held a sprig of holly, its red berries a bright promise of Christmas to come. Her son hurried to her side. 'Mother! How good to have you about!'

She wrapped her free arm around him and held him close. 'I have ignored you for entirely too long, my darling. I have neglected both the living and the dead.' She held up the sprig of holly. 'Poor Georgiana Jane has been abandoned as well.' She moved to the spot where her youngest child was buried and laid the greenery against the snow. 'My little dearest,' she murmured, 'it is the best I can do at this time of year; perhaps it will remind you of the Christmases you were too young to enjoy.'

'I am sure it is Christmas all year round where she is,' her son spoke hopefully.

Mrs Thornton stared down at the small stone. 'If dear little Georgiana had lived, perhaps she would have been a credit to her mother, as other girls are not.'

'Oh, mother,' her son consoled. 'It is not your fault.'

'Then I do not know who else's it could be. I have tried to be a good example to my daughters but have failed miserably. I fear I have been neither a good mother to my children nor a fit wife to my husband.'

'That's not true!' Edmund protested.

'What must you think of us, Mr Brontë?' she questioned, turning to me.

'My opinion of you, Mrs Thornton, is so high, you can no longer see it.'

'Bravo, Mr Brontë!' Edmund exclaimed. 'You hear how well Mr Brontë thinks of you, mother?'

'I am most flattered,' she smiled, looking deep into my eyes in a way that made me unable to look away. 'If only I deserved such estimation.'

'And Mary is still here,' Edmund added. 'I think there is no fear of her running off.'

'Except with a horse.' Mrs Thornton laughed in spite of herself, then covered her mouth because she had done so.

'Oh mother,' her son chuckled as well, 'how good to see you laugh again.'

'It is time for laughter,' she replied, removing her hand from her mouth and smiling radiantly at us both. 'It is time for decking the halls with holly. I have decided that we shall have a proper Christmas whether Mr Thornton or Alice or Elizabeth are with us or not. We shall make the best of those who are left.'

'But Mr Brontë will be leaving us for the holiday as well,' Edmund remembered sadly.

'Perhaps we can persuade him to stay.' Mrs Thornton looked at me beseechingly. 'You have become a second father to Edmund, and I, too, am in need of your company.'

I was anxious for my family to be reunited at Christmastime, yet Edmund, in his beguiling way had become part of me; and the luminous Lydia Thornton herself had requested my presence. 'But my sister, Charlotte, is coming home from Brussels,' I finally protested; 'although not until the new year.'

'All the more reason to wait until after Christmas to see her. Besides, your sister has informed me that Miss Charlotte will not be returning to Brussels.'

'That is true,' I admitted.

'Please say that you will stay, Mr Brontë,' Edmund pleaded. 'Now that mother has returned to us, we shall have such good times together.'

'Yes, Mr Brontë,' Mrs Thornton echoed her son, 'please say that you will stay.'

I looked from one to the other. How could I refuse the two people I loved most outside my own family?

'I shall stay.'

'How simply wonderful!' exclaimed Edmund, locking his arm in mine.

'We are pleased.' Mrs Thornton beamed as she put her hand through my other arm and we three tramped through the snow in the direction of the great house. 'Deck the halls with boughs of holly!' Mrs Thornton sang in a clear, pure soprano.

The Journal of Branwell Brontë

21st December, 1845

Yes, we have a small tree this year in the Parsonage. My sisters have strung garlands above the stairway railing. How appropriate, as I sit near this aromatic fir, by the warm fireplace in the parlour, that I write of quite a different Christmas.

Christmas at Thorp Green

What an extravagant Christmas was lavished on so few!

The rooms of Thorp Green Hall were resplendent with ornamentation. Garlands were strewn; holly was abundant; a hand-carved representation of the Nativity adorned the mantle-piece; candles blazed brilliantly about the great house, especially on the enormous tree that Mrs Thornton had selected from her own forest.

Mrs Thornton was determined to have a royal Christmas; although at the Brontë Parsonage we had never had a tree.

Mrs Thornton had sent to London for an assortment of baubles to decorate it. On Christmas Eve, under Mrs Thornton's direction, Edmund, Mary and I fastened them to the branches. How magnificent the collection appeared when each and every tiny candle was lit, the small flames twinkling like tiny stars in the firmament of the tree!

Also in attendance was the Thornton family surgeon, Dr John Crosby, a most agreeable man who had befriended me and with whom I felt at ease. A widower, he lived alone with his fifteen-year old son, William, and a female servant in Great Ouseburn. Young William was Edmund's sole contemporary companion and we had visited father and son in Great Ouseburn on more than one occasion. This night they were both elegant in their dark evening finery, although the freckled young William, as fair as his father, could not hold a candle to the handsome Edmund.

We gathered around the piano where Edmund played carols and, encouraged by cups of hot rum punch, we sang with vigour.

Mrs Thornton, in the spirit of Christmas, wore red satin, the strands of her luminous raven hair laced with scarlet ribbons. Mary's frock was white muslin stitched with small roses that nestled in the garden of her many petticoats, her dark hair adorned with faux flowers.

Mrs Fitzpatrick was encouraged to share a cup of punch and to lend her voice to our carolling.

Hark the herald angels sing!
Glory to the new-born King!

She sang louder than any of us!

Soon we opened the Christmas presents set beneath the tree. I had purchased nothing, but Mrs Thornton was generous to all. Edmund, with his mother's encouragement, had ordered a new suit of evening clothes for me. In contrast to my familiar black, he had selected a jacket, waist-coat and trousers in complementary shades of russet that, he declared, matched my reddish hair and ruddy complexion.

I was encouraged to try on the clothes immediately. When I returned from my quarters, I was greeted with applause and approval, for, indeed, they fitted me to perfection.

Mrs Thornton's personal gift to me was something I never would have anticipated:

'You shall paint me, Mr Brontë. I have seen enough of

your sketches to assess your skill and Miss Brontë has informed me of the brilliant painting you have executed of her and her sisters, to say nothing of your portraits of the ladies of Bradford.'

'It would be a great honour,' I stammered, 'but I wonder if I am up to such a task.'

'Nonsense,' she protested. 'I have every confidence. The portrait shall be a gift to my husband when, and if, he ever returns from Africa, and I shall pay you handsomely.'

'If I can capture even half of your radiance on canvas, I will consider myself successful,' I spoke from my heart.

'What a lovely compliment,' Mrs Thornton replied; 'but Mr Brontë, there is even more to this venture. We have yet another surprise.'

'I am already overwhelmed,' I responded. Upon the death of my Aunt Branwell, the previous year, each of my sisters had received what would amount to about £300 each. Nothing was left to me because my aunt felt my sisters stood more in need of assistance. They were saving their inheritance to open their own school. Now, at last, I thought, I might have some money of my own, and I could contribute as well.

'A proper artist must have a proper studio,' Mrs Thornton continued. 'I am having the Monks' House converted into a private lodging and studio for you. Commencing after Boxing Day, a sky-light shall be added to the upper storey so that you can have proper illumination for your endeavours.'

'It has been a secret I have been dying to share with you, Mr Brontë, but mother swore me to the strictest secrecy,' Edmund confided.

Monks' House was a deserted seventeenth-century brick dwelling on the outskirts of Thorp Green, a house in which a late caretaker had once resided. Although within walking distance of the manor house, it was a special world of its own, protected by elms and surrounded by a high stone wall.

I was somewhat surprised by Edmund's enthusiasm for my new quarters, which would, I thought, remove me from his proximity. His mother's next revelation, however, made all clear. 'Edmund's lessons will naturally continue here, but I shall have the second bedroom furnished for my son so that he may stay overnight when you are toiling away on your stories and the weather is inclement.' She took my hands and held them gently in her own. How delicious was her touch! 'You have become a second father to my son and filled a great void in his life – especially when I absented myself from my motherly duties. For this we are eternally grateful.'

Dr Crosby congratulated me on my good fortune. 'Perhaps one day, Branwell, you will paint my portrait in return for my professional services.'

'I would be honoured to paint you, Doctor,' I responded enthusiastically, 'but I hope I shall never need medical care.'

'But mother must be painted first,' Edmund persisted, 'and when the portrait is completed, we shall invite the entire county to view it.'

'I pray I shall be worthy of my subject.'

'You will not have to flatter me, Branwell,' the doctor chuckled. 'I shall expect to be portrayed warts and all.'

I wish now that there had been time to paint this good doctor. After the terrible events that transpired, this fine doctor is the only friend from Thorp Green still remaining to me.

There would never be another Christmas such as this. I knew even then that such happiness could not last. 'I am so grateful, I am at a loss for words,' I stammered. I had not been so appreciated in a very long time; not since I was as young as Edmund and showed unbridled promise.

'It is we who are grateful, Mr Brontë,' Mrs Thornton insisted, reaching for a last present beneath the tree. It was a small volume with gilt-edged pages and a red cloth cover, the title embossed in gold on the front and spine and illustrated with coloured etchings by the celebrated John Leech. She handed the gift to her son. 'We have Mr Dickens' words for our Christmas Eve. It is his new Christmas story, Edmund, which I had sent down from London. We will gather round the fireplace and you shall read it to us; and if you grow tired, we can take turns.'

We moved away from the tall tree with candles that were now starting to burn dim, and made ourselves comfortable in front of the blazing fire. Berwick was in attendance as well and we made ourselves comfortable in anticipation of the latest offering from the master story-teller. '*A Christmas Carol*, Chapter One,' Edmund began in a voice that was stronger and more assertive than when we had first met. 'Marley was dead, to begin with. There is no doubt whatever about that. The register of his burial was signed by the clergyman, the clerk, the undertaker, and the chief mourner. Scrooge signed it. And Scrooge's name was good upon "change" for anything he chose to put his hand to. Old Marley was as dead as a door-nail.'

We were gripped and enchanted by this marvellous new story depicting the redemption of the miserly Ebenezer Scrooge. The visitation of the three Christmas spirits, which we took turns in reading, unnerved all of us, especially Mrs Fitzpatrick. Later we wept for poor Tiny Tim, but rejoiced at the happy ending and Mr Scrooge's salvation.

The logs had been reduced to glowing embers when the guests departed and we finally ascended the great stairway to our separate bedrooms. Soon, as I anticipated, Edmund found his way to my chamber and crawled in beside me. 'If just for Christmas Eve...' he pleaded. 'I long to be close to you.'

I kissed his forehead and opened my arms to him. 'For Christmas Eve.'

'I can now sleep contentedly for you are beside me. I love you, Branwell.'

'And I, you.'

'I hope you are pleased with your gift.'

'To have my own small house and studio. It is something for which I have dreamed.'

'And a bedroom for me,' he added joyfully.

I smoothed his hair and held him in the crook of my body until he fell asleep, his soft breath warming my cheek. How trusting and innocent he appeared in the shaft of winter moonlight that glimmered through my window.

Was it wrong to hold this young boy in my arms so that he felt safe and protected against a world that offers little of these things?

Perhaps if there had been someone to hold me at such a tender age I would not be so hungry for love now.

The Journal of Branwell Brontë

23rd December, 1845

Dear Journal, my story resumes. As this Christmas continues in the present, I continue to describe one from the past.

Christmas Morning at Thorp Green

I awakened on Christmas morning to discover that Edmund had slipped away without awakening me. I shivered in absence of the special warmth he had provided. My room was so cold, I feared I would freeze before I could ignite the kindling and start a proper fire. The water in my pitcher had frozen. I carried it to the fireplace and warmed it, along with my frosty fingers.

Flames began to curl about the logs. I ventured to the window and observed what Christmas had wrought outdoors. Fresh snow had fallen throughout the night in such plenitude that a dazzling sea of white stretched to the horizon. The distant trees looked taller in their winter array while the fields displayed new snowy mantles. I opened the casement, and mindless of the consumption that had taken my sisters, Maria and Elizabeth, breathed the frosty air. How good it felt to be alive on this Christmas morning of 1844! I had come through the night, as had Ebenezer Scrooge in Dickens' remarkable story. How happy I was to confront such a magical morning!

After breakfast, Mrs Thornton summoned all the servants into the great hall and presented each with coins of the realm. All bowed in gratitude and accepted a glass of Christmas 'nog' with which to toast Our Saviour's birth. 'Father would never have given them so much,' Mary whispered as the last one pocketed his funds. 'Mother has become most extravagant in his absence.'

William Allison had fitted out a sleigh to convey us to the Traditionalist Holy Trinity Church at Little Ouseburn. Bells were attached to the straps of the horses and we sang cheerfully to their jingling. I was pressed warmly against Edmund under the furry protection of a lap-rug. The sky above was silver-grey and pointed icicles hung from the trees. A choir was already singing when we arrived at the small church.

On Christmas day in Haworth I would have been compelled to attend all three of father's services, but in Little Ouseburn one morning service sufficed. The vicar did not have the Celtic intensity of my father; still, in a quiet way he shared with us his evident love for the Christ Child.

On our return to Thorp Green to fetch food baskets for the less fortunate members of the estate, the snow once again descended like pale confetti. Bells jangling, the sleigh whisked us from tenant farmer to tenant farmer, even to the poorest of the farms. The Thorntons dispensed good wishes and Christmas charity to every tenant on their vast estates.

Late in the afternoon, as we basked in the warmth of the large dining-room fire, the Christmas goose was served. Ebenezer Scrooge could not have provided a more perfect bird for the Cratchet family. We lowered our heads in a prayer of thanksgiving which Edmund concluded with a plea to God to bless '...all here and away, especially Alice and Elizabeth, and father, and Miss Brontë.'

I prayed privately for all my family – Anne, Charlotte, Emily and my father – that God would keep them healthy and happy, and grant them long lives!

By January the snow had departed. What was once a seamless white blanket was now as mottled as Flossy's coat. In truth, the spaniel was happier to return to Thorp Green than his mistress – for was there ever such a large estate about which a dog could forage?

Anne, who had not yet recovered from the loss of her beloved, was filled with news of the parsonage, and especially Charlotte's return. She had sought me out in my chamber upon her return. I suspected that my youngest sister would not have returned to resume her employment at all, were it not for her strong desire to contribute her wages to the establishment of a school. 'The Misses Brontë's Establishment' was to begin slowly in the parsonage itself, Anne informed me with a trace of former animation. 'Since we cannot yet afford our own structure, Charlotte will begin the school with only five or six girls who will board in our rooms while we are here at Thorp Green.'

'But I have not agreed to this,' I protested.

'Oh Branny, this means so much to Charlotte. We were sure that you would agree.'

'And when will this school take you away from Thorp Green?'

'I would not think until next year,' she assured me.

'Then I consent,' I smiled, 'for I must have you here with me.'

'I shall write to Charlotte immediately, although knowing our sister, she will appropriate your room whether you consent or not.'

'Tell me more of this venture,' I insisted, helping Anne to remove her cloak and seating her before the warming fire, for her face was still blue with cold.

'We will offer board and a general education for thirty-five pounds a year. For an extra guinea per subject, we shall offer French, German, Latin, music and drawing. We will charge an extra five shillings for the use of papa's piano. Oh, Branny,' she said, 'it is not being governess here I mind so much; it is being away from father and Emily and Charlotte and those I love so dearly. And now that Tabitha has recovered and returned to us as well, the picture is almost complete.'

'And how do I fit into this school of yours?' Once again I felt left out of the lives of my sisters. When did this actually begin? I believe it commenced with my failed excursion to London to study at the Royal Academy. (The truth behind this botched venture is known only to myself and the dearly departed William Weightman, to whom alone I have revealed my disgrace.) Perhaps it was my failure as a portrait painter in Bradford; or my dismissal as tutor to the Postlethwaite sons in Broughton because of 'too many spirits'?; or was it my dismissal as a railway clerk for the Leeds and Manchester Railway at Luddenden Foot? Although I was not responsible for the inexplicable loss of over eleven pounds in the accounts, I was nevertheless held culpable and dismissed.

I suppose it is the sum of all these things.

At Thorp Green at least, I was determined to redeem myself. I felt certain that I could restore my sisters' faith in me.

'It is women's work, Branny,' my sister responded, attempting to smooth over my exclusion. 'Just to have you home with us so that we can all be together will be more than enough.'

But what did their school have to do with my profession and my ambitions? I was silent for a while as Flossy rubbed against my leg and licked my fingers. Anne managed a smile. 'Papa has taken such a fancy to Flossy, I believe he was more despondent at her departure than my own.' She reached low to pet the dog. 'And what of your Christmas at Thorp Green?'

'Splendid,' was the most suitable word I could think of

to describe it, but before I could continue Mary burst into my room with scarcely a knock, her dark ringlets bobbing wildly about her head. 'Miss Brontë! I was told you had returned,' she exclaimed, rushing to my sister and hugging her. 'How we have missed you. I have even missed my lessons, which shows how desperate I was for your company!'

'And I have missed you,' Anne replied, pleased by her pupil's display of affection. 'And if what you say about your lessons is true, then our lesson for to-day is not to burst into a room without rapping on the door first.'

'Edmund does so,' Mary defended. 'I have seen him barge in on Mr Brontë at all hours.'

'That does not make it correct,' Anne remonstrated, glancing at me before rescuing Flossy from Mary's over-zealous embrace.

'Miss Brontë,' Mary confessed. 'I am so desperate for your company, you may correct me to-day all you wish.'

'I would rather hear about your Christmas. Is there still no word from your father?'

'We believe that he has been eaten by cannibals.' She took my sister's hand. 'But come! I must show you the wonderful things that mother gave me for Christmas.' They were half-way to the door. 'Has Mr Brontë told you about the Charles Dickens story that we read aloud in front of the tree?'

'He has not had the opportunity.'

'You must read about poor little Tiny Tim. "God bless us, everyone!"' she quoted, pulling my sister outside, with Flossy in pursuit.

I moved to the window. Far in the distance work continued on the roof of Monks' House. In the space of a few days, the dwelling would be mine.

The Journal of Branwell Brontë

29th December, 1845

Dear Journal, I am about to describe the most sacred portion of my life, the transcribing of which no eyes must ever see. One day in the future, when I am happy again, I shall create a fiction of these events so as not to disgrace my family nor the lovely lady depicted herein. But, for now, I must guard these pages with all my life – such as it is – until I am reunited with my dearest.

Monks' House: the palette of love

Monks' House was the remnant of a mediaeval building, a timber-framed building on two storeys with small diamond-paned windows. There was a long, large room upstairs – perhaps, at one time, a dormitory for monks breaking their journey between Fountains Abbey and York. This was to be my studio and it was here that Mrs Thornton had had a sky-light installed to provide additional illumination to what would otherwise have been a poorly-lit space. My bed-chamber was immediately below and so large was the fire-place in this room that only on the coldest days did it fail to provide sufficient heat to make working tolerable in the studio above. The adjoining room on the ground-floor was furnished solely for Edmund's comfort and contained a bed so that, if he chose to spend the evening with me rather than walk home in the dark, he might do so. Needless to say, this was a temptation to which he often succumbed.

Mrs Thornton had supervised the furnishing of my private quarters, choosing such pieces of furniture as were, in her words, 'wasted at the manor house'. Needless to say, the result bore testimony to her exquisite taste, and I could only bless my good fortune. The start of February brought little warmth: but, on certain days, grey skies turned a pale blue and a wan sun appeared above the horizon.

Soon I was ready to begin Mrs Thornton's portrait.

My pictures of the ladies of Bradford had all been painted indoors. Of some of these I am proud, especially that of my former landlady, Mrs Issac Kirby, which depicts, I think, with no attempt at flattery, her sharp and sour visage.

Mrs Thornton, however, was to be my most beautiful subject. I wished to present her in the open air, sitting on the wrought-iron bench before her rose garden with the manor house looming in the background.

The roses would have to be depicted from memory, or I would wait until later to colour them. She accepted this proposal. I placed her once in the setting so that I could sketch the details of the background that would surround her, before we moved into my new studio – one that any professional artist would covet.

For her portrait, Mrs Thornton chose a blue satin gown that matched to perfection the startling hue of her eyes. It scooped low on her bosom and the puffed sleeves were hemmed with delicate lace. She wore no hoop beneath this costume, but her waist was so narrow that it billowed out just the same. About her neck she wore a small cameo bearing the likeness of her dearly departed daughter; a white lace stole was draped over her arms, and in her hands she held a matching parasol. Her hair was parted in the middle and fell in long glossy curls, a swatch of lace mingling with them. Leonardo da Vinci himself did not face a greater challenge when confronted by his celebrated Mona Lisa. I prayed that I would not fail this task, and that she would not be disappointed by the result.

Uncertain of her husband's return, we decided to complete the portrait as rapidly as possible so that it might be ready for his appearance. After the initial 'al fresco' sitting we moved inside to the warmth of my studio, where Mrs Thornton kept her beautiful dress so that she could pose in it each day. Mornings were for Edmund's lessons, but the afternoons were set aside for his mother's portrait. We were not to be disturbed until I accompanied her back to the manor house, Mrs Thornton happy to walk and stretch her limbs after a session of holding a pose.

During the concluding session of our first week a violent storm broke over the wintry countryside. Inside, however, we were snug and warm, protected from the Yorkshire elements. As I lit the candles, so dark had the sky grown, I caught Mrs Thornton, though holding her pose resolutely, yet looking – not where I had directed – but at myself, the painter. 'You are not looking where I instructed,' I chided.

'At what am I supposed to be looking?' Her soft voice, almost girlish, belied the difference in our ages. I can still hear that precious voice now; for it is always in my ear. I can still remember all that she said; every musical word of hers is embedded forever in my heart, like the notes of a great symphony.

'Something that pleases you,' I instructed. 'Something that causes you to smile ever so slightly, as you did on the first day of our sitting when we were out of doors.'

'It pleases me to look at you, Mr Brontë.' Indeed she was now smiling in the manner I wished.

'But if a subject is painted looking directly at the artist,' I protested, 'the completed portrait is unnerving to look upon.'

'Are you unnerved, now, Mr Brontë?'

'No, but I shall be shortly, if you do not hold the pose I requested.'

'Very well,' she acquiesced, looking away as she had in the garden. 'I shall think of something equally pleasant to contemplate so that you can paint me as this celebrated Mona Lisa of which you speak.'

'And of what are you thinking, Mrs Thornton?' The delectable smile had returned.

'Something I cannot yet reveal,' was her reply. How confident she had become since emerging from her self-enforced mourning, now there was no belligerent husband there to undermine and subject her. 'Do you think, Mr Brontë, that a century from now, people will see this portrait and wonder why *I* am smiling?'

'Certainly descendants of your family will. My paintings have yet to find their way to a museum.'

'Perhaps this will be the first to do so.'

'I will certainly never have a more beautiful subject.' Her smile grew even more beguiling. 'Such a lovely smile. How can I compel you to retain it?'

'Pray continue with these generous compliments, Mr Brontë. I am starved of praise.'

'There is much to laud,' I replied.

'You see that I am already smiling again.'

She held that precious smile for a long moment of silence, punctuated only by the intensity of the rain, while I continued to paint. 'You have a talent, Mr Brontë,' she said finally. 'It is obvious even in your smallest sketch; and you have instilled some in my son.'

'It was expected that I should become a painter,' I replied simply. 'We had hopes that I would follow in the footsteps of Mr John Martin. His allegorical paintings are favourites among my family.'

'Then why have you buried yourself away at Thorp Green – although I am certainly pleased that you have – where such talent cannot be properly appreciated or developed? Why have you not gone to study in London?'

‘Because…’ I certainly could not tell her the truth of my profligate journey. ‘I had letters of introduction and recommendation to the Royal Academy from my teacher, Mr William Robinson of Leeds, who studied there himself and was pupil to Sir Thomas Lawrence, but I never arrived at my destination.’

‘And why is that? Was the thought of such a city too overwhelming, Mr Brontë? It is often to me.’

‘I am a simple curate’s son who feared rejection at the hands of the masters.’

‘And I am still a country girl at heart. I have never been comfortable in a city the size of London. As soon as I have arrived I wish desperately to return home. That was what drew me to Mr Thornton: our mutual love of the country.’ She sighed. The smile faded from her lips. ‘And now he has abandoned both me and it.’ I did not know how to respond; but suddenly the smile returned to her as quickly as it had departed. ‘And I must confess, Mr Brontë, that since our wonderful Christmas, I have been quite happy and not minded his absence at all.’

‘Nor I,’ I volunteered; then regretted immediately that I had said it.

She did not appear offended. ‘One must make the best of things and that is what I have decided. You and your sister have been a great consolation to us.’

‘Thank you.’

‘My son dotes on you.’ She caught my eye again. ‘So do I.’

Abashed, I busied myself with her painting, and we continued in silence; yet I caught her eye on many occasions. Her delectable perfume brought spring into the winter chamber. It filled my nostrils and permeated the room. Her face assumed the features of those amorous gipsies who had seduced me so many years ago and I began to dare to desire her as I had desired them. My eyes continually sought her bosom as it gently rose and fell in rhythmic respiration. The blood throbbed warmly at my temples; I found it difficult to stand. The sky above had turned black and there was no longer light enough for me to work. I did not want this afternoon to end; but it was time to cease. 'I shall weaken my poor eyes,' I said finally, setting my brush down on the easel and covering the canvas.

Mrs Thornton relaxed her position, dropped her parasol and rose to her feet. 'Mr Branwell, do you remember your promise of earlier this week?'

'And what was that?'

'That at its conclusion you would permit me a quick glance at this preliminary part of your work.'

'So I did,' I responded, wishing that I had not: for I was not yet sufficiently advanced.

She moved to where I was standing, her perfume overwhelming me. It was as if I had tumbled into a bed of delicious roses. 'I wish to see it now.'

I raised the cloth covering her portrait and she examined the little that I had completed. 'But your preliminary work is excellent!' she exclaimed. 'I can well imagine the final portrait – and you have captured the colour of my frock exquisitely.'

I dared to look at her. 'It is the same as your eyes.'

'I kiss the talented hands of such a talented man.' She took my hands into her own and pressed them to her lips. How sweet and moist they felt against my warm skin! 'If Mr Brontë will not be offended, I should like to kiss his delectable lips as well.'

I needed no other invitation. I pressed my lips with dangerous ardour against her own. Soon our mouths were open and she was whispering my name 'Oh, Branwell,' she murmured. 'May I call you Branwell?' she whispered, looking dreamily into my eyes.

'It is like music to hear you say it.'

'And you must call me Lydia here in Monks' House where we can savour our afternoons together and pretend the world outside does not exist.'

'Lydia,' I moaned, rubbing my hands through her lustrous hair and kissing the tresses.

'I love you, Branwell,' she whispered. 'I have loved you since before my husband departed.'

'And I have loved you since the very first night of my arrival when I beheld you at dinner – my Artemis, my Greek Goddess of the Moon.'

'I am older than you, but not wiser. I feared you would reject me if ever I made my feelings known; that I would be nothing to you but a foolish old woman, a Phaedra spurned by Hippolytus.'

'I would sooner reject God himself.'

'How I have longed for you,' she sighed, removing my glasses and kissing me about the face. Then, putting her hand in mine and raising the candelabrum with the other, she led me downstairs. 'We will be warmer by the fire.'

I pressed my hand in hers, savouring the touch of her warm flesh against mine, not wanting ever to let go. On the ground floor she passed through the parlour and into my bedroom. She set down the candelabrum and touched the four-poster. 'This bed has been in my family since before I was born. I especially wanted you to have it.'

'I have lain beneath this canopy dreaming only of you.'

'We have had the same dream.'

She reached back and unfastened her gown so that it fell to the floor. She slipped out of the sea of blue like Venus emerging from a sapphire sea. In the candle-light her skin was as rich as cream: I could not stop touching her. She undid my clothes and marvelled at my own nakedness, for modesty had abandoned us. 'I am somewhat inexperienced,' I whispered.

'Then I shall tutor you,' she whispered.

We became intent on pleasing each other.

Afterwards, when we lay contentedly close, I felt that manhood had finally descended upon me.

'A wife should never speak ill of her husband, Branwell,' she whispered in the darkness, 'but, in truth, if *you* are inexperienced, he has much to learn.'

The rain had ceased; night had truly descended as Lydia slipped into her clothes and I escorted her back to the manor house. We walked in silence, not even daring to hold hands, both filled with the wonder of what had transpired.

At dinner we pretended that nothing had changed, that we were the same as we had been the previous evening: I believe we were successful; although my sister eyed us both suspiciously.

After dinner, when Edmund asked if he could accompany me back to Monks' House, I put him off, making the rain an excuse.

In truth, I wanted to dream in the bed where she had lain beside me; to breathe traces of her sweet perfume; to remember I was finally loved.

I wanted nothing – not even Edmund – to disturb this.

Was I being heartless? Perhaps so.

But where Lydia was concerned, nothing else mattered; nor does it still.

The Portrait is Completed

A portrait that would have been painted in haste was now laboured over painstakingly, for neither Lydia nor I ever wanted our afternoon sessions to end. Certainly we did not meet every day but, nevertheless, the afternoons when she ventured to my cottage were like precious jewels in a glittering necklace.

February surrendered to March, and March to April.

The first day of the new month brought torrential rain, but Lydia sallied forth nonetheless, protected by a large umbrella which I held over her precious head. As thunder and lightning tormented the island we had made out of my cottage, I could no longer linger over the painting. It remained only for me to sign my name, which was something I did not always do, but the large portrait of Mrs Edmund Thornton was one of which I was extremely proud.

If my work is to be remembered at all, it will be by this portrait. I would hang it unashamedly beside the paintings of Sir Thomas Lawrence, Gainsborough, or George Romney.

Love had given me the skill to achieve one work of real excellence, which is more than many in their lives achieve. It is not that I did not love my sisters when I painted them, but my love for Lydia was of an entirely different kind; one which calmed my restless nature, that filled the empty vessel of my heart until it overflowed.

It was as if the portrait literally glowed: Lydia's skin seemed translucent; her haunting smile, sharing a secret between subject and artist, hypnotised any who beheld it; the blue of her eyes and gown was mesmerising its intensity. If I could go on just painting her, perhaps I could achieve the greatness for which my family believed I was destined. I would not be the first artist to discover his greatness in the continual depiction of the same subject.

I signed my name carefully in the lower right-hand corner of the painting. The deed was done.

Subject and artist looked at the portrait together and then at each other, glad for my achievement, but saddened by what it represented: the loss of our afternoons together. We wove silently down the stairs to the bedroom that had become a sacred haven. I carried Lydia in my arms. She seemed as light as the perfumed air itself and I set her gently on the bed; undressing her first with my eyes and then my hands; savouring every inch of delectable flesh exposed by the gradual removal of her clothing. Soon we were naked, devouring each other, the rain beating against the window with a ferocity that transported us to such a plateau of love we ached afterwards from the intensity of it.

We lay, breathing each other's breath, our hands and limbs entwined. Lydia at last spoke: 'If it were not for the children, I would give everything up for my darling. I would run off with you, dearest, as my daughter did with Henry Roxby, anywhere you chose to go.'

'And I would paint you the rest of my life.'

'Mary would survive – but not Edmund. He loves you as much as he loves his mother. He would never forgive us.'

I would not hurt your special boy for anything in the world.'

'That is why I love you so,' Lydia murmured, thrusting her lips against mine for one last, long, lingering kiss. 'I could survive on just your kisses,' she sighed.

I hated to see her rise from my bed, even though I delighted in her nakedness before she slipped reluctantly into her travelling clothes. I also dressed; for I must escort the mistress back to her mansion, where I would share dinner in the large dining-room and we would pretend that nothing had occurred between us.

'To-morrow, when the rain ceases, Branwell, you must carry the portrait to the house so that all can see.'

We had scarcely sat down to supper when Lydia announced the completion of my masterpiece. Edmund was the most excited at the news. 'How I have longed to see it!' he exclaimed, 'but Mr Brontë has refused to uncover his canvas before it was finished.'

'What a blessed relief,' Anne replied succinctly.

'It is the finest work I have ever done,' I assured my sister.

'Mr Brontë has flattered me considerably,' added Lydia, her face flushing.

'There is no need of that, mother,' Edmund declared; 'for everyone knows that you are the most beautiful woman in Yorkshire.'

'My sister thought *she* was,' Mary was quick to remark.

'That reminds me, there has been a letter from Alice,' her mother said, producing the pages. 'I have been waiting to share it with all of you.'

'She never writes to me,' Mary complained, 'nor does Elizabeth.'

Mrs Thornton unfolded the pages. 'Alice's letters are for all of us.' She read silently a moment, then began aloud: ' "Dear mother, I am writing to you directly now and not through Miss Brontë, since father is away in Africa and my letters to you will not get you into trouble with the unforgiving ogre." '

'I wonder if he will ever return,' Mary sighed wistfully.

'Perhaps he has gone native,' her brother added, to taunt her.

'This is a most informative letter, as you will see,' their mother continued, reading on silently before resuming aloud. ' "You will not believe my good fortune. I have been invited to participate in the new travelling acting company of Mr Charles John Kean and his wife Ellen Tree. Mr Kean happened to catch me in our Christmas pantomime in London. He is the son of the great actor, Edmund Kean, who, you will remember, collapsed while playing Othello to his son's Iago. Mr Kean hopes one day to manage his own theatre in London as did his father at Drury Lane. Although we will be touring the provinces, this is a more prestigious company then that of the threadbare Hanlons. I am to receive a higher salary for my services and have been promised Juliet and Ophelia as well as other leading rôles; for Mrs Kean is some five years older than her husband and has graduated to playing Hamlet's mother, Gertrude. Please tell Miss Brontë how happy I am that we studied *Hamlet* even though I resisted at the time.

'"One of my conditions upon joining Mr Kean's company was that my husband be included as an artist. Henry, however, is not happy because Mr Kean, although some thirty-two years of age, feels quite young enough to portray Romeo, Orlando, Hamlet, Henry V and other Shakespearean heroes. Mr Roxby will have to be content playing companion to the protagonist. It is not my fault that I have achieved more fame as a Shakespearean actress than he has as an actor. Henry should be grateful that it was only through my persistence and obstinacy he was included in this fine new company at all; for many actors were clamouring to join.

'"Mr Kean has already formulated a schedule for our tour, and I am delighted to tell you that we will be appearing at the Georgian Theatre in Richmond, Yorkshire, for the week beginning 5th May this year.

'"If Papa returns, you will not be able even to consider coming to Richmond; but if he has not, I hope the whole family, in which I include Miss Brontë and her brother, will come to see me perform with Mr Kean. I am most anxious you should see my Juliet *and* my Ophelia so you will have to stay at least two days. The other plays Mr Kean has chosen do not feature me as strongly.

'"Rest assured I am deliriously happy when I am upon the stage. Everything else in my life has been a mere prelude to this.

'"I send my love to Edmund, Mary, Miss Brontë and Mr Brontë, Berwick, Mrs Fitzpatrick and cook, and hope all is well at Thorp Green. I miss each and every one of you and was particularly desolate at Christmas.

'"I shall inform you of our complete schedule of our week in Richmond as soon as Mr Kean advertises it.

'"Your loving daughter, Alice."'

'Oh, mother,' Edmund spoke excitedly, 'it is just a month away. We must assuredly go.'

'I should love to see Alice tread the boards,' Mary agreed. 'I am curious to know if she is as good as she thinks she is.'

Lydia folded the letter and set it beside her on the table. 'And Mr and Miss Brontë, would such a trip be agreeable to you?'

'I would be happy to accompany you,' I replied.

'And Miss Brontë?'

'Since Miss Alice seems to credit me somewhat with her interpretation of Ophelia, I would be most happy to see the result.'

'Then we shall go. April will have ceased its showering and in May we shall have a most beautiful ride across the countryside to Richmond. The wild-flowers will be blooming and we will enjoy a glorious adventure.'

'But what if father comes?' It was Mary who suddenly dampened our soaring spirits.

'Perhaps he has gone native as Edmund suggested; perhaps he has joined some ferocious tribe and taken many wives.'

'Mother!'

I laughed outright, hoping it was so, and caught my sister's suspicious eyes, as she looked curiously from mistress to tutor. Fortunately, Berwick chose that moment to serve dinner and to announce that Dr Crosby had arrived to minister to one of the servants.

A Poet's Profession of Love

I became desperate after Lydia ceased her visits to Monks' House because she no longer had the excuse to do so. She confided that she had grown fearful of detection when Ann Marshall, her lady's maid, had revealed to her mistress the suspicions of the servants and that Dr Crosby had remarked on how long it had taken to complete my painting.

Not unlike Eve, who tasted the Forbidden Fruit and wanted more, I, too, had experienced untold bliss and grew frenzied because it was now denied me. My Chippendale bed craved companionship and I welcomed the nights that Edmund crept in to sleep innocently beside me.

Now, since I could not paint my love, I wrote of her instead.

Her effort shows a picture made
To contradict its meaning:
Where should be sunshine, painting shade,
And smiles with sadness screening;
Where God has given a cheerful view,
A gloomy vista showing;
Where heart and face are fair and true,
A shade of doubt bestowing.

Ah, Lady, if to me you give
The power your sketch to adorn,
How little of it shall I leave
Save smiles that shine like morn.
I'd keep the hue of happy light
That shines from summer skies;
I'd drive the shades from smiles so bright
And dry such shining eyes.

I'd give a calm to one whose heart
Has banished calm from mine;
I'd brighten up God's work of art
Where thou hast dimmed its shine,
And all the wages I should ask
For such a happy toil –
I'll name them – far beyond my task –
THY PRESENCE AND THY SMILE.

Upon the cessation of rain and the advent of blue skies and the gentle warming of spring sun, I found myself riding in the late afternoon to York where I could drown my hunger in strong drink in the company of Henry Bellerby. A drunken discussion of the poetry of love was as close as I could come to mentioning my own 'amour', although whisky loosened my tongue enough for me to quote my hymn to Lydia Thornton, and Mr Bellerby insisted on publishing it under the title 'The Portrait'. How potent poetry can be when one is raising one's glass and one's heart is throbbing with a love that will not be stilled. I wept at my own words and moved my listener to rapture as well. The spirits are strong at the George Hotel.

Fortunately, only my sister recognised my signature, 'Northangerland', when the poem was published in the *Yorkshire Gazette* the following week. My portrait of Lydia Thornton was now hanging over the mantle in the great hall. The reaction of everyone in the household had been most favourable. Edmund proclaimed me a veritable genius and besought me to paint *his* portrait soon. How I wish that I had done so immediately and captured the fragile beauty of this loving young man before it was too late.

'Oh, Branwell,' Anne said sadly, as she opened the newspaper and pointed to my effort, Flossy at her heels.

'Only you would know the identity of this obscure Yorkshire poet,' I replied in my defence, bending to pet the spaniel, for I could not bear my sister's accusing eyes.

'Has this gone as far as I have feared?'

I could not lie; I could not deny what was in my heart. 'We cannot always choose whom we love,' I replied finally, 'nor who loves us in return.'

Anne was clearly dismayed. 'One has only to look at her portrait to know. I feared it was love for her that catapulted you to greatness.'

'Then you approve of the portrait?'

'Of the result – yes – but not of what inspired it. I never thought I would wish for Mr Thornton's return, but it would be much better for this household if he did come back ... as soon as possible!' She turned and shook her head sadly. 'Your portrait of your sisters shows much less affection.'

The Diary of Emily Brontë

6th June 1845

It is already June, and I have yet to transcribe the extraordinary events of April. Sometimes I wonder if he came to me at all. Perhaps by confiding this to this diary, he will become more real and not vanish like a dream with waking.

I dare not write this in the parsonage parlour where a persistent sister might see. Charlotte, as curious as our sadly departed cat, Tiger, is bristling with questions as to how I spent my time during her trip to Manchester, questions that I refuse to answer.

It is only here on the moors at Ponden Clough – away from prying eyes, and a good distance from the parsonage – that I feel safe to commit to paper the strange event that befell me.

On a glorious June day such as this, I need only the rolling green hills of Yorkshire, the purple heather, the magenta foxgloves and yellow buttercups as companions. They accept me as I am and return each year to comfort me: no more faithful friends could one wish for!

Since her return from Brussels – with little to occupy her restless mind – Charlotte, to my great anger, has managed to unearth an entire notebook of my poetry. Now, against my better judgement, she has convinced me that a collection of the poems of all three of us sisters could possibly find a publisher. She is so impressed with the idea of our 'collected poems', that I can no longer refuse her.

I felt some of Branwell's extraordinary work should be included as well, but Charlotte was insistent that this should be our secret venture and that only we sisters, the neglected women of poetry, should be represented, although the pseudonyms we have concocted – Currer, Ellis and Acton Bell – suggest we are not women at all.

Now I have just learned that – courtesy of Abott and Jones, Publishers, and at our own great expense, something we could afford only as a result of the generous legacy of our departed Aunt Branwell – our *Poems* are to be published sometime next year.

Even though I am hiding behind the name of Ellis Bell, and no-one beside my sisters will know that it is Emily Brontë who is displaying herself in such a public manner, I would still take my poems back if I could.

At least no prying eye will spy the haunting story that I begin upon these pages to-day.

In the midst of the torrential rains of April, for the first time in my life, I had had the parsonage to myself.

At long last my father, almost seventy years of age, and stalwart man that he is, consented to undergo cataract surgery for his failing eyes. The delicate operation was performed by Dr William James Wilson, former President of the Manchester Medical Society and a founder of the eye hospital there. Charlotte accompanied our father to the city. He was confined to a bed for five weeks with bandages over his eyes and leeches applied constantly to prevent inflammation. Father's new curate, the Reverend Arthur Bell Nicholls, an Irishman like my father, carried the burden of the parish during his absence.

Our faithful retainer, Tabitha Aybroyd, had at last come back to us, but I gave her a holiday until father's return, when she would be needed. Since Anne and Branwell were away at Thorp Green, that left only our faithful young Martha Brown who has been servant to us for some five years and was deserving of a rest too.

I was completely alone for the first time in my life. There

was nobody to answer to. I could play at the piano for hours at a sitting and disturb nary a soul.

If I chose to tramp the moors in the pelting rain and arrived back at the parsonage dripping with water and shaking with the cold, there was no-one to remonstrate or scold me for my irrational behaviour.

I missed my sisters and my brother and my father; but for this brief period of my life, their letters sufficed.

The only obligation I felt was to make an appearance at Mr Nicholls' Sunday service, because I liked and admired this man who had already been such a great help to my father.

The first replacement for our beloved William Weightman had proved disastrous. The Reverend James William Smith had little in common with my father and was not beloved by his parishioners. His departure for the curacy of Keighley was welcomed by all – especially me.

Keeper was my only company. He loved our trip through the moors as much as I, although during Christmas I believe he became too attached to Anne's spaniel, and now misses the gentle Flossy. I suppose everyone needs a mate, though there shall never be one for me!

Now I am contemplating an abandonment of poetry. I am considering a venture into the world of the novel, one which Charlotte has already essayed with *The Professor*, though she has yet to find a publisher.

When my sister had written from Manchester that she was attempting a new work concerning a governess named Jane Eyre, why did I immediately feel compelled to make my own attempt at this difficult form of writing? Are we sisters forever to be in competition with each other? Certainly Charlotte knows what it is to be a governess. Both she and Anne have had their share of that distasteful occupation. Fortunately, I have been spared. I think I should die first before assuming the care of others' unpleasant children!

Simply teaching music to the girls at the Misses Patchett's Boarding School at Law Hill was more than I could bear.

Perhaps the consignment to these pages of the haunted events of this past April will reveal whether I have a story of my own to tell.

I had been too long at Top Withens. I had fallen asleep over my poetry, my poems for Gondal, the make-believe world that Anne and I had forged out of the fantasy created by Branwell and Charlotte, a continuing saga in which I was beginning to lose interest. I had lain my head on a tuft of heather, closed my eyes, and fallen asleep to the pleasant song of a dunnock. Keeper, who had dozed as well, awoke me by licking my face. No Prince Charming he – nor I a Sleeping Beauty – but unless it were William Weightman awakening me with a blessed kiss, I would rather Keeper's warm breath upon my face than any other's.

The sun had long since set; darkness was descending. It was a long walk back to the parsonage, but I was not afraid. Keeper was with me. Besides, I knew the way home, even had there been no moon at all – but a wan orb was rising, a pale suggestion of the harvest globe that would greet us at the end of summer.

I reached a neglected stone wall that once kept white sheep from wandering from a now abandoned and decrepit farm.

At first the only sound was the wind soughing in the thorn bushes and heather. But suddenly a rude noise broke upon these fine ripplings and whisperings, at once far away and yet clear: a positive tramp, tramp, tramp – a metallic clatter which grew in intensity until the ground began to shake.

Not knowing whence the sound was emanating, I crouched low in the shelter of the stone wall and pulled Keeper close to me, the dog as perplexed as I, growling at the disturbance.

The din not only grew louder but quickened as well.

Then I realised it was a horse. A ghostly tale with which Charlotte had frightened me as a child loomed in my mind. Her North-of-England spirit had been named 'Gytrash', which, in the form of a horse, mule or large dog, haunted solitary ways, and sometimes came upon belated travellers, as this horse was now descending upon us.

I could not remain concealed any longer. I was resolved to stand at my full height and confront this creature, be it malevolent spirit or not.

The horse and rider were about to negotiate the wall when I arose. I glimpsed a startled face amidst a tangle of dusky hair. Perhaps the rider assumed I was some sort of heathen spirit myself, for he pulled back on his dark steed in an attempt to avoid me. The consequences were dire: the horse reared, stumbled and fell, crushing its front legs against the brutal stones atop the wall.

The pitiful whinney of the terrified beast rings still in my ears. The hapless rider's foot was caught and twisted in the stirrup so that he fell to one side off the horse and across the length of the wall. A sharp stone gashed his leg, making a deep wound from knee to calf from which the blood flowed freely.

'Damn you, witch!' he bellowed, hanging from the top of the broken stone wall where his steed was also pinioned.

'I am no witch,' I protested, advancing, yet uncertain what to do.

'Then free me!' he pleaded, wincing in pain as he attempted to hoist himself upward towards his boot, still pinned to the stirrup.

I silenced Keeper, who was barking ferociously, and hastened to his aid, attempting to untwist the black booting. The young man screamed in agony. 'The boot! Free me from the boot.'

The horse, momentarily stunned by its own catastrophe, was beginning to rouse itself. 'Quick!' he bellowed, fearing he would be dragged to the earth and crushed by his own steed.

Fortunately, he was suspended on my side of the wall. I reached underneath his arms and pulled with all my nerve. He pushed with his own considerable power against the stones with his free leg, moaning from the pain this endeavour was costing him. His sinewy young body twisted in my arms.

Finally he was free. As he tumbled from the wall on top of me I was momentarily trapped beneath him, his head falling across my breast, where never a man's head had rested before. Instinctively my hands found their way to his hair, and to his temples. He sighed a moment. Was it in pain or in response to my ministration? Did my touch momentarily soothe him? I do not know. I felt his warmth through his woollen coat and he felt mine through my pelisse. Then the horse freed its damaged limbs and tumbled to the other side of the wall.

The young man attempted to sit up. I managed to pull free of him. I knew nothing of nursing and medicine but I examined his brutal wound nonetheless. How warm the gushing blood! 'You are seriously injured, sir.'

'I am not the important one here,' he ejaculated. 'We must see to my horse.'

His accent was strangely foreign, though overlaid with a hint of Yorkshire. However, I was not well-travelled enough to be able to place it.

He struggled to gain his footing. 'Sir,' I protested, 'you must not attempt to walk.' Still, he persisted, but the pain was so excruciating that he sank back down in helpless agony.

'We must staunch the flow of blood immediately,' I advised, kneeling beside him and examining the gaping wound once more. I know that something must assuredly be done – and that quickly. He ignored me and, feeling inside his jacket produced a pistol, holding it by the barrel so that the curved butt faced me. 'His legs are broken. You must kill my horse.'

'I cannot kill any living creature.'

'For God's sake, put poor Yurik out of his misery!'

Hesitantly, I accepted the pistol. My father had pistols. He would carry them loaded whenever he had to make a long journey across the moors during periods of unrest such as the rising of the Luddites. When he would return home he would discharge them outside the house. The noise always sickened me. How quickly death could come with the mere flick of a trigger. I never wished to be such a messenger. Now I was holding this instrument of death in my own hand. 'Do it, for God's sake. Do it!'

I nodded obediently. I could not bear to see any creature suffer, certainly not such a beautiful horse.

The stallion remained where he had fallen. He was breathing heavily. His eyes were open, wide circles of white, each with a black dot of fear. They followed me as I approached. Trembling, I lifted the pistol, wondering where I should shoot. I aimed between the poor creature's eyes, at a spot beneath its black mane. I pulled the trigger. From the other side of the wall came a desperate cry of farewell: 'Yurik!' I was propelled backwards by the power of the discharge, but I did not miss. The horse made one last sound. Was it a whimper? Was it a sigh? Then it was dead. And suddenly it became peaceful, as if asleep, the way dead creatures look: as if they are resting contentedly on their sides and are not dead. They do not die on their backs, fighting to stay alive, gasping for air, as my mother and older sisters died; the way in which Death will surely come to me.

I returned to the injured rider. He lay on his back, staring at the moon, his handsome young face blanched and grim. 'Is he gone?' he whispered, more to the pale orb than to me.

'Yes.'

'Now perhaps you can do the same for me.'

'Isn't one death enough this evening?' I remonstrated, turning my back and ripping material from my petticoats to make a bandage for his wound. 'I am not worth saving,' he protested.

'A man who puts the suffering of his horse above his own is certainly worth something,' I responded, tearing the cloth in strips. I then ripped away the material of his trouser-leg up to the thigh in order to dress his injuries. I had never seen this part of a man's body exposed before. How white the skin! How finely muscled this hidden anatomy! I was hesitant even to touch the young man in such a private area, but necessity dictated. I removed his belt and buckled it as tightly as possible around the thigh in an attempt to reduce the flow of blood. Where had I learned such a technique? Perhaps it was from perusing father's heavily annotated copy of Thomas Graham's *Domestic Medicine*. I hoped the process would prove successful. Next I wrapped thick strips of petticoat cloth around the actual wound. The white cloth was quickly soaked in blood at first, but shortly the bleeding began to lessen and the dressing grew no damper. I had never seen so much blood.

'Are you a nurse?' the man questioned, watching my face intently.

'I am neither nurse nor witch,' I replied, completing my task. Perhaps nursing would be a suitable profession for me, even though father would never hear of it. I had heard him once say that it was disreputable and that such women were often little better than drunken prostitutes. 'I am nothing,' I replied, and realised for the first time that it was so. Could I possibly call myself a poet because we are to be published? 'Now you must rest,' I said finally, rising to my feet. 'I will seek help, and a doctor. Let me put something under your head.'

'Forget my head,' he retorted; then immediately thought better of it. 'There's a blanket under the saddle and another tied to the horse.'

I did not relish returning to the deceased stallion, but did so nonetheless. Managing to free both blankets, I covered the young man with one and cradled his head with the other. 'What is a woman like you doing walking the moors by yourself at night?'

'I am the moors,' I responded.

Perhaps this is true.

'Have you a name?' I asked, preparing to depart.

'I am called —,' he replied. Even on these pages that no-one shall ever see, even here, I cannot reveal his true appellation. It is a strange name; it put me in mind of foreign fields and forgotten forests. 'But you must not call me that,' he added quickly, 'for I have stolen this horse and have been accused of filching money into the bargain. I was traced to —, whence I have fled.'

'What shall I call you then?' I was disturbed by his honesty.

'My mother once told me I was born in Hathersage in Derbyshire. You may call me this.'

I knew of this village. It was west of Sheffield and Henry Nussey, brother to Charlotte's school-friend, Ellen, is to become the new curate there in the fall.

'I am Emily.'

I followed the route that would take me by the once-abandoned barn at Ponden Clough. It is now occupied by Ollie Firth, who took over the ancient place and fashioned the upper storey into a comfortable dwelling for himself, making the barn below a home for his gig and large horses.

Ollie used to follow us Brontë sisters about when he was just a young boy. I it was with whom he was supposed to be smitten. He scarcely ever spoke, and I had little or no interest in him, although he was exceedingly tall for his age, so that I did not appear so gangling in his company.

Ollie's horses were his true love, and his double gig which he rented from the Haworth Livery Stables. Since we Brontës almost always walked to our destination, we seldom had use for his mare or his shabby phaeton.

Many years ago, Branwell had hired a then young Ollie Firth to convey us and Charlotte's friend, Ellen Nussey, to Bolton Abbey at Birstall where we were to be met by Ellen's family. I remember Branwell displaying his brilliant memory by naming all the hills along the route and even their heights above sea-level. However, when Ellen's family arrived in a handsome carriage and pair to convey her home, it put our own humble conveyance to shame; and Ollie's adoption of some sort of blue uniform with a tall black hat that always left a dark smudge on his forehead did not lessen our mortification.

On another occasion, Ellen Nussey appropriated her brother's carriage and whisked Charlotte off to the Leeds Railway Station where they rode the train to York and then took an 'open fly' to Driffield and Burlington, where Charlotte had her first glimpse of the sea, the dramatic vista of the East Yorkshire coast that I have yet to witness.

Besides his buggy and horse, Ollie's only other interest appeared to be my father's church. He never missed a service and we sisters became used to catching him staring surreptitiously at us in our pew beneath the pulpit. He doted on my father's every word and appeared to be truly fervent in his worship of our Saviour. We hoped that he would find a mate among the woollen workers, but he appeared content to live alone, his mother having died from cholera. He was in his late twenties, as was I, and not about to change his ways.

How startled Ollie appeared to discover me standing at the doorway of his private chambers. 'Miss Brontë!' he exclaimed. 'And whet are ye in me laith?'

‘There has been an accident, Ollie, just here above the Clough. Please come with your buggy and horse.’

This was the first time I had been in Ollie’s phaeton since our trip to Bolton Abbey. He had purchased a new gig since then, but this too was now worn with wear from too many trips to Keighley or Leeds.

We rode in silence. He appeared to be pleased just to have me for company and I was grateful he had come to my rescue. ‘A bonny lass such as yerself, Miss Brontë, ought not t’ be out by yerself after t’ sun is set.’

‘I fell asleep, Ollie.’

He shook his head as if this was a foolish thing to do. ‘Ye knaw whet they call ye in town, Miss Brontë?’

‘What Ollie?’

‘Mistress of t’ Moors.’

I had heard this before and it did not displease me; but what had my perambulations that day caused but a sacrificed horse and an injured rider as well?

We soon arrived at the scene of the terrible accident. The young man was lying so still I feared his loss of blood had been too great and that he was dead. But when I leapt from the buggy and hurried over to him, he lifted his head at my approach. ‘I have brought help,’ I assured him. ‘We must get you to a doctor.’

‘I was dreaming of…’ he murmured.

‘What?’ But he did not respond.

It was with great difficulty that Ollie and I lifted the wounded rider into the buggy. Hathersage was very brave during this endeavour, but at times could not suppress a cry of pain. The bleeding had ceased, but I feared his leg was broken and that we were doing more damage by moving him; yet what else could we do?

The ride back to Haworth was torture for the young man. I was never so aware of the jostling and agitation one must endure during such a journey. Every time the horse stumbled or a wheel rolled into a rut in the narrow road, I seemed to feel our passenger's pain myself. Hathersage simply closed his eyes and did not complain.

'Un wher' will we be takin' 'im, Miss Brontë?'

I had not even thought. The doctor merely treated patients. He did not take them into his home to be nursed back to health. 'We shall take him to the parsonage, Ollie.'

He couldn't resist turning to look at me curiously. We were sitting so close together on the driver's board that his hungry eyes almost bore into mine. 'Wud tha' be such a good idee, Miss Brontë?'

'I am alone at present at the parsonage, Ollie,' I responded, for he knew my father would never approve. 'Mr Brontë is in Manchester with Charlotte. Branwell and Anne are employed at Little Ouseburn, and I have sent the servants away until father returns. We shall put the young man in Tabitha's room. It is at the back and does not have direct access to the parsonage.'

He immediately understood. 'Ay, Miss Brontë.'

When we finally arrived, the moon had retreated behind a dark cover of clouds. It was now so black I doubted anyone would have seen us approach the parsonage from the expanse of moor behind our dwelling. The only life stirring at Haworth would have been at the Black Bull Inn, not visible from the rear of our home.

Tabitha's room was reached through the backyard, by an outside stone staircase. Hathersage draped his arms over our shoulders. Ollie and I dragged him up the stairs to the freshly made bed. He sighed with relief as his head fell against the pillow. I prayed he would not die in the night. How should I ever explain it? I do not care what my father's parishioners think of me, but would be sorry to damage their good opinion of him.

The handsome young face was no longer as ghastly white as it had appeared in the moonlight. Although there was little actual colour to his sallow cheeks, the light from the candle fell warmly on his chiselled features. Hathersage appeared to have fallen asleep.

'You must fetch the doctor, Ollie,' I said.

'Ay, Miss Brontë.'

'You must not tell anyone what happened to-night. Nobody must ever know. It must be our secret.'

He understood. 'Yer trust is more sacred to me than e'vn the altar in yer father's church.'

'You're a good man, Ollie Firth,' I replied, taking one of his big rough hands and holding it in mine.

'I wud tak' yer secret to the grave with me, Miss Brontë. Ye can rest assured a that. To my grave.'

As Ollie departed, I told him of the horse that lay dead on the opposite side of the wall where we had retrieved the young man. 'Thar's use that cin be made of a dead horse.'

I had heard of people eating the flesh of this animal, but it was something I did not care to think about. 'If you would just dispose of him. There is a good saddle as well.'

'Nobody weel ev'r knew it was thar.'

I expected to see the elderly, suspicious face of Dr John Wheelhouse, but was relieved when someone entirely different arrived. Dr Wheelhouse was a staunch supporter of my father's, and would certainly have told him of my mysterious guest at the parsonage upon his return.

But Ollie had summoned a much younger man to Tabitha's doorway. 'Where is Dr Wheelhouse?' I asked.

'Dr Wheelhouse has been called away to Edinburgh on business. I am presently assistant to Dr Pritchard in Harrogate. He has spared me to attend to Dr Wheelhouse's patients while he is absent. I am Thomas Haxby.'

'And I am Emily Brontë,' I responded, accepting the man's hand. He appeared almost too young to be a doctor. His hair was blond and tousled, his complexion ruddy from the night air; yet there was an authority in his erect posture and compassion in his grey eyes.

'I observed you on my morning walk,' he spoke, his eyes almost smiling, 'tramping ahead of me as if there was no-one else about.'

I realised now that I had glimpsed him as well, but paid little heed to the stranger. As usual, my mind was elsewhere. 'There seldom is.'

He moved to the bed. 'And is this the patient?'

I stood beside him at Tabitha's pillow. 'I fear for his life.'

I related the facts of the unfortunate accident. Dr Haxby sent me to the kitchen to boil water and set immediately to work. As he removed the blood-soaked cloth I had wrapped around Hathersage's leg, he advised me that my petticoat may have saved the young man's life, for it was likely he would otherwise have bled to death.

He set about cleaning the gaping wound and dressing it in a more professional manner. Hathersage had awakened and was observing every medical act performed upon him. As the doctor completed the dressing he surreptitiously indicated an area of the wound at the calf that already bore a suggestion of discoloration, but shook his head slightly to indicate I should not remark upon it.

The wound attended to, Dr Haxby then felt gently about the exposed leg to determine if there was a break. Hathersage was able to tolerate pressure about his thigh, but when the physician squeezed his calf, he emitted a cry of pain.

'If there is a break I think it is here, probably the fibula.'

I know nothing of the bones in our bodies, except that they can break and cause great distress.

Dr Haxby gently caressed the patient's calf. 'The fibula is the bone that runs through the back of the leg from the ankle to the knee.'

'What can be done?' Hathersage demanded anxiously. It

was *his* leg that was injured and *he* who must live through the agony of it.

'It must heal itself. The process can take six weeks or more,' the young doctor advised. 'The important thing is to put no weight on the leg, for that will cause even more damage.'

Standing over the bed, he placed a cool hand over the patient's heated forehead. 'You are warm, Mr Hathersage, but I detect little fever.' Turning to me, 'Miss Brontë,' he said, 'is there perhaps a clean night-shirt the patient could put on?'

'There is my father's,' I answered, and hurried to fetch it.

Dr Haxby was considerate enough to dress the young patient out of my presence. Soon Hathersage was sleeping beneath Tabitha's warm covers. I snuffed out his candle and led Dr Haxby down the stone stairway with a small lantern. All was black. The moon had set. It was as if nothing existed beyond the dim light of my lantern and the doctor's face which it lit. The air had turned colder. The doctor donned his coat. I shivered without my pelisse.

He spoke softly. 'The bone will mend, but I fear the onset of gangrene. There is already some discoloration, which I indicated to you.'

My heart sank. 'Is there nothing that can be done?'

'There are two types of gangrene,' he explained as if, indeed, I were his nurse. 'Dry and wet. In dry gangrene there is usually no bacterial infection. The deprived area dies and blackens because its blood supply has been blocked. That type of gangrene does not spread.'

'And the wet?' I was already fearful of his response.

'Amputation is the only method of stopping its spread.'

I shuddered at the very sound of the word. No doubt my eyes betrayed my horror for the doctor attempted to reassure me. 'We will hope for the best. We must bathe and clean the wound continually.'

I led the way around to the front of the parsonage. Opening the parsonage door, I lit the hallway candle and handed Dr Haxby the lantern. 'You will need this on such a dark night.'

He accepted the lamp gratefully. 'I shall return it on the morrow.'

I hesitated, not knowing if he would understand what I was about to say. 'Haworth is a small village, Dr Haxby. Although I have never been there, I am aware that Harrogate is much grander. I would be most pleased if no-one in Haworth knew I have taken in a patient. You see, for the present I am alone here at the parsonage. I doubt anyone would understand the responsibility I feel.'

It was evident from his benevolent expression that he well understood. 'As I have not disturbed your reverie upon the moors, I shall not betray your privacy here. I come from a small village as well. I understand perfectly.'

I have read somewhere that a nurse should read to a patient and write letters home for him. Where did I gain this information? I do not remember. Has it something to do with the nursing of soldiers during the Napoleonic Wars? The Duke of Wellington has always been a hero in our household. He is the inspiration for Charlotte and Branwell's Angria stories and for Gondal tales which Anne and I wrote, although I think Branwell, perhaps on account of his own short stature, identifies more with Bonaparte.

I know now that it is time to move beyond this world of make-believe. Yet it was this very world that I depicted to my patient in hope of distracting him while he lay helpless in Tabitha's bed.

At first he tolerated my special kingdom, something I never dreamed I would share beyond my sisters, but then, as he grew a little stronger, he rejected the fanciful stories and desired only the poems – my Gondal sonnets which Charlotte has appropriated for publication.

He relished particularly my moor poetry. He said the Yorkshire countryside was in my voice and that I could make him see what I was describing. I do not know if this is true. Perhaps it is merely because he was my captive audience. Nevertheless, I shared this feral part of my life with him in a way I have never shared anything with anybody before – and possibly never will again.

For the moors, for the moors where the short grass
Like velvet beneath us should lie:

Charlotte may have criticized this effort, but my young listener committed it to memory.

In truth, I confess that I enjoyed this nursing. I took a pleasure in cooking and washing which, hitherto, I never had. I derived satisfaction from cleaning and dressing his wound. The touch of my fingers against the white flesh of his leg, or along the sparse forest of hair upon his skin, gave me an exquisite thrill that I blush now to confess.

I was not in love with this young man as I had loved William Weightman, but there was an attraction that I will not deny. Had it been reciprocal, I can only speculate as to the results.

Tabitha's room is decorated with examples of our attempts at drawing and painting. She is partial to our depictions of the animal kingdom; all manner of creature can be found gracing the walls of her chamber. There is my water-colour of Nero, my pet merlin, the hawk which I rescued from an abandoned nest on the moors and who flew away when I was abroad with Charlotte in Brussels – perhaps in search of me.

Ah could my hand unlock its chain
How gladly would I watch it soar
And ne'er regret and ne'er complain
To see its shining eyes no more.

Hathersage appreciated this poem too. 'I am like this hawk,' he ruminated, studying my depiction. 'Chained to this bed, but wishing to fly away.'

There are other winged creatures represented on Tabitha's walls: Charlotte's depiction of a mountain sparrow and Branwell's of a goshawk. There are representations of our present pets: mine of my beloved mastiff, Keeper and a colouring of Anne's spaniel, Flossy, gleefully pursuing a sparrow. There are also reminders of past habitués of the parsonage: my study of Gaspar, our gentle Irish terrier, and, lastly, my pencil drawing of Keeper, Flossy and Tiger, the last sadly departed from us earlier this year and recently replaced by a black tabby I have named Tom. This feline followed me up to Tabitha's room and slept on Hathersage's bed, where Keeper also kept guard, for there was something in this young man to which my animals responded.

Even though little colour returned to his sunken cheeks, the hollows of which appeared almost to have been sculpted by God himself, Hathersage was still a darkly handsome man. I have seldom seen such perfect symmetry in the human head, commencing with a rich tangle of wild hair that fell in dark ringlets above his fine brow; then thick black eyebrows sheltering penetrating brown eyes; strong nose and full lips that turned neither upwards nor downwards, but persisted in a set look of determination. His voice was in keeping with his physiognomy. It poured forth like the hill torrents in spring-time, a moor voice, softened by sunshine and heather, but with rich, peaty depths.

I respected the privacy of this patient – as I wish my sisters would respect mine. I asked no questions and he volunteered little information.

Our special world was the animal kingdom hanging about the walls. These pictures awakened in him special memories of horses, hounds, cats, chickens, domesticated rooks, badgers, hedgehogs, and even voles for which he had cared as a young man.

I felt that I could love this man. Indeed, I think I did during those precious moments when he drew me into his special menagerie, so warm and vivid were his memories. I feel I could sketch these creatures now from his mere description of them.

Instead, I painted him. Could this possibly be my finest water-colour, though far from skilful, for I have had little experience with portraits? Branwell is our portrait painter. Still, when I examine now my rendering of the young man – when I remove it from the secret place where I have hidden it – I feel that I have indeed captured something special. Hathersage bursts forth from that canvas, as dramatic as when he lay back against Tabitha's pillow.

The blackness of his wound persisted but did not significantly spread. I hoped this was an indication that the gangrene would not be fatal. There was little pain. The tissue had died and the diseased area had grown numb; but there was bacterial infection, indicated by redness, swelling and an oozing pus around the darkened area.

Dr Haxby, out of respect for me, took to visiting the patient at night. He feared that the gangrene was wet, even though I bathed and cleaned the wound twice daily – this operation being repeated by Dr Haxby at night. There was an unpleasant smell to the wound that did not bode well for the patient. This odour is difficult to describe. Indeed, I cannot – but it persists in my nostrils.

More than a few days had passed and the patient's wound was getting neither better nor worse. Haxby feared that gas gangrene, the most virulent form of the disease, indicated by the foul odour, was arriving like some Grim Reaper. Amputation was the only way of preventing the condition spreading.

Hathersage accepted the doctor's pronouncement with deceptive equanimity. It distressed me more than the patient.

Was it not my fault that he was injured? I wished to take his strong hands and press them to my lips and murmur my apologies.

Dr Haxby, still hoping to protect my reputation, scheduled the surgery for the following evening. Under cover of darkness, I was once again to secure Ollie Firth's services and deliver Hathersage to Dr Wheelhouse's surgery where the amputation could be safely performed.

Hathersage said little. He simply closed his eyes and pretended to sleep.

I accompanied the doctor downstairs. He stood holding his lantern at the level of his chest. The night was filled with stars. Desultory rain had departed earlier in the week. In its wake, on the horizon, there was the promise of May.

'Is there no other way, Doctor?' I feared the answer.

'I have waited too long as it is. The longer I delay, the more of his leg I will have to remove.'

'What if he is better to-morrow? What if the wound is truly beginning to heal?'

He sensed my distress and reached out to touch my arm. 'You have done everything you can for him, Miss Brontë.'

I gazed into his gentle eyes, responding to the kindness of his touch; yet I did not feel the same as when I touched Hathersage in dressing his wound. 'Thank you, Doctor.'

I watched him depart.

Inside the parsonage I moved to my father's study and removed the key to his church. A candle sufficed to lead my way through the graveyard to the door of St Michael's. How strangely quiet was this edifice in the dead of night. I was seldom inside, except when I felt obligated to attend father's services; now I was there of my own volition. I wanted to pray, close to the niche where my mother and older sisters were buried. I wanted to pray for the young man, pray that he would not die, pray that he would not lose his leg because of me.

I besought God with anguished voice. The sound pierced the all-pervading stillness like a pebble dropped into water. So my plea to our Heavenly Father rippled into Eternity.

Did God hear me?

Will I ever know?

He lay awake later that evening when I crept back into Tabitha's chamber, his face a study of consternation in the candle-light. I sat by his bed, took his hand and kissed it. 'It is such a terrible thing I have done to you.'

'Terrible things have been done to me long before you.' He squeezed my fingers in response. This was the rough hand of a man who has bridled and ridden many horses. 'It is my own damn fault for running away in the dead of night.'

'Perhaps you should sleep now,' I suggested, still clasping his hand. 'You will need as much rest as possible.'

'So I'll be fresh as a daisy for him to cut my leg off to-morrow?'

'Perhaps to-morrow will have a better outcome.'

'He'll never take my leg! I won't let him!'

I did not know how to respond. Instead, I pressed his hand to my lips again.

'I could never go back there half a man – some pathetic peg-leg.'

'Where?' I could not resist asking. Was it time for him to tell me something of himself.

'——,' he answered.

I cannot reveal the location, even here on these private pages.

He, who had said so little before, now wished to speak, to tell a story that I remember as clearly as when he related it. The words tumbled effortlessly from his lips, sentences sometimes so bitter that he spat them out as if they were rancid seeds. I kept hold of his hand and listened with equal ferocity, the words singeing my ears, burning and haunting my memory of him.

'It is true that I came from Hathersage, but it is not an association of which I'm proud. My mother was in service to a family there that I will not name. I still detest each and every one of them. They have a grand manor house and enough money to fill it with servants. My mother – I'll call her Mary – in truth, that was not her name – was the upstairs maid.

'It was the youngest son of the lord of this manor who had his way with her. He professed his love, and my mother believed him and loved him back. Yet when she began to show that she was with child, my young lordship denied he had had any knowledge of her and she was dismissed in the seventh month of her pregnancy. They had given her enough to make her way to London where I was born in a charity hospital. Afterwards my mother secured work as a chambermaid at an hotel. I did not feel deprived for she loved me dearly and filled me full of stories about how one day I would take my place as the lord of a very fine manor. She had foolish hopes that I would be the only heir.

'She worked herself to the bone – that good, fine woman – and before I was six years of age her lungs filled with fluid and she breathed her last breath.'

A solitary tear started in his eye; he ignored it and continued.

'They put me into an orphanage, a foul place where there was never enough to eat and too many to the bed. Most of us were put out to labour, I to a miserable blacking factory. My work was to stir and cover the pots of paste-blacking, to tie them round with string and then clip the paper close and neat. After that it was my duty to tidy up after everyone else had departed. I was nearly dead with exhaustion each night before I crawled into bed.

'What did I have at the end of the day but a meal of thin gruel and a sound beating if I ever seemed less than grateful?

'I must have been twelve when I ran away. You can't be sure how old you are when they never celebrated a birthday in that loathsome place. Many died there. I vowed I would never again wake up to find one of my companions dead beside me.' He stopped and turned to look at me; for hitherto he had been staring into the void created by his past. 'Do you wish me to continue, Miss Brontë? It is not a pleasant story.'

'I wish to know all,' I responded. 'I have a great curiosity about you.'

'Have you not read Mr Dickens' *Oliver Twist*?'

'We have all read it. Your childhood resembles that poor boy's, I agree.'

'There was a Fagin in my life as well. He kept a house of young boys, but we were not taught to pick pockets. Perhaps I should have resisted, but I had no place else to go.' He stopped then, studying me, unsure whether to proceed further. 'You are far removed from London in a secluded parsonage such as this. Perhaps I should cease now and not offend.'

'I am not as sheltered as you may think,' I replied.

His eyes left me then and he continued to speak. I report his account here as accurately as I can remember. His voice is in my ear as if it were yesterday.

'We were maintained purely for gentlemen's pleasure, disgusting old men who had their way with us – there in our Fagin's brothel or at their own domiciles. As debased and depraved as this life was, it was better than the drudgery of the blacking factory or being beaten and starved to death at the orphanage. At least our Fagin kept us well fed and healthy so that his customers would find us attractive.'

I had never imagined that such things could be possible. Indeed, I did lead a protected life at my father's parsonage. In my wildest nightmares, I had not envisioned that man could stoop so low as to corrupt an innocent child. However,

I endeavoured to conceal my dismay and revulsion, for I feared this would silence him, and I was desperate to learn all the particulars of his history.

'One can remain in such a life for only so long. I soon felt that I would rather die than be debased any further.'

Had not this unnaturalness been demonstrated in the tragic life of the great poet, Lord Byron? I have read of his strange fondness for a young Greek boy, whom he bought as a page from Cephalonia and to whom he addressed his last agonized poem:

> If thou regrett'st thy youth, *why live*?
> The land of honourable death
> Is here: – up to the field, and give
> Away thy breath!
>
> Seek out – less often sought than found –
> A soldier's grave, for thee the best;
> Then look around, and choose thy ground,
> And take thy rest.

Hathersage freed his hand from mine and reached for the cup of water I had placed beside his bed; he sipped slowly before once again speaking. 'I lived in the streets, stealing what food I could, but I could not survive so I went back to my Fagin who, out of spite, would not take me in.' He set the cup back down and took a small breath, an indication that his story would now take a different direction. 'Out of desperation I resolved to sell myself to the first bidder. Have you any idea what it is to starve?'

I shook my head slowly and sat patiently waiting for him to continue.

'The despair is so great one looks on death as a blessed reprieve.' A wan smile played on his lips, then died. 'I chose a distinguished looking gentleman who was strolling along the Thames. "Would you be liking some company, sir?" That was how I put it.

'"And what would a handsome young lad like you be offering an old gentleman like myself?"'

His mimicry was masterful.

'"I beg your pardon, sir," I apologized. "I did not mean to offend."

'"Is there no-one to take care of a plucky lad like yourself?" he demanded.

'"I am alone in the world and must make my way." It was a truthful reply.

'"Have you nary a relation in the world?"

'"No, sir."

'"And where will you sleep to-night, laddie?"

'"By the river, the same as last night and the night before. It is my icy bed." He was a Lord, and the kindest, most decent man I ever encountered.'

He spoke the man's name then, but I shall not divulge it here. I shall call him Lord Browning, after our special poet, and the names of the others involved in Hathersage's history shall be changed also. This is a tale I shall never share with another.

'He not only fed me that evening, but took me back to his palatial hotel, where I was given a room all to myself, and in the morning we travelled by train back to his ancestral home in —. Such a grand place you never saw. I never dreamed that such a fine home as that ever existed.

'Lord Browning was a widower and was raising his children as best he could alone. There was a boy, Spencer, two years older than I, who resented my appearance bitterly, and a girl, Colleen, my very same age. You never saw such a beautiful lassie, with hair and eyes as dark as coals and a wild streak in her character as deep as a country well. She was a child of nature, as I soon learned to be. We lived to ride and roam the countryside, to lay traps for furry creatures and then raise them as our own. I think I loved her from the very first moment I set eyes on her.

'Lord Browning, observing that I had a way with horses, apprenticed me to Dudley Collins, who was the stable-man. He was a kindly old gentleman, who taught me to love and care for the animals.

'I was given my own room in the grand house and although I was fed in the kitchen, I received lessons with Spencer because Lord Browning said that man must have an education and improve his station in life.

'Spencer never accepted me into this household and was constantly jealous of my closeness to his sister. We avoided him as much as possible and were never happier than when we rode about the moors and fashioned a secret hide-away from the stones at Cranston Crag.

'We were more than brother and sister, truly happy only in each other's company. It was enough for me just to hold her hand or run my fingers through her hair, though we both knew that one day we would want more. We trembled in anticipation of it.' He paused a moment, lost in his own reverie, the memory of this girl softening the contours of his face. I was reminded of the way William Weightman had looked at my sister. Perhaps Ollie Firth looked at *me* that way. Poor Ollie!

'Everything changed upon Lord Browning's death. Spencer became the new Lord and moved me out of the house and into a squalid room over the stables. I became simply the groom and was not allowed in the grand house beyond the kitchen. Sometimes he even struck me with his whip. I endured his harshness because I could not bear to be parted from his sister. She came to the stable daily; and in her company I could forget her brother's humiliating treatment.

'Spencer insisted that Colleen be introduced into society. She became a regular lady, attending balls and spent days at the country estates of wealthy neighbours. She did not have much time for me, yet she always returned to the stable and then we would go riding and she would declare she could be herself only with me and that one day we would run away together. But I feared that day would never come.'

He stopped a moment and shook his head sadly. 'One night I overheard what she truly thought of me. Earlier in the day she had brought one of her "superior" friends to go riding with her. He wasn't fit to wipe her boots! I was jealous and, in consequence, was surly and insolent to her guest and rude to my beloved as well. I refused to saddle the horse he desired and put him on one of our lesser nags.' He took a deep breath, as if what came next would be the most painful thing of all to tell. 'Later that afternoon she stomped into the kitchen. I was in the adjoining scullery. She did not see me; I heard her every word. She told cook that she detested me; she was ashamed of me; I would never be fit for polite society. She complained that I was an "unwashed embarrassment" and she would stay away from — as long as I was there. "He'll never make anything of himself!" were the last words I heard from those beautiful, precious lips.'

A look of determination galvanised his features. 'If it's a gentleman she wants, a gentleman I shall be!' He sat up a little straighter in Tabitha's bed. 'I took Yurik, the horse Lord Browning had given me, all my wages hidden away in the stable and set off to make something of myself. The next morning Spencer raised a hue and cry, declaring that I had not only stolen a horse, but *his* money as well. I was apprehended at —, but managed to escape.'

He looked directly at me, his piercing dark eyes burning through me with the fire of his conviction. 'As God is my witness, I took nothing from that house that was not mine!'

'I believe you.'

'*She* knows that Yurik is mine.'

I attempted to calm him.

'What you overheard her say – I am sure it was spoken in great anger. We all say things we don't mean when we are angry. How could one who had spent so many happy hours with you change so much?'

His jaw was still set in fierce determination. 'If it's a gentleman she wants, it is a gentleman I will become.' He gazed forlornly down at his wounded leg. 'But I'll not come back to — with half a leg, half a man. She'll never have me then, will she? I'm coming back in one piece or not at all!'

The Journal of Branwell Brontë

7th January, 1846

I continue to write of love. My quill moves across the paper of its own accord because my fingers still pulsate with the passion I am describing.

I hate this month the most of all. Cruel winter holds us in her relentless grasp; there is nothing to look forward to but February, which promises to be even more severe.

I write this from my bed. I remain beneath the covers as long as I dare. I am nearing the end of my story and I must continue until it is all written; even though it seems I transcribe less and less because I dread re-living its conclusion.

I wait desperately for just one letter. When there is nothing for me in the post, I hurry to the Black Bull to drink away my sorrow and hope for a letter to-morrow – a missive that will make all the difference to my life.

On this bitterly cold January morning, I shall remain in bed, free from the icy winds that buffet the parsonage and rattle the window panes; free from the outdoors where the remaining few leaves on the thorn trees are whisked to the graveyard and lie frozen on the ground.

A Journey to Richmond

At Thorp Green, a little less than a year ago, spring was not late. It arrived precisely when expected and in glorious array.

Lydia had given orders for an open carriage to be prepared

to convey us to Richmond where her daughter was to appear on the stage. The sky above was a blue bonnet with small white clouds for a brim. The air was fresh and fragrant and loud with birdsong.

Our coach took us across the River Swale, and we stopped in Ripon for a light lunch before journeying on to Richmond, eager now to reach our destination.

Anne sat between Edmund and me, facing Lydia and Mary. Lydia's eyes would meet mine and we would share a secret smile, before allowing the glories of nature to divert us. She held a flowered parasol that matched her frock: but was there any flower as fair as she? I longed to be sitting beside her, feeling the warmth of her precious body, but I had to content myself with furtive glances.

In Richmond we took rooms in the Star and Garter Hotel, an attractive establishment on Richmond Hill. After a hearty supper we were conveyed to the Georgian Theatre, an intimate hall with every seat offering a superior view of the stage. I was as excited as Edmund at the prospect of attending a theatrical performance, for I had seen so few in my life.

Mr Kean's presentation of the evening was to be *Romeo and Juliet*, with the celebrated actor-manager himself portraying Romeo and Miss Alice Roxby, Juliet. As the curtain lifted and gas-lights at the foot of the stage illuminated the proceedings, Edmund squeezed my arm in exhilaration. The Chorus entered:

Two households, both alike in dignity,
In fair Verona, where we lay our scene,
From ancient grudge break to new mutiny,
Where civil blood makes civil hands unclean.
From forth the fatal loins of these two foes
A pair of star-cross'd lovers take their life;
Whose misadventur'd piteous overthrows
Do, with their death bury their parents' strife.

Later, young Alice, a vision of convincing innocence, made her entrance as Juliet.

How now! Who calls?

How well she enunciated the Bard's glorious words! Her voice, that I had so often heard raised in defiance to her father, filled the theatre and was now most pleasing to the ear. She was doubtless the most beautiful Juliet to grace any stage; and Miss Ellen Tree, wife to Mr Kean, although not unattractive, had been wise to yield the rôle to one so young and content herself with endearing herself to the audience in a finely judged performance as the Nurse.

Mr Henry Roxby comported himself admirably in the part of Benvolio, while Mr Kean, though certainly not as young as his Juliet, possessed a theatrical youthfulness that sufficed to make the audience believe in his Romeo, although I could not help but imagine young Edmund in the rôle. What a handsome Romeo he would have made! And, having read the Bard aloud with him, I had no doubt that he possessed Thespian talents the equal of his sister's.

At the play's conclusion, when the young lovers lay lifeless in each other's arms, there were tears in all our eyes. Even Mary had given herself over completely to the theatrical experience.

For never was a story of more woe,
Than this of Juliet and her Romeo!

Afterwards we swarmed backstage and, amidst a confusion of scenery, actors, and costumes, found Alice who fell into her mother's arms and wept as we had wept for her tragic heroine. 'I wondered if I would ever see you again,' she sobbed.

'Although I still hold reservations about the profession of

an actress,' her mother confessed, 'you are indeed to the manner born. I cannot fathom whence such talent has flowed.'

'Certainly not from papa,' Mary was quick to put in. 'Although in his own way he is most histrionic!'

'There is no news of him?' Alice questioned.

'We have heard nothing,' her mother replied.

'We think that he has been eaten by the cannibals,' Edmund volunteered.

'What a hearty meal he would make!' Alice laughed.

Henry Roxby, still in his costume as Benvolio, slender and youthful in orange tights and tunic, appeared from a dressing room and put his arm around his bride. 'What a pleasure it is to see Mrs Thornton and her fine children once again.'

'When you performed at Thorp Green,' Mrs Thornton responded, 'I had no idea that you would be taking our daughter away from us.'

'Nor I,' he replied simply, looking lovingly at his bride, 'though I think Alice would have found her way to the stage with or without my assistance.'

'Perhaps you are right, Mr Roxby,' Lydia acquiesced. 'To-night Alice has demonstrated admirably that her life is here in the theatre.'

'It is true, mama,' Alice agreed, wiping away the tears that had stained her make-up. 'Nothing else can compare with the exhilaration I feel when I am performing.'

'You must take off your guise as Juliet and return with us to our hotel for some refreshment.'

'Is Henry to accompany us?' she asked timidly.

'But of course,' her mother replied. 'You are Mrs Roxby now, are you not? Even your father cannot deny that.'

Later, as we were retiring, Edmund asked if he might come to my room after everyone had gone to sleep. Deep in the chambers of my beating heart there was the hope that Lydia would come to me one more time, so I could press my lips against hers for a last taste of rapture. I put him off with the admonition that such intimacy as we had should be confined to Monks' House. He nodded reluctantly.

I had scarcely settled beneath the warm counterpane when there was the slightest tapping at my door. My heart raced in the hope that it was she. I had not yet extinguished my candle. I opened the door quietly and Mrs Thornton, my beautiful Lydia, was standing before me, her finger to her lips. I could scarce catch my breath. She walked '...in beauty like the night', as she took my hand and led me to her chamber.

Safely inside, I plunged safely inside her world – a region I wanted never to leave.

On the morrow, Mrs Thornton spent the day with her three children while Anne and I busied ourselves in exploring the town which we had never previously visited. Life was no longer the same between us because of what she had observed at Thorp Green, but nevertheless, we attempted to ignore what was left unsaid and make the most of our outing. We spent much of the morning lost in the literature of a book-seller's. Over lunch at a nearby tavern, we discussed our literary aspirations. I was no longer content to add more adventures to the denizens of Glasstown – or Angria, as it was now called. I hoped one day to write my very own novel in the style of Mr Dickens or Mr Scott.

'I, too, have the desire to create a novel,' Anne confided.

'And of what will you write?'

'Should I not write of what I already know: the story of a governess who must toil for other people's children, serving their lives and not her own?' Her blue-grey eyes held my own, not in accusation, but perhaps in divining.

'I too shall call upon my experiences at Thorp Green.' I met her penetrating gaze and did not flinch. I had discovered love at Thorp Green and would not be made to feel ashamed for it. Perhaps one day I could share my rapture in the disguise of literature. I shall make such an attempt when this journal is completed.

'Perhaps I will write of William and what might have been,' she said wistfully, finally lowering her eyes.

I took her hand across the table and squeezed it. 'There may yet be another to come into your life, Anne. Perhaps when you and our sisters have begun your school ... perhaps a parent of one of the children ... perhaps a widower who ...'

'I have had enough of taking care of other people's children.'

That evening we attended a performance of *Hamlet*. This was a more difficult rôle than Romeo and Kean, though admirable, could not compare with the greatness which reputation ascribed to his father in this part; although his delivery of Shakespeare's verse was admirable. He was still a young man and there would be ample time for his performance to develop. Perhaps he would eventually surpass his father.

It was Alice we had come to see and her Ophelia once again brought tears to all our eyes. How lovely and poignant was her mad scene, her radiant blonde hair entwined with spring flowers!

> *There's a daisy. I would give you some violets, but they wither'd all when my father died. They say he made a good end.*

These words touched every heart.

Mr Roxby was splendid as her brother, Laertes; but it was Miss Ellen Tree who was most arresting as Gertrude, Hamlet's mother. Although not a completely admirable character – indeed, she marries her brother-in-law in unseemly haste – I wept for her when she drank the poison, as I weep for all mothers – even my own, whom I had scarcely known.

I would not have minded if the play had gone on forever; except for the fact that later in the evening I hoped once again to be invited into Lydia's room.

This last night, after we had tasted secret pleasures, we lay helplessly in each other's arms, not wanting the moment to end. 'Oh Branwell,' she said finally. 'I cannot bear the thought of losing you.'

'Nor I you.'

'What are we to do?'

I had no answer, except to kiss once more those precious, sweet lips.

The Diary of Emily Brontë

2nd July, 1845

I have too long neglected these pages.

I have not completed the singular story I set out to relate. Sometimes I wonder if the young man called Hathersage ever existed.

Was he some figment of a desperate lonely imagination?

Did I conjure him up to compensate for the loss of my precious William?

Had he truly lain in Tabitha's bed and told me the haunting story of his life?

If I did not still possess his hidden portrait, I would surely believe that I had invented him.

I have been spoiled by everyone's absence from the parsonage in April. Now there seems to be no privacy for me at all.

Father returned from Manchester with his eye-sight greatly improved, so now I catch him looking at me curiously and his eyes following me about the house.

Charlotte, scratching out her *Jane Eyre*, is as inquisitive as ever about what I may be writing. Hence I am compelled to carry my note-book here to Penistone Hill so that I may complete this tale in secrecy.

Anne has returned suddenly from Thorp Green, having tendered her resignation with no explanation to any of us. We fear that this may have something to do with Branwell, who is still employed there, and will accompany the Thorntons to Scarborough for their summer holiday. Anne, who does not seem her usual placid self, refuses to discuss any particulars – even with me.

Instead, she busies herself with thoughts of writing a novel, yet she is not yet certain what fashion the story will take.

Meanwhile, I must complete my own tale, although I fear it is a story that will never have a proper ending.

Will I ever know if I have made the right decision?

Has a young man died because of me – because I have a foolish, romantic desire for love to be fulfilled, if not for me then, at least, for somebody else?

The young man slept. He had mustered all his energy and strength to relate the particulars of his life and was now exhausted.

I watched him doze until dawn, as did Keeper beside me, while Tom lay curled up contentedly on the bed.

With the first light of dawn, I took Keeper for a walk. I passed workers making the descent to Bridgehouse Mills. Although I did not acknowledge them, I could hear them murmuring amongst themselves. I care little for what the villagers think of me: to see me out walking so early, must have added fuel to the fire that branded me an eccentric.

There was no sunlight for Haworth, yet the clouds were thin and did not threaten rain. The air was crisp and invigorating; the heather trembled with dew. How beloved was my valley on that solitary morning! How fortunate I was to be able to keep pace with the always curious Keeper, while the young man in Tabitha's bed, facing the certain amputation of his leg, would never be able to tramp the moors unaided again.

Ollie Firth had already risen and was grooming his horses. A few wisps of smoke floated from the chimney at the upper storey. He must have risen as I, with the dawn. 'Gut mornin', Miss Brontë. Ar' ye out fer yer mornin' stroll?'

I stood in the doorway of his stable and watched him gently brush his two horses. They were cared for better than his gig, their coats as shiny as armour. 'An how be th' young man this mornin'?'

'You have been such a help already, Ollie. Would your gig perhaps be for hire to-day?'

'Mrs Turpin is ridin' it t' Keighley to-day.'

'And this evening?'

'Miss Brontë, it is a' yer disposal.'

I turned away because he was looking at me with obvious affection. The citizens of Haworth are right when they speak of me as a misanthrope. Perhaps I am only fit for beasts such as Keeper, and no mortal man. Ollie deserves better.

Earlier in the week, late at night, the usual hour of his visit, Dr Haxby had delivered a pair of crutches so that Hathersage could slowly accustom himself to their use.

Often, after tending to the patient, I would invite the good doctor into the parsonage and prepare him a light supper. We would sit at the parlour table and I would burn just one candle and pester him with questions about his medical training, and his life in London and Harrogate.

Sensing my own reticence, he asked me little about myself. Perhaps he knew enough already. The denizens of the parsonage are often discussed in Haworth.

He was a fine young man. I should have liked him better. I should have loved him. The impecunious daughter of a simple parson in the Yorkshire countryside could not aspire higher than to be the obedient wife of a doctor in a town as grand as Harrogate.

Why did he not ignite the same spark as dear William – and yes, Hathersage, who lay above us in Tabitha's room and was foremost on my mind?

We cannot choose whom we love, I suppose. The men I chose did not choose me.

As for the doctor, he could certainly do better than a curate's daughter. The finest gentry took the waters at Harrogate – even members of the Royal Family. I have read that Lord Byron partook of these baths and resided at the Crown Hotel. How I would have enjoyed seeing him. He is my brother's idol, but I am equally fond of his poetry. There is something to be said for dying in one's youth, as he did at the age of thirty-six, when one still has one's creative powers. I do not condemn his style of life, as others do.

I wish I could write as well.

Again I am delaying the completion of this tale.

Why?

I shall hesitate no longer but put an end to it … not today, however, for Keeper is anxious to make his way home to the parsonage and I am weary of writing.

The Journal of Branwell Brontë

2nd February, 1846

I am alone in the parlour.

I sit at the dining-table.

My sisters are about their own activities and do not disturb me.

There is no excuse not to continue.

I must hurry before I am interrupted – or feel in need of a whisky.

The Master Returns

How well I remember our happy return to Thorp Green from Richmond! The weather was as delicious as upon our day of departure; if anything, the sun shone even more brightly, the clouds were fuller and more billowy as they floated lazily above us, buoyant as balloons.

I doubt that any of the others suspected the depth of despair into which Lydia and I had fallen. We had become excellent dissemblers: smiling and talking gaily, commenting upon the vast landscapes of Yorkshire spreading before us. How empty would our beds seem now upon our return!

Dusk, when the afternoon has not yet surrendered to night, had fallen as our carriage wove through the woods that fronted Thorp Green.

This was my favourite time of day: this last gasp of mysterious light before the sun surrendered to the moon. Soon a solitary star would rise and complement this orb with a twinkling incandescence.

We were near the house when we spied a tall figure standing resolutely in the doorway. 'It is papa!' Mary shouted, the first to recognise the familiar defiant stance of her father. Lydia and I exchanged apprehensive looks. Edmund appeared stricken as well. Anne surveyed us all. She could well imagine what his return would portend.

As we drew closer to the manor and better surveyed the figure, I was shocked, as were the others, by the radical change in Mr Thornton's appearance. His clothes now hung loosely upon him, as if draped over a skeleton. He was a mere shadow of his former self.

'He looks perfectly dreadful!' Mary exclaimed bluntly, voicing what each one of us privately felt.

'I would not have recognised him,' Edmund whispered softly to me.

Lydia's hand had gone to her mouth. Before any of us could speak, Mr Thornton was upon us.

'You have disobeyed me, Mrs Thornton!' he bellowed. His voice, at least, was almost as strong as before.

'We had no news of your return,' his wife responded, ignoring his accusation.

'I strictly forbade you to have any contact whatsoever with that runagate daughter of yours.'

'Alice has become a most brilliant actress, and although I do not relish her life in the theatre, I am proud of her accomplishment.'

'You dare to champion such deceitful and scandalous behaviour?'

'She has discovered more happiness on the stage than Lord Broughton ever would have provided her in his silly greenhouse.'

'You condone the reprehensible behaviour of one daughter and doubtless you will champion the reprehensible behaviour of the other!'

Lydia's handkerchief returned once more to her lips. 'The other?' she questioned. 'Elizabeth?'

'Upon my return from Africa I have visited our daughter in Paris and she has informed me that she has not only embraced the Popish faith but is contemplating taking the veil as well.'

'What was I to do, with you so far away and my responsibility here in Yorkshire?'

'The Grisborne side of the family has tainted all my children!'

'We should never have sent her to a Catholic convent. If you recall, I was always against it.'

'When I demanded that Elizabeth return home with me, she defiantly refused to accompany me. When I informed the Mother Superior that I would make no further pecuniary contribution to Elizabeth's education, that person had the effrontery to say that her order would take none, having now secured a convert to the true Faith.'

'Mr Thornton, I doubt our Elizabeth will actually go so far as to become a nun; as for her turning Catholic, I can think of worse things that could befall her.' She alighted from the carriage, her husband reluctantly assisting her.

'You defy me as well?'

'Perhaps that is too strong a word.' His wife no longer seemed as fearful of him as she had been prior to his departure when she would have been reduced to tears by this altercation. I chose to believe that it was my ardent love that had so bolstered her courage.

'It is a most proper word!'

'Mr Thornton, what has happened to you?' she questioned as we all alighted from the carriage. 'You have lost so much flesh I would scarcely have recognised you.'

Indeed, upon closer inspection, he looked positively emaciated. There were deep circles beneath his eyes which had sunk deeper into his large skull; and his cheeks, that once only suggested creases, were now deep ravines. 'It is some damned parasite I picked up on the Ivory Coast. I have refused to let the blasted doctors bleed me one more time and have come home to Thorp Green for some of Frieda's good cooking, which will set me right in no time.'

'I am most distressed at your appearance.'

'Oh, papa!' Mary exclaimed, hugging her father. 'I scarcely would have recognised you.'

'Nor I you!' he returned, embracing his daughter. 'How lovely you have grown in my absence. Perhaps you, after all, will become our most beautiful and obedient daughter.'

'Oh, papa,' she protested, smiling at the compliment.

'Perhaps our own Mary could win the affection of the distinguished young Lord.'

'I would rather run off and join the circus and become a bare-back rider than marry him!'

'What?' he thundered, pretending to be angrier than he actually was. 'Another one defies me!'

'The theatre is bad enough,' her mother remonstrated.

The master turned his attention to his son.

'I have brought you a splendid hunting rifle. When I return to Africa, you shall accompany me – although if it pains you to hunt a fox, no doubt you would develop an attachment for lions and elephants too.'

'I believe I would, father.'

'And are the Brontës still with us?' he questioned, surveying Anne and me as we stood in attendance. 'Our children must be most accomplished by now.'

Berwick appeared in the doorway, doubtless pleased with the return of his master; but one could never be sure whether Berwick was pleased or not – he was a man of such few words. 'Perhaps madam would like tea after her long journey?'

'Oh, yes, Berwick, that would be very nice.'

'Where would Madam wish it served?'

'In the parlour, I think.'

'Very good,' and the butler withdrew.

Inside we were confronted by a quantity of massive crates strewn about the lower gallery. 'What is this?' Lydia exclaimed.

'My trophies,' her husband boasted. 'I have brought half of Africa to be hung on the walls of Thorp Green.'

'Is it to become a menagerie then?'

'Remembrances of a man's finest moments – the life-long struggle between man and beast. To the victor the spoils!'

'Oh, papa, can we see them right away?' Mary asked excitedly.

'First sip your blasted tea. I have only returned this afternoon and I must take a rest.'

Mr Thornton turned and began to drag himself slowly upstairs. The defiant determination had departed from his stride and he was now, suddenly, a much older man. We could not help but exchange worried glances; but those between Lydia and me conveyed much more.

'Mr Thornton,' his wife called up to him. 'I have a surprise for you.'

He turned and looked down at us, leaning on the bannister for support. 'I have seen your portrait.'

'And?'

'I would marry you all over again at sight of it,' he said graciously. 'You have glowed like a candle in my absence.'

'It is the artist who flatters me.'

He surveyed me curiously. 'There is more to you, Mr Brontë, I fear, then meets the eye.'

'He has begun a painting of me,' Edmund added proudly, for indeed I had made preliminary sketches of the handsome lad.

His father proceeded upstairs without responding, then turned back one more time to address us. 'When I have regained my strength we shall have a proper unveiling of this portrait and invite all those who attended the not-to-be engagement of our disgraceful daughter. We shall display all my African trophies as well.'

'We are most anxious to learn of your trip, Mr Thornton.'

'In due time. First I must rest.'

The Journey to Scarborough

Despite Frieda's abundant cooking and daily visits from Dr Crosby, Mr Thornton's condition showed little sign of improvement. Whatever the parasite that had invaded his sturdy body in deepest Africa, it continued to bring severe bouts of dysentery which left him progressively weaker, so that he took to using a cane when walking about the estate. Although the warm days of June brought abundant sun and skies as blue as berries, the salubrious weather did little to heal the master of this house.

August had been the customary month for the family's journey to Scarborough; yet suddenly Mr Thornton, feeling the sea air might be the tonic he needed, declared that we would travel on the 1st July and stay perhaps the remainder of the summer.

Anne, who had been to Scarborough with the Thorntons on previous occasions, looked forward to what she declared would be her last visit there as governess to their children, confessing that the sea lifted her spirits and brought a peace and tranquillity she had discovered nowhere else, not even in father's church. Perhaps in Scarborough she could finally accept the loss of the man she loved.

As preparations were being made, I grew excited at the prospect of such a journey. I was the only Brontë who had never actually seen the sea. Both Charlotte and Emily had crossed the English Channel to Brussels.

Edmund came to me the evening before our departure. His father had softened with illness and now craved not only the company of his only son, but that of God. The boy often read to him from the Bible late into the night, so that his visits to Monks' House were less frequent.

It was an unusually warm June night, hardly Yorkshire weather at all. Not expecting Edmund, I had left the door ajar and the windows open to the unusual humid atmosphere. I had unbuttoned my shirt and was reading by candlelight when Edmund slipped inside and moved behind me to kiss me on the top of my head. 'I have missed you, Branwell. I am pleased that father needs me now, but I need you.'

I rose to my feet and gave him a hug of welcome. 'May I kiss you, Branwell?' the boy begged. 'I have missed you these summer days.'

'You may,' I acquiesced. I had been too long without his mother and was as desperate for affection as he. What began as a gentle kiss became more. Hungry for passion, I opened my mouth to his. How innocently his tongue explored my teeth. I responded in kind as his hands moved inside my open shirt and stroked my bare skin.

Perhaps that warm summer night we would have proceeded further, so great was his young passion and I so desperate for affection. I shall never know. At that moment, I glimpsed my sister's face. She was standing in the shadow of the window. I will never be able to erase the memory of the horror that distorted her lovely features in a way I had never seen before. As quickly as she was there she was gone, vanished into the moonlight. Edmund had not seen her. I will never know why she had ventured down to my cottage that evening. Perhaps it was the warm weather and the special moon that drew her outside for a walk.

I pulled free of Edmund. Passion inflamed his handsome features; his eyes questioned my sudden coolness. 'I would love you, Edmund, the way you desire and hold nothing back,' I whispered, 'but we would be sorry afterwards.'

'Not I.'

'This is not the proper conduct for a tutor here at Thorp Green.' In truth, my conduct had hardly been proper with his mother either.

'And if we were on a voyage and shipwrecked as in our story?'

'Then I would love you more than anyone else on this earth.'

'Then I shall pray for rough weather.'

He stole one more quick kiss, but I would not respond and firmly led my student outside. 'It is a perfect evening for a stroll. I shall accompany you back to the manor.'

I had hoped to overtake my sister, keeping a good pace with Edmund beside me, so that she would be satisfied that nothing more compromising had occurred between us than an innocent kiss – but she had fled.

When I reached the manor house, Anne had already retired. I had not the heart to disturb her, for what could I say in my defence? A kiss such as mine with a young boy is never innocent. Men have been prosecuted for less.

In the morning, when I entered the manor house kitchen, I found my sister had already taken Flossy and fled, proffering her resignation and departing in haste. When the Thorntons demanded of me an explanation for this unreasonable behaviour, I feigned ignorance, suggesting that there must have been a family crisis of which I would later be made aware.

Would I ever be able to meet my sister's gaze again? She had been made deeply uneasy by her suspicions of my affair with the mother; now she would believe she had evidence of an improper involvement with the son. What other recourse did she have but to leave the premises immediately?

I should have done likewise, but I could not bear to tear

myself away. I loved two of the Thorntons and could not leave either.

I should have departed Thorp Green in pursuit of my sister and thrown myself upon the mercy of my father's Saviour: *He* may have forgiven me then.

I was powerless to do so.

I would accompany the Thorntons to Scarborough.

Tragedy would ensue.

The Diary of Emily Brontë

10th July, 1845

I have come to the place where it all began: Top Withens, whence I commenced my solitary journey home on a dimly pale night, from which emerged the mysterious rider who haunts my waking hours and my dreams.

I shall complete the tale here. Then I shall hide it away somewhere in the parsonage.

Years from now – when I can no longer remember or believe that he existed – I will read these pages once more before consigning them to the fire.

It was my decision as much as his.

I could no more bear the loss of his leg than could the victim himself.

Who was to say for sure if his leg would mend or the infection spread as the doctor predicted?

Such matters are not in our hands but in those of some higher power, a power that reaches beyond my father's church and engulfs the universe – a power that frightens me.

Ollie arrived at the parsonage soon after night-fall. Outside was black and bitter. The wind was a ferocious animal, tearing the summer leaves and shaking the very grave-stones above the sleeping dead.

The only illumination was the lantern attached to the side of his phaeton swinging to and fro in the turbulence.

With great difficulty Hathersage descended the staircase from Tabitha's room. He was not used to the crutches and on more than one occasion almost stumbled and fell. I held onto him with all my strength and delighted in the feel of my arm around his waist.

He wore the black jacket in which he had first appeared. I had supplied him with a thread-bare pair of my father's trousers that I hoped would not be missed. His wild hair was buffeted by the wind, his face was as turbulent as the elements. This was clearly a young man who should never be confined to the cruelty of a sick bed. He was a creature of the outdoors.

When we reached Ollie's gig, Hathersage turned and engulfed me in his arms. I had never been held like this – with so much strength and ferocity. I had never been kissed by a man before. When I had touched my lips to William Weightman, he had not responded. Hathersage's burned with fiery passion; my own mouth felt singed in response. This was indeed a man born to love. I still wish – this very moment, in the lonely desolation of Top Withens – that I was his beloved, that I could have been the object of his desire.

'I'll never forget what you've done for me, Miss Brontë.'

'I shall never forget you, Hathersage. I pray God will make you whole and bring you safe home once again.'

The rest of our words were taken by the wind – swept away, as was my last view of this shadowy phantom, almost hidden inside the gig.

I walked through the darkness. I know these Haworth streets as well as I know my own soul. There were lighted windows to lead me the way to Dr Haxby.

He was awaiting my arrival.

How warm and safe and comfortable he appeared standing in the doorway. 'I thought I saw Ollie's buggy. I have everything prepared. Is he bringing Mr Hathersage?'

I did not shake my head. I simply looked at his handsome trusting face. 'Mr Hathersage is gone.'

'What?'

'He does not wish to lose his limb.'

'He may die.'

'It is a chance he wishes to take.'

He did not protest further. If it had been Dr Wheelhouse there would have been great remonstration. He would have pursued the patient to the Bradford Railway Station.

Dr Haxby was from Harrogate. He had a life beyond our village.

'May I accompany you back to the parsonage, Miss Brontë?'

I shook my head. My skirt was victim to the wind, and my spencer, which is not trimmed with fur as are the more expensive models, did not provide enough warmth. 'I wish to make my way alone, Dr Haxby.'

He did not insist. This was a man who could not only detect illness but was sensitive to the inner workings of the spirit as well. 'Perhaps one day you will visit Harrogate. There is much to see there.'

'Perhaps.'

I think we both knew that I never would. I have been to Brussels; that is enough. Haworth is where I belong. 'Thank you, doctor. You have been most kind.'

I turned and left. It must have seemed to him that I vanished into the darkness.

I wonder now if Dr Haxby existed as well.

Could this whole episode have been but a figment of a demented imagination?

I am no longer certain.

The Journal of Branwell Brontë

12th February, 1846

It is very late at night. I have made my way home from the Black Bull.

I sit in bed and scratch these lines into my note-book. My father snores unevenly in his bed beside me. My candle is burning low and will soon flicker out. How far away Scarborough seems now. It is almost as if that restless sea had never existed.

Summer at Scarborough

Anne's fondness for this coastal paradise was not surprising. It is a haven by the sea. I feel guilty that, on my account, she was denied its dramatic beauty.

The Thorntons were in residence at Wood's Lodgings. The house was part of an impressive Georgian terrace, situated on the summit of a cliff overlooking the white, sandy beaches of South Bay. Far in the distance, on a headland, stood a medieval castle, reminiscent of the sites described in our Glasstown stories; stories that had bound us together as children, but stories, I fear, in which I can no longer take refuge.

Our lodgings consisted of a drawing room, a dining-room, eight bedrooms, a housekeeper's room and a kitchen; large enough for each to enjoy a degree of privacy. Edmund's room was next to mine.

The boy's ailing father demanded his son's constant

attention, appearing to depend upon him in a manner he never had previously demonstrated. Illness creates desperate needs, even in such a formidable character as the Reverend Mr Thornton.

For those of us who were healthy, there was much walking to be done. Edmund and Mary introduced me to every nook and cranny of this charming seaside retreat. Although we were lodged immediately overlooking the water, the actual town of Scarborough is a considerable distance from the sea. It is separated from the water by a labyrinth of new streets and houses and stands atop a hill that breathes deeply of the pure sea air. There are shops and inns and dining establishments, but it is the sea beyond that beckons. Each day we answered its siren call.

On one occasion, as Edmund, Mary and I made our descent to the beach, the girl betrayed her distress at my sister's abrupt departure. 'Will Miss Brontë resume her position after our return to Thorp Green?'

'I don't know,' I replied; but, in truth, I felt certain that she would not.

'But why did she go away so suddenly?'

'I am certain the reason will be made known to us.'

'I was so looking forward to showing Flossy the beach and watching her run in and out of the waves.'

'Perhaps you should find your own puppy.'

'I have become quite attached to Miss Brontë's.'

Edmund touched my arm as we turned to face the great North Sea. 'I should be most distressed if *you* ever left us so suddenly, Mr Brontë.'

'It is not my intention,' I assured him. In truth, I was powerless to leave, and I trembled to think what reception might await me in Haworth; although of all my family, Anne was the most secretive and her sensibilities the most delicate.

If Anne had accompanied us, might events have been different?

In Which Tragedy Ensues

How can one determine when one awakes on a tranquil morning in July that the day will end unlike any other and will haunt one for the rest of one's life?

The weather continued to warm the sandy beaches; the wind off the sea was bracing. On this morning there was a discernible improvement in the condition of Mr Thornton. Colour had returned to his rough cheeks and some weight was now visible on his bones. He had begun to take walks with his son, excursions that grew longer with each sunny day.

Lydia Thornton looked as fresh as a Scarborough day in her flowered summer cottons, her matching parasols protecting her flawless skin from the summer sun. As her husband grew stronger, I despaired of ever possessing her. I had only to look at her to understand that her desire for me was as great as mine for her, but we were powerless to alleviate our hunger.

Finally on 14th July an opportunity presented itself. It was Sunday and we all attended church. The servants were given their free Sunday afternoon. Mary was spending the afternoon with a girl whom she had befriended. Mr Thornton declared he would take a walk with Edmund.

I stood in the doorway of No. 2, The Cliff, as our lodging was called, watching Thornton father and son depart. I moved to the edge of the bluff to observe them until they grew smaller in size and were no bigger than crabs along the shore. When I returned to the house, I could scarcely breathe with the knowledge that Lydia and I were now alone. Somehow I calmed myself, afraid to make the first move lest, with the return of her husband, she had resolved to remain true to him. Instead, I entered my own bedroom and took off my clothes in the hope that she would seek me out. Finally, there was a gentle tapping on my door. I opened it in all my nakedness to crush my Lydia in my arms. 'I cannot survive without you,' I whimpered, anxiously pulling off her garments.

'Nor I, without you,' she moaned.

We were so sensitive to each other's touch that we almost spent ourselves from the sensation of merely holding each other.

'Come to my bed,' I breathed, pulling her down with me.

'I have slept with no-one since you,' she confided. 'Mr Thornton has made no demands on me.'

There was no other world for us but that bed and my room. We shut everything else out; we forgot the world outside. The only sounds were of our own making: sounds of ecstasy – sounds that carried us to a place from which we never wished to return.

We had no inkling that outside the skies had quickly blackened. We did not hear the mutterings of distant thunder nor observe the first flash of summer lightning that lit the darkening sky.

My curtains were drawn. Inside our own storm raged – one in which our pent-up emotions burst from us like cannon blasts. We did not hear the first drops of rain as they splattered across the roof of our dwelling.

The walk to the beach had tired Mr Thornton. Taking shelter in a colonnade of shops he sent Edmund to fetch a carriage to convey him home.

How ugly we must have appeared in our nakedness when he burst excitedly into my room.

There is no way to describe the shock and anguish that twisted Edmund's features as he beheld what to him was a hideous betrayal; nor the shame his mother and I felt at this discovery. He stood frozen a moment, unable to move or speak. Lydia attempted to pull free of me and cover our nakedness. It seemed an eternity before her son turned and fled the room. 'You must stop him!' she shrieked. 'Somehow you must explain! If he speaks to his father, we are doomed!'

I leapt from the bed and pulled on my clothes.

Outside the rain was pouring from the heavens; the wind whistled along the bluff, lightning sundered the sky, thunder cracked like a giant whip. Beneath me, Edmund was running frantically down the traverse to the sea, ignoring his father's carriage bearing Mr Thornton up the hill. I sped after him.

Reaching the shore Edmund leapt into a small fishing vessel and immediately cast off before I could stop him. The wind licked its sail hungrily and carried it quickly out to sea. I called desperately from the shore, begging the boy to turn back. 'I love you!' I shouted over and over. I did not care who heard. 'I love you, Edmund!'

The sky grew darker as the wind circled about the small craft. This way and that the boat was thrown, buffeted by waves, tossed from one to the other, dragged further out to sea. I had one last glimpse of the vessel and its lone occupant amidst an explosion of lightning before it disappeared in the darkness and blinding rain.

I remained transfixed upon the beach, praying that the storm would cease.

Night had fallen when I gave up my vigil and walked back through the pelting rain to the house on the bluff.

Lydia was awaiting me at the entrance. My valise was packed; an envelope contained the last of my wages. 'Have you explained to my son?' she asked anxiously.

'He has … gone off. A boat is missing. They will search for him as soon as the storm ceases.'

'Dear God!'

She seemed ready to faint before my eyes. I reached out

to stop her from falling. She pushed me away. 'Don't touch me! Never touch me again.' She collected herself and leaned against the doorway. 'It is a promise I have made to Mr Thornton – in hope of gaining his forgiveness. I have confessed to him what surely his own son will reveal. May God forgive us both!' She indicated the valise and envelope. 'Everything is here. You must leave this dwelling and never return to Thorp Green. Your belongings at Monks' House will be sent to you.'

I looked into her eyes, wet from tears, searching for a last sign of love. She averted her gaze. I retrieved my valise, but not my wages. She picked up the envelope and stuffed it into my pocket.

'Now I must prepare to face my son!' She withdrew and closed the door. I forbade myself to look back, but could not resist and observed Lydia watching me from the window: when she saw that I had detected her, she dropped the curtain and her lovely features were lost to view. The rain stung my face, but I welcomed the assault. It was a punishment.

Where was I to go? I had only home – the parsonage.

Would my father and sisters welcome my return?

Truly this time, I *was* the Prodigal Son.

The Journal of Branwell Brontë

14th February, 1846

Dear Journal,

Is this how an author like the great Walter Scott feels when he reaches the conclusion of his work? Is he both sad and relieved at the very same time?

My heart is heavy as I begin to transcribe what will be the last sentences of my peculiar history.

My only solace is that I am seated in my comfortable chair at the Black Bull Inn and I shall empty a tankard to mark the conclusion of this effort.

It does not seem possible that I am finally reaching the end of my story, at least for now, unless I can provide a happy ending to these sad histories. I have persevered until it is all written down. Perhaps I am a writer after all and one day I shall return to you and convert you into a work of romantic fiction, a work that will catapult me into the ranks, not only of my sisters, but of the more celebrated names of literature. Only time will tell; for, indeed, I am a Brontë and we are all writers.

The Conclusion

In the morning the storm lifted and the azure sky of an English summer returned in all its warming glory. The sun beat once again upon my back, the birds sang and dried their wings. One would almost think there was a God in heaven after all.

I had meant to walk the entire way home to Haworth as a penance, but my flesh is weak. I quickly grew tired and boarded a post-chaise at Bridlington.

Our family was finishing supper when at last I appeared in the doorway of the parsonage. My sisters had ways of keeping things from my father. When he rose to greet me, I felt he had little inkling that anything untoward had transpired. His cataract surgery had worked miracles. He studied me with eyes as clear as this summer day. 'What?' he demanded, surprised, but pleased, to see his only son. 'Have you handed in your resignation at Thorp Green as well?'

'I have been dismissed,' I replied honestly; but the true explanation for this dismissal was more than I could bring myself to relate.

'On what grounds?'

'The loss of my young charge.'

'What?' Anne exclaimed, her napkin flying to her mouth.

'He has been lost at sea.'

'Oh, no Branwell!' She shared a look with Charlotte and Emily. I wondered how much she had told them.

'How did this happen?' Anne asked, for she loved the boy as well as I.

'It is … we are still hoping he will be found,' I finally responded. 'Please do not ask me more.'

Fortunately, our faithful retainer, Tabitha Aykroyd, chose this moment to enter from the kitchen. How wonderful it was to see her wrinkled old face once again. Her smile for me warmed my heart. 'Is it Master Brontë come home?'

'So your leg has mended and you have returned!' I exclaimed, delighted to see her.

'My dancing days are over,' she said, smiling somewhat ruefully, 'but it is good enough to take care of my Brontës. There is food left in the kitchen for your supper.' She hurried off. 'I'll just fetch a plate.'

'Was this the sole reason why you were dismissed?' Charlotte demanded. I knew it would be she who would enquire most deeply. Her voice cut as it always did, like a knife through butter. The features of my younger sisters were slightly more pronounced in Charlotte: her nose somewhat sharper, her eyes darker, and her mouth set in fierce determination.

'We have not seen each other, Charlotte, in well over a year,' I remonstrated. 'That is all you have to say to me?'

'Welcome home, Branwell,' she replied, attempting a smile. 'Anne will not tell us why she left Thorp Green. Perhaps you can enlighten us? Is this boy truly lost, or are there matters you are keeping secret?'

This was a different Charlotte from the loving sister who had raised me. I knew she was losing faith in her younger brother and I realised then that nothing I did could now change her. Perhaps disappointment in her love for the Belgian Professor Heger – of which I learned more later – had hardened her. I felt that she no longer loved me at all.

'Oh, Branwell, what of young Edmund?' Anne persisted. 'Please tell me.'

There was nothing I could say. Only Emily's face appeared sympathetic.

I suddenly felt the need of whisky, none of which my father kept in the house. 'I think I shall go to the Black Bull for I am more thirsty than hungry.'

'Are you back to that disreputable place already?' my father demanded.

'Just for this evening, father. The loss of my charge has been a great ordeal and I am in need of a proper homecoming.'

'Can you not receive one here?' he persisted.

'Just for this evening, father.'

'Just for this evening,' he muttered, looking uncommonly old.

'I shall take my leave of you.'

I turned quickly and fled outside. At least there was money enough in my pocket to buy my fellow customers several drinks. How happy they would be to see me back!

Inside the familiar smell of spirits set my mouth watering. Drinking companions circled me at the bar. I quickly quenched my thirst.

Perhaps this really was my home. Perhaps this was where I belonged.

My love for Lydia is an even greater hunger, but I have hope that it too can be satisfied.

Neither the sailing craft nor the body of young Edmund Thornton was ever recovered.

In my fondest dreams he has sailed to safety and is living the life of adventure we depicted in our stories together.

My own world has narrowed considerably. It is confined to the space of a stool at the Black Bull Hotel, where I await word from my beloved.

PART THREE

From the Author

My Dear Readers,

This is the conclusion of Branwell Brontë's Journal and his sister, Emily's, Diary, but their sad story does not end here, as the following extracts and fragments attest.

Letter from Charlotte Brontë to her Schoolgirl Friend, Ellen Nussey

November, 1845

All of Branwell's hopes for a return to employment with the railway co. have been dashed. The place (a Secretaryship to a Railway Committee) is given to another person, and I am not surprised. Anne persists in her silence as to what took place at Thorp Green, while Branwell, in his drunken moments, raves of his love for the disgraceful Mrs Thornton. Emily, meanwhile, refuses to deny or confirm the rumours of a late night rendezvous here at the parsonage with a certain mysterious doctor from Harrogate while I was attending to father in Manchester and all others of this household were away. There is also talk of Ollie Firth's nocturnal appearance at the parsonage as well. He is our feckless local gig driver and has always been enamoured of my sister. She has nothing to say on the subject, and when I questioned him, he pretended not to know of what I was talking.

This is a troubled household, dearest Ellen. Branwell remains at home and while *he* is here, *you* shall not come – I am more confirmed in that resolution the more I know of him. I wish I could say one word to you in his favour – but I cannot: therefore, I will hold my tongue.

A Letter From Branwell Brontë to his Greatest Friend, Joseph Bentley Leyland

January, 1846

I have, since I saw you at Halifax, devoted my hours of time snatched from downright illness, to the composition of a three volume *Novel* – one volume of which has been completed – and, along with the two forthcoming ones, is really the result of half a dozen past years of thoughts about, and experience in, this crooked path of life.

My sisters do not know that I have secret knowledge of their forthcoming publication of a collection of their poetry under assumed masculine names, and at their own expense – the published proofs of their efforts were delivered to me by mistake. That they did not deign to include samples of my own work – I, who have seen my poetry published in the local newspapers – is the most dire form of rejection.

Now Charlotte is toiling away on her work of fiction, something she is calling *Jane Eyre*, a mysterious work of fiction, and I have a suspicion that Anne is contemplating something of the sort as well.

It is I who shall conclude my effort first and reveal to them that it is Branwell who is to be respected as an author.

I felt that I must rouse myself to attempt something to assuage my torment while roasting daily and nightly over a slow fire. And I knew that in the present state of the publishing and reading world a Novel is the most saleable article, so that where £10 would be offered for a poetic work, the production of which would require the utmost stretch of a man's intellect, £200 would be the least offered for three volumes whose composition would require the smoking of a cigar and the humming of a tune.

My Novel is the result of years of thought and if it gives a vivid picture of human feelings for good and evil – veiled by the cloak of deceit which must enwrap man and woman – if it records as faithfully as the pages that unveil man's heart in *Hamlet* or *Lear*, the conflicting feelings and clashing pursuits in our uncertain path through life, I shall be as much gratified (and as much astonished) as I should be if in betting that I could jump over the Mersey I jumped over the Irish Sea.

Letter From Charlotte Brontë to Ellen Nussey

April, 1846

I went into the room where Branwell was about an hour after I returned from an outing. I was determined to speak to him but it was very difficult. I might have spared myself the trouble as he took no notice and made no reply – he was stupefied. My fears were not in vain. Emily tells me that he got a sovereign from papa, while I have been away, under pretence of paying a pressing debt. He went immediately to an inn, and has employed it as was to be expected. She concluded her account with saying he was 'a hopeless being'. It is too true – in his present state it is scarcely possible to stay in the same room with him. What the future has in store I do not know–

Branwell Brontë Composes a Poem Titled 'Lydia Grisborne', the Maiden Name of his Beloved

May, 1846

LYDIA GRISBORNE

On Ouse's grassy banks, last Whitsuntide,
I sat, with fears and pleasures, in my soul
Commingled, as 'it roamed without controul',
O'er present hours and through a future wide
Where love, methought, should keep my heart beside
Her, whose own prison home I looked upon:
But, as I looked, descended summer's sun:
And did not its descent my hopes deride?
The sky though blue was soon to change to grey –
I, on that day, next year must own no smile –
And as those waves, to Humber far away,
Were gliding – so, though that hour might beguile
My Hopes, they too, to woe's far deeper sea,
Rolled past the shores of Joy's now dim and distant isle.

Obituary in the York Newspaper

May, 1846

'The Reverend Edmund Thornton of Thorp Green died on Tuesday, 26 May, 1846, at the age of forty-six. He died as he lived, in firm and humble trust in his Saviour.'

Letter from Branwell Brontë to Joseph Bentley Leyland

June, 1846

I should not experience such joy and elation at the demise of another human being, but I cannot contain myself. I have reason to hope that, ere very long, I shall be the husband of a lady whom I love best in the world and with whom, in more than competence, I might live at leisure to try to make myself a name in the world of posterity, without being pestered by the small but countless botherments, which like mosquitoes sting us in the world of work-day toil.

Letter from Charlotte Brontë to Ellen Nussey

June, 1846

I am sorry to say I have been somewhat more harassed than usual lately. The death of Mr Thornton – which took place about three weeks or a month ago – served as a pretext for Branwell to throw all about him into hubbub and confusion with his emotions, &c. &c. Shortly after came news that Mr Thornton had altered his will before he died and effectually prevented all chance of a marriage between his widow and Branwell by stipulating that she should not have a shilling if she ever ventured to reopen any communication with him. Of course he then became intolerable: to papa he allows rest neither day nor night – and he is continually begging money from him, sometimes threatening to kill himself if it is withheld. He says Mrs Thornton is now insane – that her mind is a complete wreck, owing to remorse for her conduct towards her husband (whose end it appears was hastened by distress of mind) and grief for having lost him. I do not know how much to believe of what he says but I fear she is very ill–

Letter from Branwell Brontë to Joseph Bentley Leyland

July, 1846

Mr Thornton has left his widow in a dreadful state of health. She sent the coachman, William Allison, over to me yesterday, and the account he gave of her sufferings was enough to burst my heart.

Through the will she is left quite powerless, and her eldest daughter, who married imprudently, is cut off without a shilling and the next as well if she dares to become a popish nun.

The executive trustees detest me, and one declares that if he sees me he will shoot me.

These things I do not care about, but I do care for the life of the one who suffers even more than I do. Her coachman said it was a pity to see her, for she was able only to kneel in her bedroom in bitter tears and prayers. She has worn herself out in attendance on him, and his conduct during the few days before his death was exceedingly mild and repentant, but that only distressed her doubly. Her conscience has helped to agonise her, and that misery I am saved from.

I have got my finishing stroke at last – and I feel stunned into marble by the blow.

I have this morning received a long, kind and faithful letter from the medical gentleman, Dr Crosby, who attended Mr Thornton in his last illness and who has had an interview with one whom I can never forget.

He knows me *well*, and he pities my case most sincerely for he declares that though used to the rough vicissitudes of this weary world, he shed tears from his heart when he saw the state of that lady and knew what I should feel.

When he mentioned my name she stared at him and fainted. When she recovered she in turn dwelt on her inextinguishable love for me, her horror at having been the first to delude me into wretchedness, and her agony at having been the cause of the death of her husband – who, in his last hours, bitterly repented of her – and the certain demise of her missing son.

Her sensitive mind was totally wrecked. She wandered into talking of entering a nunnery; and the doctor fairly debars me from hope in the future.

The Journal of Branwell Brontë

25th July 1846

What I shall do I know not – I am too hard to die, and too wretched to live. My wretchedness is not about castles in the air, but about stern realities. My hardihood lies in bodily vigour, but my mind sees only a dreary future which I have as little wish to enter on, as a criminal to meet his executioner.

A Newspaper's Critical Response to the Publication of the Brontë Sisters' Book of Poetry

July, 1846

Who are Currer, Ellis, and Acton Bell, we are nowhere informed. Whether the triumvirate have published in concert, or if their association be the work of an editor, viewing them as kindred spirits, is not recorded. If the poets be of a past or of the present age, if living or dead, whether English or American, where born, or where dwelling, what their ages or station – nay, what their Christian names, the publishers have not thought fit to reveal to the curious reader. Perhaps they desired that the poems should be tried and judged upon their own merits alone, apart from all extraneous circumstances, and if such was their intent, they have certainly displayed excellent taste in the selection of compositions that will endure the difficult ordeal.

The second book on our list furnishes another example of a family in whom appears to run the instinct of song. It is shared, however, by the three brothers – as we suppose them to be – in very unequal proportions; requiring in the case of Acton Bell, the indulgences of affection . . . and rising, in that of Ellis, into an inspiration, which may yet find an audience in the outer world. A fine quaint spirit has the latter, which may have things to speak that men will be glad to hear, – and an evident power of wing that may reach heights not here attempted.

The Diary of Emily Brontë

10th August, 1846

This is the last time I shall darken these pages.

Our poems are published, but have so far only garnered two pitiful sales.

Ellis Bell has not yet found her public.

Perhaps the tale I wish to tell now will meet with more success. I have not decided on a title, but the setting is always with me. It is one I know intimately: the Yorkshire moors.

I shall set my story at the beginning of this century, during the stark reign of George III, before the civility of our Queen Victoria.

The tale festers in my mind like the young man's gangrene and must be told.

My novel begins.

I shall close these pages with a poem. It shall be my final entry and last attempt at poetry.

Oh, thy bright eyes must answer now,
When Reason with a scornful brow,
Is mocking at my over-throw;
Oh, thy sweet tongue must plead for me
And tell why I have chosen thee!

Stern Reason is to judgement come
Arrayed in all her forms of gloom;
Wilt thou my advocate be dumb?
No radiant angel, speak and say
Why I did cast the world away:

Why I have persevered to shun
The common paths that others run
And on a strange road journeyed on;
Heedless alike of Wealth and Power –
Of Glory's wreath and Pleasure's flower –

Letter from Charlotte to Ellen Nussey

August, 1846

You say I am 'to tell you plenty'. What would you have me to say? Nothing happens at Haworth – nothing at least of a pleasant kind. One little incident indeed occurred about a week ago to sting us to life – but if it gives no more pleasure for you to hear than it did for us to witness, you will scarcely thank me for adverting to it.

It was merely the arrival of a Sheriff's Officer on a visit to Branwell – inviting him either to pay his debts or take a trip to York. Of course his debts had to be paid. It is not agreeable to lose money time after time in this way but it is ten times worse, to witness the shabbiness of his behaviour on such occasions. But where is the use of dwelling on this subject? It will make him no better.

Letter from Branwell Brontë to Joseph Bentley Leyland

September, 1846

This last week an honest and kindly friend, Dr John Crosby, has warned me that concealed hopes about one lady should be given up, let the effort to do so cost what it may. He is the family medical attendant, and was commanded by Mr Evans, M.P. for North Derbyshire to return me, unopened, a letter which I addressed to Thorp Green and which the Lady was not permitted to see.

I have received to-day, since I begun my scrawl, a note from her maid, Miss Ann Marshall, and I know from it that she has been terrified by vows which she was forced to swear to, on her husband's deathbed (with every ghastly addition of terror which the ghastly dying eye could inflict upon a keenly sensitive and almost *worried* woman's mind), a complete severance from him in whom lay her whole heart's feelings. When that husband was scarce cold in his grave, her relations, who controlled the whole property overwhelmed her with their tongues, and I am quite *conscious* that she has succumbed in terror, to what they have said.

I have been in truth too much petted through life, and in my last situation I was so much master, and gave myself so much up to enjoyment that now, when the cloud of ill health and adversity has come upon me, it will be a disheartening job to work myself up again through a new life's battle from the position of five years ago to which I have been compelled to retreat with heavy loss and no gain. My army stands now where it did then, but mourning the slaughter of Youth, Health, Hope and both mental and physical elasticity.

The last two losses are indeed important to one who once built his hopes of rising in the world on the possession of them. Noble writings, works of art, music or poetry now instead of rousing my imagination, cause a whirlwind of blighting.

Sorrow sweeps over my mind with unspeakable dreariness, and if I sit down and try to write all ideas that used to come clothed in sunlight now press round me in funeral black; for really every pleasurable excitement that I used to know has changed to insipidity or pain.

I shall never be able to realise the too sanguine hopes of my friends, for at twenty-eight I am a thoroughly *old man* – mentally and bodily – far more so indeed than I am willing to express…

My rude rough acquaintances here ascribe my unhappiness solely to causes produced by my sometimes irregular life, because they have known no other pains than those resulting from excess or want of ready cash. They do not know that I would rather want a shirt than want a springy mind, and that my total want of happiness, were I to step into York Minster now, would be far, far worse than their want of a hundred pounds when they might happen to need it; and that if a dozen glasses or a bottle of wine drives off their cares, such cures only make me outwardly passable in company but never drive off mine.

I know only that it is time for me to be something when I am nothing – that my father cannot have long to live, and that when he dies, my evening, which is already twilight, will become night – that I shall then have a constitution still so strong that it will keep me years in torture and despair when I should every hour pray that I might die.

Letter from Charlotte Brontë to Ellen Nussey

January, 1847

I expect from the extravagance of Branwell's behaviour and from mysterious hints he drops (for he will never speak out plainly), that we shall be hearing news of fresh debts contracted by him soon.

Mary Thornton has begun a correspondence with Anne, these six months after her father's death. Elizabeth Thornton, the older sister who was in Paris, has come to her senses, abandoned her popish convent school and returned to Thorp Green. She has written to Anne as well. Why they have suddenly begun to flood my sister with letters is a mystery to us all. Perhaps the duplicitous Mrs Thornton no longer fears that Branwell will return to Thorp Green and cause trouble, and hopes that he has accepted the inevitable – that he will never become her husband. Her daughters have announced that they are on the point of departing Thorp Green for Birmingham, where they intend to live at Great Barr Hall with Sir Edward Scott. They plan to visit Anne sometime in the interim.

Letter from Charlotte Brontë to Ellen Nussey

March, 1847

Branwell is quieter now – and for a good reason: he has got to the end of a considerable sum of money of which he recently became possessed. It is my belief it was a sum advanced by the scurrilous Mrs Thornton to buy his silence. You must expect to find him weaker in mind and the complete rake in appearance. I have no apprehension of his being at all uncivil to you. On the contrary he will be as smooth as oil upon your visit here. Needless to say, papa has been beside himself over Branwell's erratic disgraceful behaviour and we can only hope that matters improve.

The Journal of Branwell Brontë

12th June, 1847

I have scarcely darkened your pages.

I have been occupying myself with a novel, which I still hope to complete; for I have observed my sisters sitting at the dining-room table and scratching away like busy birds into their note-books.

Do they truly believe I am unaware that not only have their novels been completed but accepted by a publisher?

They do not show me these labours, but I have stolen a look at them nevertheless. It is the title of Emily's *Wuthering Heights*, that intrigues me the most; but I will not ask to read the entire volume if she does not volunteer.

What has happened to the precious closeness we once all shared?

Will we never again write our stories together?

My sisters have closed ranks against me, like soldiers to an invader.

I am an outsider in my own home.

From *The Life Of Charlotte Brontë* by Elizabeth Gaskell, Published in March, 1857

Branwell had attacks of delirium tremens of the most frightful character; he slept in his father's room, and he would sometimes declare either he or his father should be dead before morning. The trembling sisters, sick with fright, would implore their father not to expose himself to this danger; but Mr Brontë is no timid man, and perhaps he felt that he could possibly influence his son to some self-restraint, more by showing trust in him than by showing fear... In the mornings young Branwell would saunter out, saying, with a drunkard's incontinence of speech, 'The poor old man and I have had a terrible night of it; he does his best – the poor old man! but it's all over with me'; (whimpering) 'it's her fault, her fault.'

Branwell did little to court his family's approval. Not only was he hopelessly entangled in debt, but also he was driven to the abuser's extremes of duplicity in his desperation to feed his habit. He would often steal out of the house while the family was at church to cajole the village druggist out of a lump of opium.

Letter from Charlotte Brontë to Ellen Nussey

January, 1848

Branwell is now always sick and has two or three times fallen down in fits. Once he even managed to set his bed-clothes on fire while lying in a drunken stupor. Fortunately, Anne happened to be passing his open door and tried to rouse him. When she could not do so, she ran to get Emily who dragged her brother out of bed, flung him into the corner and the blazing bed-clothes into the middle of the room, dashed to the kitchen for a large can of water and doused the flames.

The Thornton girls, Mary and Elizabeth, continue to amaze me by the frequency and constancy of their correspondence to Anne. Even Alice, who is now appearing on the London stage, writes as well. The poor girls – they still complain of their mother's proceedings. That woman is a hapless being; calculated to bring a curse wherever she goes by the mixture of weakness, perversion and deceit in her nature. Sir Edward Scott's wife is said to be dying. If she goes, I suppose they will marry – that is if Mrs Thornton *can* marry. She affirmed her husband's will bound her to remain single – but I do not believe anything she says.

The Journal of Branwell Brontë

20th August 1848

Was I foolhardy to hope when Mr Thornton died that my Lydia would be free to marry me?

I did not know then that he had constructed a will which denies me all hope.

I am doomed to live without her.

I cannot!

I have destroyed my worthless pathetic attempt at a novel.

I will resume again.

I shall beat my sisters at their game yet!

Perhaps my new attempt will depict the neglected wife of a husband who did not appreciate her. A romantic tutor assigned to her household will enliven her life and that of her son.

Perhaps my novel will have a happy ending.

Love will conquer all!

I will commence writing to-morrow.

It is late now. All have gone to bed.

I cannot sleep as soundly as they.

I write sitting here alone in the parlour and am in desperate need of whisky.

The Black Bull is too close. I can almost smell the fragrance of its liquor.

I shall join my friends and sit in my special chair and raise a toast to my beloved Lydia. Only whisky can lessen my desire for her.

To-morrow I shall begin my new novel.

To-morrow.

A Description by Francis Grundy of Branwell Brontë, his Former Fellow Employee on the Railway at Luddenden Foot

September, 1848

I ordered dinner for two in a private room at the Black Bull and then sent word up to the parsonage for Branwell. While I waited I was surprised to receive a visit from Branwell's father, the Reverend Patrick Brontë, who informed me that he was touched by the kindness I was showing his son. He wished to prepare me for a dramatic change in Branwell's appearance. Much of the Rector's old stiffness of manner was gone. He spoke of Branwell with more affection than I had ever heretofore heard him express, but he also spoke almost hopelessly. He said that when my message came, Branwell was in bed, and had been almost too weak for the last few days to leave it; nevertheless, he had insisted upon coming and would be there immediately.

Presently the door opened cautiously, and a head appeared. It was a mass of red unkempt hair, wildly floating round a great, gaunt forehead; the cheeks yellow and hollow, the mouth fallen, the thin white lips not trembling but shaking, the sunken eyes, once small, now glaring with the light of madness – all told the sad tale but too surely.

Letter from Charlotte Brontë to her Publisher, William Smith Williams

September, 1848

My brother, Branwell, breathed his last breath this past Sunday morning, the 24th day of this month, victim to consumption.

I myself, with painful, mournful joy, heard him praying softly in his dying moments, and to the last prayer which my father offered up at his bedside, he added, 'amen'.

How unusual that word appeared from his lips – of course you who did not know him, cannot conceive.

After a struggle of twenty minutes, which seemed an eternity to his distressed family, Branwell started convulsively almost to his feet, and fell back dead into his father's arms. He was thirty-one years old.

When the struggle was over – and a marble calm began to succeed the last dread agony – I felt as I had never felt before that there was peace and forgiveness for him in Heaven. All his errors – to speak plainly – all his vices seemed nothing to me in that morning, every wrong he had done, every pain he had caused, vanished; his sufferings only were remembered; the wrench to the natural affections only was felt.

He is at rest – and that comforts us all. Life had no happiness for him.

Branwell was his father's and his sisters' pride and hope in boyhood, but since manhood, the case has been otherwise. It has been our lot to see him take a wrong bent; to hope, expect, wait his return to the right path; to know the sickness of hope deferred, the dismay of prayer baffled, to experience despair at last; and now to behold the sudden early obscure close of what might have been a noble career.

I do not weep from a sense of bereavement – there is no prop withdrawn, no consolation torn away, no dear companion lost – but for the wreck of talent, the ruin of promise, the untimely dreary extinction of what might have been a burning and a shining light. My brother was a year my junior; I had aspirations and ambitions for him once – long ago – they have perished mournfully – nothing remains of him but a memory of errors and sufferings. There is such a bitterness of pity for his life and death – such a yearning for the emptiness of his whole existence as I cannot describe – I trust time will allay these feelings.

My poor father naturally thought more of his only son than of his daughters, and much and long as he had suffered on his account, he cried out for his loss like David for that of Absalom – My son! My son! And refused at first to be comforted.

Aftermath

The Misses Brontës' Establishment, the school for young ladies that was to begin at the parsonage, never commenced owing to the lack of response to a circular advertising the school, but the publication of the Brontë sisters' novels brought them other consolation.

In 1847, Mrs Lydia Thornton moved to Birmingham to live at Great Barr Hall with Sir Edward and Lady Scott, distant relatives. Not long afterwards, Lady Scott died and on November 8, 1848, the widow of Edmund Thornton married the widower and became Lady Scott.

Mary Thornton married Henry Clapham, a manufacturer, residing at Aireworth House just beyond Keighley.

Elizabeth Thornton also married.

Branwell Brontë's portrait of Lydia Thornton has never been discovered. Perhaps upon his return to Thorp Green from Scarborough, Mr Thornton destroyed it. Not long after his death, Thorp Green was sold. It is now a convalescent hospital.

Emily Brontë died from consumption on the afternoon of Tuesday, December 19, 1848, at the age of thirty. She is buried in the family vault, as was her brother. Her water-colour of her mysterious visitor has never been unearthed.

Anne Brontë, ill with consumption, begged that her sister, Charlotte and Charlotte's school friend, Ellen Nussey, convey her to Scarborough for one last look at the sea. Her wish was granted and she died peacefully in Scarborough, where she is buried, on Monday, May 28, 1849, at the age of twenty-nine.

On learning of her illness she wrote these lines:

For thou hast taken my delight
And hope of life away,
And bid me watch the painful night
And wait the weary day.

Keeper, the mastiff, forever mourning his Emily, died in his sleep on December 1st, 1851.

Flossy followed in 1854, almost three years to the death of Keeper. She drooped for a day and died quietly in the night without pain.

In February, 1855, as Charlotte lay dying, Tabitha Aykroyd, who had been in service to the Brontës for over thirty years, died at the advanced age of eighty-four. She was buried in the Haworth Churchyard, just beyond the parsonage garden wall, in sight of her room where Hathersage had convalesced.

Charlotte Brontë married her father's curate, Arthur Bell Nicholls, on June 28, 1854. One year later, in 1855, just three weeks before her thirty-ninth birthday, weakened by violent nausea from the early stages of a difficult pregnancy, she succumbed to phthisis, a progressive wasting disease. Her body was committed to the Haworth family vault.

Patrick Brontë outlived all his offspring, dying on June 7, 1861, at the advanced age of eighty-four. He was buried in the family vault alongside the remains of his wife and five of his children, Anne's body remaining in Scarborough.

ACKNOWLEDGEMENTS

To Joanna Bentley and The Book Guild for their impeccable professionalism, to Gareth Vaughan for his brilliant job of editing, to Coreen Turner and her novel *Dear Saucy Pat*, for steering me to The Book Guild, to Juliet Barker for writing the definitive biography of the Brontës, a great help in preparing this book; to The Brontë Society for keeping this extraordinary literary family alive; to the Brontë Parsonage Museum for keeping the flame burning; to Liz Robertson and Ruth Davis, and Steffi Sidney Splaver, always there to read first whatever comes off my typewriter, and lastly, to my typist, Bonnie Petros, who truly sees anything I write first and is always the first to give my writing encouragement.